All Points Imagination

Short Stories from Bounds Green
Book Writers

All Points Imagination
Short stories from Bounds Green Book Writers

Publisher: Green Bounds Books
Editor: Susie Helme
All rights reserved.

The moral rights of the authors have been asserted.
First published in Great Britain in 2025 by Green Bounds Books

Cover design: Gregory Motton
Layout: Charlotte Harris of Rose Editorial

No part of this book may be reproduced or transmitted in any form or by any means without written permission from the publisher, except by a reviewer who wishes to quote brief passages in connection with a review for insertion in a magazine, newspaper or broadcast.
A catalogue record for this book is available from the British Library.

Printed and bound in Great Britain.
https://boundsgreenbookswriters.com

About Bounds Green Book Writers

BGBW is a writers group with a difference. We don't just sit around drinking tea. We meet monthly at my house (in Bounds Green) and swap beta-reading. But we also, at each meeting, have a presentation by one of us on some topic or skill relating to writing. These presentations are then repackaged and posted on our 'Writing advice and comment' blog on creative writing techniques (https://boundsgreenbookwriters.com/category/writing-advice-and-comment/). During the ensuing month we swap chapters of our books in progress and do 'homework', exercises practicing the skills we learned from the presentation, which we also post on our blog.

During the Covid pandemic, we were lonely, so we published the online *Lockdown Lit*—'a collection of creative writing inspired by the coronavirus experience' (https://bounds-greenbookwriters.com/lockdown-lit-2/), for which we solicited contributions from all over.

In 2025, BGBW agreed to form a publishing venture called Green Bounds Books. *All Points Imagination* is our first venture into self-publishing. We hope you enjoy our stories.

Susie

Contents

I: Friends and Family　　　　　　　　　　　　6

Real Men by Rajes Bala　　　　　　　　　　　7
Tokyo, Here We Come by Susie Helme　　　　20
First Date by Rajes Bala　　　　　　　　　　22
Uncle Charlie by Brian T. Marshall　　　　　28
He Will Be Home, Always by Rajes Bala　　　36
Untethered by Susie Helme　　　　　　　　　39
Ringo by em.thompson　　　　　　　　　　　41
Glacial by Elaine Graham-Leigh　　　　　　　52
So Beautiful by Susie Helme　　　　　　　　56

II Snows of Yesteryear　　　　　　　　　　　66

When Our Boys Come Home by Susie Helme　67
The Lost Battlefield by Elaine Graham-Leigh　74
Piano Lessons by Kay Towers　　　　　　　　76
Die, Die, Die by Susie Helme　　　　　　　　80
The Round Up by Rajes Bala　　　　　　　　83
El Dorado and the Potato Curse by Susie Helme　92
The Jews' Garden by Elaine Graham-Leigh　105
Chocolatl by Susie Helme　　　　　　　　　115

III Funnybones　　　　　　　　　　　　　　119

The Curious Case of the Kitnapped Cat
by em.thompson　　　　　　　　　　　　　120
My Moon Landing by Susie Helme　　　　　143
The Cat's Story by Elaine Graham-Leigh　　144

Greaper at the Pearly Gates by em.thompson	160
The Cremation of the Goldfish by Rajes Bala	177

IV Beyond the Bounds	191

The Wild Man by Elaine Graham-Leigh	192
Cunntrahayam by Susie Helme	210
Footprints by Brian T. Marshall	219
The Concierge by Marie-Lise Mullen	227
The Widow's House by Brian T. Marshall	245

Or Bios, Our Books	227

I: Friends and Family

Real Men

by Rajes Bala (Rajeswary Balasubramaniam)

Summer, 1997, London

Putting on her make-up, Janet was pleased with her appearance. The red lipstick made her look sexy, seductive. As she perfected her lips she recalled the remarks of the young man at the corner shop. His eyes would sparkle as he spoke to her. He'd said her lips were 'voluptuous'.

He and many other men made these comments, and she was well aware of her beauty.

She would have preferred a slightly different shade, but looking through her make-up, which although plentiful was dominated by the cheaper brands, and finding nothing quite right, she thought, 'Well, I am beautiful, anyway'.

'Janet!'

Peter, standing in the doorway, was ready to pick an argument; he would probably say something about the way she looked. Ignoring him for the moment, she continued to study herself in the mirror.

At twenty years old, Janet's feminine charm was more striking now than it had been at seventeen, more striking than when she took up with Pete and became the mother of their child Melanie. A slim young woman with an attractive figure, she dressed according to her simple taste—jeans and a t-shirt, usually. Peter adored and was jealous of her. Twenty-one, unqualified, unemployed, the tallish, attractive young man often lashed out at her without reason.

Their flat, on the eighth floor of a tower block on the neglected estate where they were both born and grew up, was poorly furnished. Janet did her best to keep it clean and decent with the limited resources of their state benefits. She felt she was too young to be caught in this life; a night of passion and a burst condom had led them both to this present struggle of parenthood. She hadn't imagined this would happen to her. A never ending round of housework and looking after a lively toddler, no time for going out. Still, they had stuck together, that was something, even though each was unhappy, frustrated, disappointed—hopeless, even.

Gazing at her, Peter thought of what his friend Darren had been saying.

'What's your Janet doing, hanging around that Paki shop half the day?'

His face habitually scowling and aggressive, Peter's former school friend was a short, oversized tough guy; a wheeler and dealer, a prison recidivist, always returning to 'business as usual'.

Peter had avoided Darren's gaze. He wasn't an idiot. He saw how she was. Always smiling, just popping in to the 'Paki shop', to buy a jar of baby food, washing powder, whatever, always in and out of that shop with that young guy grinning at her with his, 'Hello, darling'.

It made Darren's blood boil; Darren had told him to lay off. 'She's not your darling, you little shit.'

'Don't speak to her like that, you bloody Paki,' Peter yelled at times to the shopkeeper.

'Janet!'

'You've been flirting with that Paki from the shop, haven't you? I know you have, don't think I don't know all about it,' Peter screamed at her many times.

She often ignored him when he was like this, when his voice was venomous.

She ignored him, now; calmly regarding herself in the mirror, after all, as she often said, an answer from her wouldn't change anything.

Peter waited. Repeating the accusation again, he drew a response from her.

'So, you're jealous? Jealous of that? Jealous of nothing? Are you a real man? A real man wouldn't even think of it, a real man would be thinking about giving his woman and child a decent life. What do I get from you, big man? A crummy old council flat and no money for our little girl,' She didn't need many words.

Still calm as she spoke, looking at him as though he were a piece of dirt.

Peter felt himself losing his temper. That could see him end up in prison like Darren.

Fuming, he left the flat behind, escaping to an aimless day by means of the urine soaked lift that, today, was not smeared with excrement.

Dr Kathirgamer, as a little boy in Sri Lanka, had dreamed of being a pop star or a famous actor in Indian cinema. The medical profession, so well respected, was what his family urged him to take up, and now, middle-aged and married, he was a GP in East London.

Rathiga his wife was angry with him today. 'You're not a real man at all, are you?'

Before coming to London, the doctor had had a good, profitable position in a private hospital in Sri Lanka's capital, Colombo, where wealthy people paid him handsomely for his services; he was a 'God-sent healer', they said. Often he had attended important functions as one of the honoured guests.

The political situation there had led to him running for his life with his wife and two daughters. Here in London, everything was different. The impossible workload, the diseases of poverty, the clinical depression, the homelessness, the refugees, the scarcity of resources, the ignorance he found, were a shock, at first. Now, it was depressing, defeating him.

His wife Rathiga did not understand this about his work. Indeed, she wanted to live here in the same way as they had done at home, with servants. They should be acquiring properties, accumulating wealth as the rest of her family did. He could never have matched up financially to her family, and now, she was embarrassed by him; she felt demeaned by their life, and she was holding him responsible.

So, she was angry, and she nagged.

Rathiga, from a wealthy family and bringing a handsome dowry to her husband, was a demanding woman, expected Dr Kathirgamer, who came from a humble background, to prove himself. Dr Kathir's father was a farmer. On his few acres he cultivated long beans, melons, bitter gold, okra, aubergines and gram sticks. As a young man, the son had gone with his father at dawn to market with the vegetables. His memories of those mornings, with their gentle breezes and the smell of the fresh vegetables, were still strong. In the evenings after tuition he would water the garden or turn the soil. It was hard physical labour, which enabled him to save up the money to go to further education. As one of the poorer students, he struggled through university and got to the finals.

At university parties he would sing Beatles songs, and there had been the chance to act in the student productions; a small way of fulfilling his boyhood dreams.

After qualifying, he was considered a good catch, and there were many proposals of marriage. His family chose Rathiga for him; she was from a wealthy family, and the dowry would be substantial. Kathir did not like to be bartered like this, knowing he would become a slave to his socially superior wife's demands. He did very well in Colombo; the private practice brought plenty of money, and they had a prosperous lifestyle.

Rathiga had nothing to complain of, then, rather she was proud and boastful.

Now, in London, their two lovely daughters were growing into young women, taking classes in Indian Classical dance and playing the Veena.

'Oh, God only knows how much we will have to pay for the Veena and Bharatha Natiyam debuts,' she sighed.

'It is expensive to get this extra education in London,' muttered Kathir, ' but it is not the girls who ask for these lessons. It is you, who want to show off to your family and friends, and it is I who must work overtime to pay for them.' His voice was subdued; she was capable of screaming at him for taking such an attitude toward paying for things.

'As far as I can remember, art is a gift, and those who have the gift for dancing and music will learn with love and passion—not by going to expensive lessons, just so that they can call themselves 'classical dancers',' he continued.

'How do you expect them to learn if they don't have lessons?' Rathiga was hardly even interested in Kathir's opinion. She was more interested in having the money to pay for these things that were so essential to her self-importance—the dancing lessons, the properties abroad.

Today, Dr Kathirgamer was working overtime as a locum

doctor, doing home visits. He walked slowly to the car where the driver was waiting. He had a number of visits to make, and the driver was there to make sure there was no trouble. Kathir didn't feel safe in some areas of East London.

He really wasn't feeling too great, today. He suffered from diabetic mellitus, high blood pressure and angina. He was aware of this; Rathiga was not—why worry her?

Still, he felt uneasy, today. He wanted to make his wife and daughters happy, and he worked too hard. To him his daughters were like Saraswathy and Luxmy, powerful Hindu goddesses of wisdom and wealth. His daughters should have the best education, the brightest future. They were beautiful, kind, intelligent girls.

The day was windy and chilly, rain lightly coming and going. He sat in the car and took a deep breath. The air he inhaled was cold, but he felt hot and sweaty. 'I must check my blood pressure,' he mused. He thought of going to Yoga classes, but where would he find the time? 'I am only fifty; I will have many more good years of life,' he assured himself.

'Good evening, Doctor,' the driver said. Kathir mumbled his response, preoccupied with his thoughts.

'Are you OK, Doctor?' the driver asked, noticing the doctor's laboured breathing.

'Yes, I'm fine,' the doctor responded firmly.

He looked at the driver as he started the engine; Jacob was a West Indian with old fashioned manners. 'He has more kind feeling toward me than my own wife does,' he thought.

Janet was calling Peter's mobile phone once again, angry and anxious that he didn't answer. It was about six-thirty in the evening, and she hadn't seen him since the morning. Their little girl was not well; she had a fever, and the liquid paracetamol had done no good. Suddenly, she had vomited and screamed as though she was being stabbed. Right now, she was sleeping, but she had not eaten or drunk anything nor shown any interest in playing her usual lively games.

Janet looked at Melanie, wondering at this small carbon copy of herself. She even had the same mannerisms, the same way of hunching up her little shoulders when she laughed, the same way of biting at her lower lip in concentration. 'It's probably just a cold making her fretful,' she thought. But her usually bright eyes had become dull.

'Sod Peter, I bet he's with Dodgy Darren, chasing after school-girls or something to smoke—why can't he ever be here to do something for us?'

Perhaps she should call Mum, she thought; but she probably wouldn't be home, yet. Janet had two brothers and one sister—until her brother Mark died in a car accident. He'd been fifteen and in the wrong place... so now, there was only an older brother, always in trouble with the police; they never seemed to leave him alone; and Lisa, a dancer of sorts.

Their parents, a quiet ordinary couple, had been glad when Janet had fallen pregnant and Peter had stayed with her; they were happy that she had settled with someone.

Peter's family was large; Irish Catholic, and Pete sometimes promised they would have a big family, too. Janet wondered what that would be like. Would she drown in kids while he disappeared to the pub? She could see him becoming just like the dads in some of the families on the estate. They stuck by their families, certainly—coming home on a Friday night with empty pockets and raising hell. Maybe it would be different. Maybe not. Peter's family looked as though they managed okay, but Pete wasn't getting anywhere, despite his parents' regard for education and family responsibility. He took more notice of Darren's opinions than anyone else's, always had done.

Darren was different, he'd never really gone to school, except to cause trouble. Since being expelled at the age of seven for aggressive behaviour, it had held no attraction for him—and his family, comprised of mother and sister, either couldn't cope or didn't care. No one knew where the father was, and no one had ever asked. At the age of twenty he had spent more time at 'Her Majesty's Pleasure' than anywhere else; if anything, that was his most stable environment.

Janet gazed down from her eighth floor window. A drizzling cold English summer evening, still light for a few hours, yet. She felt interminably lonely, as though she would be here alone forever, while the rest of the world carried on better, brighter, cleverer and more impressive lives. 'Everyone in the world is enjoying life except me, the fool stuck with a child in this prison block,' she thought.

Melanie woke up and cried feebly. Janet, feeling her hot forehead and body, experienced prickles of alarm and fear—this didn't seem at all right. The fever had not gone away, it was worse than before. She wished Peter would walk through the front door, even if he were drunk or angry, it would be better than being on her own and not knowing what to do. The local doctor's surgery would be near closing, now, and she knew it would be a miserable wait if she were to go there—they might even refuse to see her. Casualty would be no good, either. Today was Friday, and even this early in the evening it would be like a madhouse. 'Oh, where's Pete?' she cried. Then she dialled the number for the doctor on call.

Peter had cruised around for a while and then headed for the street corner where he knew Darren was likely to be, near their local pub. He was there, and in a good mood.

'Business is looking up,' he grinned, his bald misshapen head bare. Even in a good mood his air was one of readiness—for a scuffle or an opportunity. His motivations in life centred around his cash-flow and his neighbourhood; particularly around the imposition, as he saw it, of the foreigners whom he saw as his duty to harass and intimidate whenever possible. His opinions were well known in the area, and they were shared by many other young white men. He felt hatred toward anyone who was in England and was not English. Darren was a good and generous mate, often pressing, as he did now, a couple of pills into the palm of Pete's hand.

In the near empty pub, Darren ordered a lager. The place would gradually fill throughout the afternoon, and by early evening it would be packed.

Seating himself in a corner with a good view of the place, staring at Peter's dejected face across the table, Darren said; 'What's the matter?'

Peter's eyes strayed around the pub, avoiding his questioner's eyes.

'What, did you lose something?'

Pete sighed and gazed into his glass, as though it might make a reply for him.

'Listen, Peter,' said Darren, leaning forward, keeping his eyes fixed intently, 'I hate seeing your Janet sucking up to those filthy Pakis, why do you let her do it? She ought to know better, the mother of your own little girl.'

Peter felt himself sinking into a slightly woozy emotional acquiescence to whatever his good friend was getting at, and a sullen, dull, moody ire at the world that allowed his girlfriend to look at him as though he were dirt, after giving her smiles to that slimy, grinning shop boy.

'I love Janet,' was all he could muster.

'Well, of course you bloody do, I know that, you don't need to tell me, mate—after all, how long have I known you two? Forever.'

A poster in luminous paper on the wall at the bar advertised the evening's entertainment; striptease from nine o'clock, DJs till late.

A couple of young Asian men came in, immediately joined by two pretty white girls that looked as though they'd been waiting for them; the greetings were light-hearted and flirtatious.

'What's going on with our girls, what makes them want to go after that lot of shifty bastards?' Darren's fist clenched in anger. 'Even the Princess of Wales Diana, look at her. An Englishman of royal blood isn't good enough for her, she prefers that short-arse greasy A-rab Dodi. That Dodi Fayed—his family runs a bloody grocer's, as well, don't they? Why do our girls go with them?' He glared meaningfully at Peter. One of Darren's sisters had married a Muslim.

For Darren, anyone with brown skin was a 'Paki'. He did not grasp that the presence of statuettes of Lord Rama, Sita and Hanuman around the corner shop indicated that the Patels were Hindus. Even if he had, he would have said, 'Dirty Pakis worshipping monkeys'.

'Well, I guess they have all the money, with their businesses and all that.' Suddenly, the boy at the corner shop appeared to be part of a conspiracy of ruthless, shady foreign businessmen, who were anxious to pick out the best of Englishwomen and corrupt them into their strange practices and make them bear their own children—not English kids like Peter's.

And Janet hardly let Peter touch her, nowadays.

'Bloody Janet,' he muttered.

The small group of young people before them were excitable

and happy; their laughter could almost have been timed to mock Darren's speech.

'Just look at those foreign idiots, they were allowed into this country to clean our toilets—see what's happened, now, with all that tolerance shit? They can take anything they fancy. A nice house? Certainly, you black bastard, here, have a swanky job; and hey, why not a white girl, too—you like them, don't you?' The hate-filled words spilled easily from Darren's mouth; they were words he repeated frequently at the meetings which he attended with a punctuality and dedication that would have astonished the would-be teachers of his youth.

'Dogs, they are... dirty low-down mutts, they don't deserve to be here... they shouldn't be here at all,' mumbled Peter, discontent and unrest fermenting in his head.

'It's up to people like us you know—who else is there to be strong and stand up to them? Do you think the government is going to do anything but roll over for the bloody whining social workers who just want to eat in stupid 'ethnic' restaurants and get paid fat money for figuring out how to make our dark friends feel more at home? No chance! They're all mates together. Look at our MPs. How many of them are lesbians, gays or whatnot? Who knows? They may have Paki or Black lovers. It's only people like you and me that see what's really going on, Pete, and I'll tell you something, those Pakis are spineless... they go running for their poor little lives if you so much as say 'boo' to them, you'll see.'

Darren saw himself as a defender of British culture and tradition. His expression was one of deep emotion—love for his country, for the land of his forefathers. He imagined a country peopled only by his white kinsmen This fatherless man's only real sense of family came from the warm, accepting camaraderie of the men he met in far right meetings, with their airs of confidence, strength and superiority. There was little else Darren encountered that seemed solid—except for the might of the establishment that incarcerated him and disapproved of him. The family of his white kinsmen embraced him and encouraged his pride; to them he was worth something.

The two friends left, slightly unsteady, but filled with pride and determination.

Peter thought, 'Janet has to stop showing me up like that. She has to. I've got to tell her that she's going to be more respectful of our family, of me... Not a real man? I'm more of a man than that snivelling Paki thief. She's being fooled like the others, stupid bitch.'

Peter took hold of his mobile to call Janet, to put her straight.

Jacob, the driver, parked the car at the entrance to the estate. On this overcast evening it seemed to be getting dark too early, and the ground was shining wet as he watched Dr Kathir making his way along a concrete-walled walkway toward the entrance to the third block and turn out of sight.

The two men, Peter and Darren, had turned the corner ahead of the doctor and rescrutinising him fixedly.

'Hey! You! Old Paki bastard! What do you want here? Do you think you'll get yourself a white piece around here? Is that what you're after, you dirty old bugger?'

The men's faces were taut with rage, rage against the foreigner on their territory.

'Your Paki friend from the shop tell you to come here, did he?'

Their fists and feet gave the doctor no chance to speak, kicking and punching him with animal ferocity. Blood poured from the doctor's nose, they kicked him in the back, as he slumped and curled up in agony.

Peter's phone was ringing as he stepped back from the bloody mess on the floor. Staring at the old man, he answered the phone, breathless.

Janet wailed at him, crying hysterically. 'I've been waiting and waiting, and the doctor hasn't come, the lazy black bastard. Mel's really ill, Pete... do something, for God's sake, do something. Please! Oh, she won't die, will she?'

Peter, irritated by Janet overreacting as usual, shut off the phone.

He feels relieved, powerful. An injured old man—Dr Kathir is on the floor, bleeding.

Darren is excited. There is no-one around; no need to escape quickly. They look at each other, judging that they may as well get what they can out of this. The man is wearing a good suit, he probably has money in his pocket, and the case he was carrying could be a laptop. The old man is disgusting, filthy, pathetic. And he owes them. All people like him have stolen from them, well—time to take something back.

Peter turns his attention to the case, lying on the floor near the inert body. He bends down and opens it. There is no laptop.

There are, instead, bits of equipment such as a stethoscope, and a notepad on top, some kind of form.

It says, Visiting: two-year-old child with high fever. Name: Melanie Peter Williams.

Tokyo, Here We Come

by Susie Helme

They lay beside each other at the bottom of the chest in the children's room, underneath the box of Christmas ornaments, the two war mementos, my father's folded US Marine flag and his father's Japanese Navy pilot's helmet.

My father-in-law's helmet is soft brown leather with a furry lining and flaps that fasten down over the ears, of such cheap materials and manufacture that now after so many years it's coming to pieces in my hands. My husband calls it a '*kamikaze* hat', but *Ojiichan* (Granddaddy) wasn't a *kamikaze*. These two children are testament to the survival of the gene pool.

He went to Manchuria to fight the Russians. Here was hope for a small, poor country to compete with the West, to expand by military might and *bushidō*, the spirit of the samurai, to glorify the Emperor, to subjugate the 'lesser peoples of Asia'. He spent the war in a Siberian prison camp, where most other prisoners starved to death.

I unfold my father's Marine Corps flag. It is white with a *Hi-no-maru* red rising sun of the Japanese flag in the middle and the words 'Tokyo, Here We Come'. Around it in the white parts, his Marine buddies had written in the names of their military victories—Okinawa, Wake Island, Midway. Granddaddy didn't pilot the planes; he was an intelligence officer, a spy. It was his job to scout out targets for the bombs they dropped on my husband's land, to make the world safe for democracy, to be the world's policeman, to 'carry a big stick'.

His father came home with enough life left in him to win the heart of a pretty girl in his hometown, and they started a family in the constant shadow of the pawn shop. My husband's childhood photos reflect the poverty of post-war Japan.

My father came home with crates of Oriental antiquities to fill his bride's living room, purchased at fire sale prices in the wake of defeat.

The quiet of the room still echoes with the memory of noisy bedtime rituals. I look at the children in their beds, their father's slanted eyes closed in sleep, my light brown hair falling in damp curls on their pillows. I watch the living ones as I remember the dead ones.

'*Oyasuminasai* (goodnight)', I whisper to their sweet sleeping heads, and I say a prayer for world peace.

First Date

by Rajes Bala (Rajeswary Balasubramaniam)

March, 1968, Trincomalee, Ceylon

It is a beautiful evening. They just got off the bus from their first date in the big city. The evening breeze touches her face gently with a pure smell of the sea next to the bus stop.

He is taking his leave, and she can feel his urge to stay longer with her. His eyes reflect the pain of separating. He looks at his watch, his train will be leaving in thirty minutes.

'I'll miss you, Rathi,' he said lovingly, his eyes sinking deep into every cell in her body.

Despite their brief acquaintance, Rathi rather expected him to say, 'I love you.' Yet, his words carried unspoken feeling. She felt herself melting into him.

'I'll miss you, too,' she said in a voice which she hardly knew, a taste of honey on her lips and a smell of her favourite jasmine flower in the air. Her body trembled with an unfamiliar feeling as they both looked at one another.

She watched him until he turned the corner. She stood, wishing him to run back to her and say, 'I'd love to have spent more time with you.'

A few minutes later she was walking into the house where she lived with three other young women of the same age. They would be asking her lots of questions about her first date, as none of them had had such an experience, yet.

So, she told them about her relationship with Siva up to now. Six months ago she'd attended a function at her old school organised by the students' union. He was there with a friend who was an alumnus of the school and now working in Colombo, the capital city of Ceylon. She sang a song at the event.

A few days later, she received a tape recording of her singing, accompanied by a note. 'A love letter!' her roommates acclaimed with gossipy glee.

It was a turning point in my life when I attended your old school function other day. Your voice took me to heaven, the melody got into my soul. Your simple, innocent beauty fills my thoughts; even when I am sleeping it is as if you are here with me. Please forgive my bold words, as you do not know me at all. I am sending a recording of the song you sang. You may have made a recording yourself, which you may have in your collection, yet I would be very happy if you'd like to keep this one.

By the way, I am a friend of your former classmate Rajah. My name is Siva, I live and work in Colombo. I was visiting him in Trincomalee and came with him to the party at your school. Thank god for that, as it provided me with the opportunity to see you and listen to your song.

Thank you,
-Siva.

She was amazed that a person was so impressed by her song that he would write and send her a tape, and she felt uncomfortable to read his comments about her beauty and her voice.

She wanted to ignore it as being a bit childish. Nevertheless, her thoughts had been interrupted by the words in his letter, and a few days later, she wrote a letter to say thank you.

He sent a few pages about himself in reply, saying, 'Please do not think I am one of those young men who is after pretty girls, but you and your voice just got into me as if I had known you all my life.' He wrote about his family, his life in Colombo and his limited knowledge about her place. Trincomalee was a British naval base during the second world war, due to its natural harbour, a God given blessing for docking warships for the battle against Japan who were bombing British ships relentlessly.

He cited in his letter what he had learned about her village, reading his travelogue almost as a poem.

> 'The sea's treasures of a multitude of corals.
> Ancient temples, people from various religions
> and cultures. Tasty seafood.
> Magnificent historical navy dockyard, buildings
> and houses'.

Her friends in the house were as excited as she was when he asked her for a date. They were Tamil girls and were never allowed to be with a young man until they married. But Mina had been in love when she was at school, 'a baby love', she told them.

But the world was changing. Western music and attitudes were influencing them, and the lives of young people were taking a completely different direction, now.

Of the other two, Mary and Kala were teachers like Rathi. Mina worked at the bank.

When she opened the door, all three friends practically swamped her with questions.

'How was it?' Mary asked. She attended a Christian girls' college and had very little to do with boys except within her family.

First Date

The others, too, waited for Rathi's answer.

'Did he kiss you?' Kala's voice was so sexy, as she mimicked the English films she loved. She especially loved the kissing scenes.

'What?' Rathi's voice screeched with confusion. 'People don't kiss on the first date, do they?' she asked naively.

'Did he hold your hand?' Mina's eyes almost pierced Rathiga's face.

'No.' Now, Rathi was feeling uncomfortable.

'He did not touch you?' all three chorused together in loud voices.

'No.' Rathiga looked at them sternly.

'No touching, no kissing, then what did you do?' Kala seemed disappointed with no sexy bits on the first date.

'We went to lunch.' Rathi's face lit with delight when she informed them that Siva had asked her, 'Do you prefer a vegetarian meal?'

Rathi said firmly, 'Not really, I like non-veg, but one of my sisters always eats vegetarian. Amma (Mother) cooks a lot with vegetables, but I am free to choose my meals.'

Siva smiled at her said, 'Thank you for telling me. I am a vegetarian, but I do not expect anyone to follow me.' She was happy that he did not say, 'I do not want to sit in front of the fish and chicken curry'.

'What are you grinning about?' Mary asked, expressing her displeasure on hearing of the non-saucy outing.

'So, you went to lunch, then what else were you two up to all these six hours?' Mina questioned irritably.

'He said he wanted me to understand him.' Rathi stopped talking for a minute and looked at them proudly. She wanted them to understand how lucky she was to have a boyfriend like Siva. Who was not in a rush to force his feelings on a young girl who does not yet understand the meaning of love.

'What did he do or say for you to understand him?' Kala's face seemed a bit bored.

'He read me a book,' Rathi smiled as if remembering Siva next to her.

'What book, the Kamasutra?' Kala smiled naughtily.

'What is Kamasutra?' Rathi asked them.

'A book about sex, a book that will tell you about the sixty four positions for having sex,' Kala whispered sexily into Rathi's ear.

'No, he said he wanted to see an equal society.' None said a word; they even seemed a bit annoyed. This was not the juicy gossip they had hoped for.

'What did he read to you?'

'The Communist Manifesto.'

'The Communist Manifesto?' all three girls chorused in unison, then were silent for a moment. What man would spend a first romantic day out together more interested in a book than the pretty girl?

'Well, did you understand it?' said Mary. 'Did it help you to understand him?'

'I did not understand at first, but I began to understand it bit by bit.' Rathi said she was a good student and wanted to 'please the teacher'. She looked at her friends' faces and said, 'I was not concentrating on his reading. I was looking at his handsome face, very closely listening to his beautiful voice.'

This was more like the account Kala wanted to hear, and she clapped her hands eagerly. 'And? And? What else?' she asked.

'I just wanted to sit next to him; it gave me a sense of being in heaven. Every time he turned to explain something I desperately wanted him to kiss me.'

'Oh my god, you're in love,' said Mina.

All three sighed rapturously, wishing for such an experience to happen to them.

'I suppose I am,' said Rathi. 'I never knew how romance could change a person's feelings. By being next to each other, smelling one another. From time to time we unexpectedly touched, and it gave me a kind of electric vibration in my body and mind, it just took me into another world.'

'Oh, being in love is beautiful,' pronounced Mina.

Uncle Charlie

by Brian T. Marshall

Everyone deserves an Uncle Charlie. In my case, I actually had one.

Still, growing up, it took me a while to appreciate my good fortune. To comprehend what an uncle could be. A window into another world. A peek at the big what-if. A glimpse of who my father might've been, if he hadn't been my father.

Maybe it was that time Charlie showed up at a party, my sister Anne's twelfth birthday, clutching a bottle of off-brand scotch and sporting a five o'clock shadow. Or maybe the way he'd commandeer the stereo sometimes, lose the ticky-tacky stuff my parents would play, Herb Alpert and Julie London, and sneak in the latest album from Miles or, God forbid, Ornette Coleman. Not that he ever got loud or obnoxious, or prove an embarrassment, but he always brought it with him. A whiff of something dangerous. A smoke alarm going off.

He was the youngest of three children, with my father being the oldest, and perhaps it was that fact alone, the primacy of rank, that determined their personalities. Or maybe it was just the name. Charlie. Never Charles or Chuck, and certainly not Chas, and I often wondered, if you were to dig up his birth certificate, would those same seven letters be typed right on it, for all the world to see. Because some names are hard to live up to. Thaddeus or Rex. But Charlie came with a wink and a nod. Nobody here but us chickens. The kind of name you could loan five bucks and not care if you ever got it back.

Plus, he was a bachelor. One who liked to play the field. Which meant that part of the fun of having Charlie show up was seeing who he brought in tow. Tawdry girls, a good decade younger, with a run or two in their hose, chattering away, Winstons burning, trying so hard to win us all over. Interspersed at least twice a year with some glacial, well-heeled matron, already regretting her choice of men, her attempt to walk on the wild side. Younger, older, rich or poor, Charlie treated them the same. As if they were lucky, being there with him. As if they'd won the lotto.

And what did my father think of all this? I never quite managed to ask. Sometimes he'd get a certain look, wise and beneficent, and you could tell how much it meant to him, having Charlie in his stable. And other times you could see him wishing, just once, he could haul off and pop him one. Because my dad was someone who'd always toed the line, slogging his way through school, then the army, and finally marrying a sensible girl. And having someone like Charlie around was a reminder. A repudiation. This wasn't the world they'd both grown up in. Good guys now finished last. And, really, who would you rather be? The poor fool who actually owned the bank, or the one who'd just slipped out the back, bag in hand, bound for parts unknown.

But whatever they shared, love or hatred, it doesn't matter anymore. Because, about five years ago, my father died. And apparently now, Charlie has, too.

I first heard about it through my sister, Anne. She always did love bad news. Charlie had been off my radar for a while, living in a trailer down south, scraping by on Social Security and cheap booze from CVS. Being a bachelor had proven, for my uncle at least, to serve as both blessing and curse. For twenty, almost thirty years, he'd been the envy of every married man in the neighbourhood. Only to wake up one morning, a lonely old fart, instead. I'd been meaning to get down there since forever, but like most things in life, I'd stalled, and fretted, and run down the clock, and finally won the big prize. One less goodbye to face.

Only it turned out that just like always, Charlie would have the last word. Maybe he'd scored his own winning ticket, or pinched pennies over the years. By whatever means, foul or fair, he'd saved up enough to finance one last indulgence. A funeral. With a big black hearse, and a handmade casket, and a hole carved into the ground. Hearing this, I had to smile. Admire his audacity. Because when was the last time you went to a real funeral, instead of some hokey celebration? Had a chance to wear your one good suit before they were burying you in it.

I ended up making the journey alone. An eight-hour drive, give or take. With a small pint bottle tucked in my lap, in honour of the deceased. I own a new car, or close enough, but I'd left it in the garage, opting instead for my battered old Chevy, far more suited to the occasion. Radio stations fading in and out. Ragged clouds that harass the horizon. Sometimes when we count the miles we travel through time instead. Once or twice, I would feel a hand on my head, a Dutch rub softly rendered. The gentle perfume of whiskey breath, unless it was my own I was smelling. As dusk finally hit, the walls closed in, and I'd entered a narrow tunnel, the cone of my headlights a static place that the Chevy never quite reached.

Until it finally does.

Bleary-eyed, I spot some neon. What they once called a motor court. Sad stucco walls and fading palms and a tear in the window screen. Lying back, the road's still there, and I'm way too wired to sleep, and then somehow there's light streaming into the room and another day has begun. It's a half-hour drive to the funeral home and I get there way too early, then kill some time in a crappy little diner that insults me with their coffee. Why am I here, I wonder. What debt do I hope to repay? Or have I shown up out of spite instead, a thumb in my father's eye. If Charlie were around, he could probably tell me, maybe turn it into a joke. One from Column A, to go. White rice on the side.

When I wander back to the funeral home, the scene is way past depressing. A big white room that they're calling a chapel, with five people waiting inside. One of them claims to be a priest. The rest are older, weathered men who have showered, shaved, put on what they have in the way of good clothes. And, of course, there's Charlie. I stare straight ahead at the gleaming wooden box as the priest finds his place at the lectern. Starts to speak, in Hallmark tones, of some guy whose name is Charles. Charles? For a moment I want to rush the riser. Launch a full body tackle. But of course I just sit there, a silent lump, enduring this indignity. Hoping that if my uncle has heard, he'll count this as one more joke.

The easy thing would be skipping what follows. No trip to the cemetery. But then I think about all the money Charlie has wasted, and the hearse that waits outside, and how pathetic the procession will already look, let alone with another car missing. It's bad enough that I'm first in line, right behind the hearse, lending it, too, a look of squalor, of life's hopes now derailed. From behind the wheel, I watch heads spin, then quickly snap back into place. Angry, resentful at this reminder of the journey they'll take soon enough.

The cemetery is on a rise, at the very edge of town, the only speck of green for miles, except, of course, for the golf course. In the few brief minutes of our drive, the sky has started to darken, and as I step outside my car, I can feel a breeze from the east. A presentment of rain, just in time for his funeral. Does Charlie really have that much clout?

Ignoring the clouds, I stare past the hearse, towards a hole up on the hill, and a mound of sandy soil, spilling out onto the grass. It looks like someone, a worker most likely, is already waiting for us, or perhaps he's another friend of my uncle who wasn't at the chapel. And then I pause. Look more closely. Realize it's a woman, not a man, who's standing there by the grave, dressed in black slacks and jacket. All at once I understand what's been nagging away at me. Not just the depressing turnout, or the mangling of his name, but the fact that not a single woman would be on-hand to send him off. Even though women—the pursuit of them, the pleasing of them, the sometimes defiling of them—was the one thing that gave his life meaning.

With my three fellow mourners lagging behind, I work my way up the hill. Use that ascent to check out the stranger who's somehow beaten us there. She's tall. Slender. Almost waifish, except the years are wrong. No tender colt, fresh to the game, but probably in her late fifties. I'd always been drawn to older women, that poignancy they bear, the loamy scent of autumn soil in lieu of spring's brash flowers. And if I'm right about her age, then it's possible that we've crossed paths before. That she might have been one of those tart young things hanging off his arm. Putting up with all his nonsense.

Feeling my gaze, she nods back once. Returns her eyes to the ground. Soon enough we're joined by the others, panting and huffing away. And, it turns out, they're not the only ones hard at work. Down by the hearse, I see them gathered, six men and a single dark box, enacting a dance that's older than time, one final waltz before closing. With slow, measured steps they start to climb towards us. Our friend, our priest, takes the rear. The sky is now a solemn grey, a lid pressing down on us all.

Eventually they mount the hill. Their burden is placed by the grave. Some kind of portable metal stand that protests against the weight. The six men take a few steps back while the priest, in turn, strides forward, and then it's a whisper of brittle leaves as he paws away at his Bible.

Mark. Matthew. Thou and Thee. All that gilded claptrap. So lulling, so hypnotic, I almost don't hear it, the sound of footsteps behind me. Not wanting to turn my head or stare, I can only sense a new presence, catch a telltale whiff of perfume, a jangle that could be a bracelet. And then a few seconds later, from my left side this time, comes something else; a cough. Or I don't know, maybe a sob. I can see the priest's eyes dart over that way, and for a second his voice stumbles. The word of God not quite as enticing as whoever he sees standing there.

Another minute, and he wraps things up. The six men are granted an encore. Three nylon straps, a deep, shocking crimson, are slung around the casket. Lowering it down into that hole, it's got to be a workout, but all half-dozen do their best to hide any sign of strain. The straps are retrieved, but one catches a little, a perilous hint of slapstick, and then the men, their duty fulfilled, all shuffle off downhill.

Or at least they try.

Because as we've stood there, all grim reflection, a sea change has occurred. A miracle as grand, as gaudy, as any loaves or fishes. Below us, around us, filling the slope, there is now a horde of women, more than mere dozens, maybe close to a hundred, too numerous to count. Some are so frail they can barely stand upright. Some so young they're more like girls. The only thing they all have in common being their gender and a fondness for black.

My eyes, unbelieving, scan the crowd. Find more eyes staring back. Some dry, even hostile, or at least resolute, some all but lost to tears. Sobs. Hiccups. Quiet moaning. A starburst of ululation.

The wringing of hands, and the slumping of shoulders, and the protestations of the flesh. They can't all be his, I tell myself. Not even spread over a lifetime. And besides, a good third, they're way too young, unless...

Unless as Charlie grew older, the women grew younger still.

And then my thoughts, my speculations, they're all blown straight to hell. The morning air is rent in two by a scream of desolation.

It's her, the woman by the grave. The very first one to arrive. Staring down at that hole carved into the ground, demanding an explanation. But of course, there is none. We live. We die. There's nothing else. Nowhere to go but in there.

In there. As if she's read my thoughts somehow, or I had foretold hers, she suddenly leaps forward. Finds the grave. Sends herself hurtling down, feet first, into that patch of darkness.

Motionless, I keep on watching, waiting for something to happen. The sound of her body hitting the casket. A second scream, this one from pain. The sight of her standing back up again, clawing her way to the grass. But instead there is nothing. Nothing. Dazed, I stumble a few steps forward. Peer into the grave. Am greeted not by her or the coffin, but instead by an absolute darkness. A passageway to nowhere.

For a lifetime or two, I stand there, staring. This can't be happening. And then a hand grabs at my shoulder, shoving me to the side, and another woman goes hurtling past, aiming for the grave. Instinctively my own hand reaches out, tries to snag her jacket, but I'm too slow, too numb and stupid, and so watch her disappear.

By now they're all at it, surging forward. Scrambling towards the grave. Lemmings, or harpies, or God knows what, all bent on their own destruction. Do some of them, a handful even, hesitate for just a moment? Struggle against that pull? Or is what Charlie gave them, what they gave in return, stronger even than death? An end unto itself.

At some point I must get knocked to the ground. Mashed into the trampled grass. Spiked heels flailing away at my back, black pumps finding my ribs. And of course, by then, I'm barely conscious, what with all that pounding away, but I'd almost swear I can feel the earth, seething away beneath me. As if it's hungry for this meal. For this sacrifice.

After a while, it finally stops. The panic, the tumult, is over. A gentle rain, little more than a drizzle, cascades down from above. Sitting up, I glance around. Realize I'm alone. The women in black, the few scattered mourners, the priest and his six strong men. All gone. Fled perhaps to some kind of safety, or sucked into the grave.

The grave.

Without even thinking, I force myself up. Stumble my way on over. Interrogate that hole in the earth, or else it interrogates me. And then, ever so faintly, a voice.

Mikey.

I start a little, hearing this. A voice I haven't heard in years.

Mikey. I know you're up there.

Charlie? I ask back. Is that really you?

Come on down, the voice tells me.

No, I insist. I can't.

C'mon, Mikey. I promise that I'll share.

I stare at the hole.

Take a deep breath.

What else can I do but jump?

He Will Be Home, Always

by Rajes Bala (Rajeswary Balasubramaniam)

Geeta was angry. 'Why can't Latha see the situation she is in?' she asked herself many times.

Geeta was an honest person and did not care much about her looks or money. She did what she wanted to do and had no hesitation in saying exactly what she thought about politics, books or art. And she was worried about her sister.

Latha was a beautiful, tolerant, smart, dutiful married woman with two lovely small kids. She was married to doctor Ravi, who was an excellent dermatologist doing very well in private practice in London. There were no problems with him regarding money, managing the family or loving Latha.

According to Latha, they were 'suitable partners' and 'very good parents'. They had expensive family holidays in fascinating faraway places. Both their parents visited them alternately every other year. They visited and invited family members for birthdays or Divali and had frequent parties with friends.

'We're a happily married couple,' Latha would state, with the widest smile spreading across her face when she saw Geeta's questioning look.

Geeta did not see them as perfect nor suitable. She knew and so did practically everyone close to Ravi that he had a 'bit on the side'. The Eastern way of saying, 'we knew but we chose not to see IT'.

He Will Be Home, Always

Geeta thought that she should do something about her brother in-law's affair. She didn't want her sister to be taken for a ride. 'Ravi, I'm going to tell your wife,' she wanted to scream at him when she saw him in central London. He was coming out of a posh restaurant with an exceptionally beautiful and elegant young woman, who was holding his hand as one does when in love.

That day Geeta was coming out of a women's rights meeting, at which she'd expressed her view. For their own betterment, she'd told the room, 'women must come out and express their problems within their marriages. We're often prevented from doing that because of societal norms.' Geeta was a writer, dedicating her life to equality and fairness in the world. It broke her heart to see her sister being taken for a fool.

At first, when Geeta saw Ravi with the young woman, she was confused for a minute or so. Then she was shocked, upset and angry. How could he? He was the father of her niece and nephew. Her blood boiled. She looked at him, angrily and wanted to insult him publicly, but she saw one of the women who had been at the meeting coming towards to her.

When she went to visit her sister at their expensive house in Chelsea, Latha was busy organising a dinner party. Geeta told her what she had seen. Geeta was in tears when she described the scene where the couple had locked hands.

Latha did not seem to react in shock or anger. 'Aren't you going to ask him?' Geeta yelled.

'No,' Latha said calmly, not looking at her sister. Busy arranging plates. 'We're one of those couples who don't ask each other a lot of questions.' Latha continued as though nothing had happened. Geeta wanted to shake her.

'Geeta, whatever he does out of this house is none of my business, as he always comes home on time, unless there's an emergency. When he's here, he does whatever a father and a husband should do.'

Latha picked up one of the plates and gave it a quick polish with her sleeve. She examined her face reflected in it with a satisfied smile. 'What more do you think I want? she said.

Untethered

by Susie Helme

You lie immobile on your back, one eye teasingly open a tiny bit, but there is no awareness in it. Your left leg, paralysed in the fall; lies heavily at the corner; you'll never walk again.

Every part of your body is anchored to some machine by cords or tubes; beeps and whistles call nurses to medication that needs renewing. In your lucid moments, you've pleaded, 'get all this stuff off of me', but the stuff cannot be taken off. What's keeping you tethered to that bed is keeping you tethered to this life.

Now, you can't even talk. A great plastic tube is shoved down your throat into your lungs, and a tube through your nose goes down into your stomach. A tube comes out your side to drain your lungs.

Tubes come out the other end to collect your eliminations, which nurses measure every hour. Your body is tethered to the bed; all your bodily functions are monitored by machines.

People send me in with books, radios—but there's no point. You can't read; you can't speak; you can't push a button. You are a vegetable. I push your part-open eye open and call your name twice. A muscle moves in your face. You can hear me. Underneath the vegetable is the man. He is not tethered. His spirit roams the cosmos.

Your fingers don't work to use your phone. No matter, you'd told me, your eyes have established an internet connection. You're watching *Doctor Who*. There's Peter Capaldi behind the nurse's desk.

I urge you to travel to the Matrix where you can get a new heart, new lungs, a new left leg. But once you're done, come back, come back.

Sitting across from you at work, drinking real ale down the pub, sharing a Large Lamb Shish at the Turkish restaurant, doing the cryptic crossword, watching *Doctor Who*. These kept me tethered; you kept me tethered.

If you don't come back, my spirit, too, will roam.

Ringo

by em.thompson

I ran across him on Hampstead Hill. Out for a leisurely stroll, I was happily minding my own business when I saw him step into the road in front of a bus, raise a hand and nod at a nearby layby. When the bus pulled up at the kerb, he broke into a supercilious smile, stuck up a thumb and gestured for the driver to move on. Pointedly ignoring the conductor's two-fingered parting wave, he sat down on a municipal bench, took out a paperback book and turned to the last page.

Not having much else to do, I sat down beside him and watched the world go by. Maybe I hoped that he would comment on the weather or the state of the nation or somesuch. No such luck. He seemed preoccupied with passing traffic. Odd, I thought.

When another bus drove around the corner, he said, 'excuse me, young man,' entrusted his book to my care, strode purposefully into the road and raised a hand. When the bus—a number twenty-nine, as I recall—pulled up, he gave the driver a nod, then sent him on his way with a flick of a wrist. Pleased as Punch, he returned to the bench.

I gave him back his book and, to make conversation, asked, 'wrong bus?'

'No idea,' he said. 'Looked much like all the others to me.' He opened the paperback, flicked through the pages, asked, 'read it?' and when I shrugged, said, 'don't bother. It's a waste of a dead tree.'

'But didn't it win that prize?' I clicked my fingers in an attempt to dislodge the name from the tip of my tongue. I failed, so settled for, 'the Whatchamacallit Award.'

'Probably,' he said. 'Most of her novels do. The only reason I buy them is to impress the likes of you. Can't abide her pseudo-intellectual claptrap. Between you and me, I am more of a Beatrix Potter aficionado. Gripping stuff, what?' Lost in a literary daze, he sat back with his hands behind his head and stretched his legs. 'Nice weather for the time of year,' he said for no apparent reason.

Well, it wasn't raining, but I would hardly have called the weather nice. Cold and overcast, there was a distinct chill in the air. Nevertheless, to be polite, I smiled and nodded.

All of a sudden, he gripped my knee, said, 'don't go anywhere, son. Won't be a tick,' jumped to his feet, ran into the road and flagged down a double-decker. When it screeched to a juddering halt, he scowled at the driver, shook his head and wagged a finger. Then, as it drove off, he resumed his stewardship of the bench.

'Where was I?' he asked, not that I greatly cared. 'Oh, yes. Thing is, the crux of a novel is the denouement, so stands to reason that the logical place to start is at the end. Let's face it—why waste valuable time reading literary vomit penned by an opinionated halfwit who knows less about the ways of the world than your average earthworm? So...' he said with a purposeful clap of the hands. 'Where are we having lunch?'

'We?' I said, not sure what he had in mind.

'Yes,' he said. 'I will let you decide.'

Although taken aback by his presumption, not having anything better to do, I pointed to a pub some way down the road. 'Does the Boar's Head do food?' I asked.

'No idea,' he said. 'Let's find out.'

As we walked, I studied him from the corner of an eye. A good deal older than me, he had an upright bearing—an officer and a gentleman once upon a time, I suspected. Clean-shaven with straggly shoulder-length grey hair, I fancied his club blazer, top pocket handkerchief, bow tie, waistcoat and silver handled cane a mite incongruous with drainpipe jeans and blue suede shoes. Being a polite sort, I introduced myself expecting a handshake, or at the very least a nod of acknowledgement, but he just looked me over, head to one side, and asked, 'have you always been so tall?'

'Not when I was little,' I quipped.

'Well, I never.' He seemed surprised. 'Ah, here we are.' He paused outside the pub and studied the menu. 'So,' he said. 'What are we having?'

I must admit that I was feeling peckish. Breakfast at the O'Leary household usually consists of a mug of black coffee—two, if I'm hungry. 'Must say, the shepherd's pie looks tempting,' I had to say. 'But so does the spaghetti Bolognese.'

He peered through the window and whetted his lips. 'Make up your mind, son,' he said. 'What's it to be?'

'Think I'll plump for the shepherd's pie,' I said after weighing up the odds. 'What about you?'

'Ah, you might well ask. But that's for another day,' he said with a wistful sigh. Stoically stiffing his upper lip, he pushed through the door, strode up to the bar and hammered a fist on the counter. He ordered two shepherd's pies, told the barman that I was paying, added, 'think I'll have a pint of whatever my friend is having. Put it on his tab,' and gave me a nod.

Glass in hand, he led the way to a table by the fire, sat down, took a sip of beer and raised an eyebrow. 'I say,' he said. 'How very quaint. What is it?'

'Real ale,' I told him. 'The local brew.'

'Taste's foul. Still, dare say it will lubricate the tonsils. Ah…

here comes the shepherd's pie.' He looked about and frowned. 'No sign of sheep, though, unless my eyes are playing up.' He gave his lunch a circumspect prod. 'Funny sort of pie. I mean, forgive me if I'm barking up the wrong tree, but from what I can tell, it is topped with potato, not pastry. Hardly a pie, is it?'

He sampled a forkful and raised an eyebrow. 'Not bad,' he said. 'Not bad at all. If I'm not wrong, there is some kind of meat under the potato. Well, I'll be blowed.'

By and large, we ate in silence. When he finished, he mopped his plate with a slice of bread then raised a hand to attract the barman's eye. He called, 'second helpings if you would, my good man,' turned to me and said, 'how about you?' When I shook my head, he said, 'please yourself,' drained his glass and asked, 'another?'

'Don't mind if I do,' I said.

'No. What I mean is, you are welcome to buy me another pint of this bilge water if you like. I won't object.'

Now, as it happens, I had had an unexpected windfall that morning. The portable garage I listed on eBay fetched shedloads more than I expected, so I was in a generous mood. 'Go on, then,' I said. 'Feel free.'

'In that case,' he said. 'I'll have a double whisky, a gin chaser and four Havana cigars. No—make it five.'

I proffered a parsimonious smile. My beneficence did not stretch to Havana cigars. So, I stonewalled him with, 'mind if I ask you something?'

'Depends,' he said. 'Is it personal?'

'No. Not at all.'

'Oh.' He sounded disappointed. 'Fire away, then.'

'Why did you stop all those buses?'

'What the devil do you mean?' He stared at me as if I was

demented. 'Didn't you see the sign?'

'Sign?'

'On the lamppost by my bench. Bus Stop, it says in large letters.' He emphasised the word stop, imbuing it with an almost mystical significance.

'Well, yes. But...'

'There are no ifs or buts about it, laddie. Bus Stop it says, so I regard it as my duty as an upstanding citizen to make sure that they do.'

'Aha,' I said. 'I see.' Although I didn't. Not really.

'The problem with this country is that nobody pays the slightest heed to the letter of the law. You know, I have lost count of the number of buses I have seen drive past that sign without stopping. And this...' He waved his fork at his plate. 'I ask you—anyone in their right mind can see it isn't pie. Should be called meat mash. It's like that book I'm reading...'

'Hang about,' I said. 'You turned straight to the last page. I would hardly call that reading a book.'

He ignored me. 'That book,' he said with a note of contempt in his voice, 'is not worth the paper it was written on. Utter tripe. Boy meets girl. Boy and girl fall in love. Boy abandons girl and joins the Royal Navy. Girl throws herself under a train. So what? I ask you, where is the drama, the tension, the riveting suspense? From what I could see, there was no mention of car chases, Napoleon Bonaparte, submarines, boy wizards or alien invaders. Not a dickey bird.

'Anyway. when push comes to shove, what does it matter if the silly girl couldn't cope with rejection? If you want my opinion, she was better off without him. Reading between the lines, he was a wimp. More to the point, what about the train driver, eh? You tell me that. Let's face it, you don't expect a total stranger to jump in front of your train just because an ambitious hack in a snooty suburb of North London wants to sell a bunch of books and win a prize that no one has ever heard of. Yes indeed—the train driver was the true victim. But did the author give a damn? Did she, buggery.

'She doesn't mention all the sleepless nights he must have had, reduced to a nervous wreck by the rattle of her word processor. Wouldn't be surprised if the poor chap didn't develop post-traumatic stress disorder, lose his job, become an alcoholic and—cruelly abandoned by family and friends—go to an early grave. Seems the author was only too happy to ruin the poor wretch's life—and to what end? I will tell you. Because she did not have the gumption to come up with a more bombastic ending for her hogwash.

'Outrageous. The long and the short of it is, her sorry excuse for a novel doesn't hold a candle to Squirrel Nutkin or Peter Rabbit. Now they are true icons of literary fiction. And as for Miss Potter's illustrations... top notch. Hardly surprising that F.R. Leavis hailed her as a seminal influence on Georges Remi... Hergé to the man on the Clapham omnibus. Ask yourself... would Tintin have seen the light of day without Mrs. Tiggy-Winkle? I think not.'

At a loss for anything meaningful to say, it struck me that I had not the first idea who he was, so I held out a hand and said, 'sorry, but I didn't catch your name.'

'Winston,' he said. 'Winston Churchill.' When I laughed out loud, he barked, 'find that funny, do you, sonny?'

'Oh, come on. Pull the other leg. Winston Churchill died years ago,' I said.

'Ah, that is where you are wrong, young fellow, me lad.' He put down his knife and fork, tucked his thumbs into his waistcoat pockets, puffed out his chest and looked me squarely in the eye.

'It was just a ruse to put them off the scent.'

By now, I had heard enough. More than enough, I dare say. 'Good grief, is that the time?' I nodded at a clock behind the bar. 'Must dash. I'm late for an important meeting.'

'Think I'll join you,' he said. 'Haven't been to an important meeting since Yalta.' He got to his feet, buttoned up his waistcoat, pocketed his book and tucked his cane under an arm. 'So who else will be there?'

'Julia Roberts,' I fibbed. Fact was, I hadn't seen her since she ran off with that bloke from the bookshop. To be honest, if I never saw her again, it would be too soon. These days I buy my books online.

'Jolly good. Maybe the three of can go for a wander. How about Regent's Park?' he suggested. 'Feed the ducks. Then we'll pop back to your place for a quick snifter before you take us out to dinner. I know...' He stuck a finger in the air. 'How about we catch a show in The West End? I'll let you pay.'

Highly unamused, I said, 'now look here, Winston or whatever your name is, I have plans, and you don't figure in them.'

'Well, that's a fine to do,' he said, bristling with indignation. 'So, this is all the thanks I get for letting you buy me lunch. I will have you know that I was perfectly happy minding my bus stop until you dragged me along to this ghastly pub. Now if you don't mind, I need to powder my nose.' Without another word, he unzipped his flies and headed for the toilet.

'Quite a character, isn't he?' the barman said as he cleared the table.

I smiled politely. 'You mean Winston? He's a bit... well, batty, I suppose.'

'Who is Winston?'

'Winston Churchill.' I nodded in the direction of the gents.

'That's his name.'

'Don't take this the wrong way, mate,' the barman said. 'But if you believe that, you'll believe anything. Don't you recognise him? That's Ringo Starr, that is. Mind, he's older than he used to be. And thinner. Something to do with fame, he reckons. Doesn't surprise me. Look what it did to Elvis,' he said with a shudder and a grimace.

'Never carries cash,' he added matter-of-factly. 'Doesn't believe in it. Don't suppose you would either, if you grew up in Liverpool. Likes to stay under the radar. That's what he told me, anyway. It's why he always demands drinks on the house.' Ignoring my incredulous expression, he returned to the bar, tray in hand, humming, 'we all live in a yellow submarine.'

'Fit to make a move,' Winston asked when he returned from his ablutions, tucking in his vest.

'That bloke…' I pointed to the barman. 'Thinks you're Ringo Starr.'

'Preposterous,' he scoffed. 'Do you honestly think that I would let you buy me lunch if I used to be a Beatle? Give me some credit, please.'

We were about to make tracks when a flustered nurse ran in—blue scrubs, hair tied back, clipboard under an arm. Moments later, she was joined by two burly men in white coats.

Winston ducked under the table, tugged my trouser leg and whispered, 'if they ask, say you haven't seen me. Mum's the word.' He pressed a finger to his lips and held his breath.

The taller and balder of the whitecoats checked the toilet while the other cased the joint. The flustered nurse, whom I took to be in charge, clicked her fingers at the barman and said, 'seen Ringo?'

'Depends,' the bartender said, nonchalantly polishing a squeaky glass with a beer towel.

'Watch your lip,' nursey said. 'I asked you a simple question. Yes or no.'

'Yes,' he said. 'But then again, no.'

Underneath the table, Winston pumped a fist and whispered, 'that's my boy.'

I raised a hand. 'Excuse me,' I said. 'This Ringo chap. Why are you looking for him?'

The flustered nurse glanced at her colleagues. 'I'd rather not say,' she said guardedly. 'Patient-doctor confidentiality.'

And that was when a veritable mint of pennies dropped. 'You wouldn't be from the local hospital, by any chance?' said I.

'And what, may I ask,' said she, 'does it have to do with you?'

Ignoring a muted whimper by my ankles, I shrugged and said, 'there's a chance I might be able to help.'

'This is highly irregular, but as we're in a hurry, I can't see it will do any harm.' The flustered nurse pulled a chair up to the table, sat down, frowned and said, 'what's that?' when she heard a muffled grunt below decks.

'The landlord's Labradoodle,' I said with my fingers crossed. 'So tell me, why are you looking for Winston?'

The flustered nurse gave her colleagues a pertinent glance. 'Winston, eh?' she said. 'So, I take it that you have seen him. He has a habit of introducing himself as Winston Churchill when he's had a tipple. Likes nothing more than a whisky and a cigar after lunch, does Ringo. Don't suppose he mentioned buses?'

'As it happens, I met him at a bus stop just up the road. Ouch…' I bit my lip as Winston buried his teeth in my leg. That was the final straw. I said, 'tell me why you're looking for him, and I may be able to point you in the right direction.'

'He's needed on the ward. It's an emergency. Code red,' the flustered nurse said with a hint of desperation in her voice. 'We've turned the hospital upside down and checked every bus stop north of the Thames, some of them twice. If we can't find him, my job will be on the line.'

Hardly had the flustered nurse finished panicking than, to everyone's surprise, Winston crawled out from beneath the table. He shuffled to his feet, dusted himself down and brushed the sawdust out of his hair. 'My dear Nurse Jabberwocky,' he said sheepishly. 'I assure you that I had no intention of causing you any grief. Heaven forbid.'

'You naughty, naughty boy,' the flustered nurse scolded, more Nursey McPhee than Florence Nightingale. She checked her watch and said, 'right you are... the ward round starts at three. If we hurry, we should be back in time.'

Winston hung his head, a perfidious picture of penitence—solemn and contrite—as Nanny McNurse took his arm and frogmarched him out to a waiting ambulance leaving the orderlies to lubricate their tonsils at the bar.

When he saw me staring at him, the shorter and the hairier of the two put down his glass and said, 'tragic,' with a sorrowful shake of the head.

'Indeed,' I said. 'If you don't mind me asking, what is the prognosis?'

'Prognosis?' He seemed puzzled. Then he broke into a grin and said, 'you don't think... ' Slowly, very slowly, the grin grew wider until it stretched from ear to ear. 'No, no—you've got the wrong end of the stick. Professor Starr isn't a patient. He is a consultant. Head of the Psychiatry Department, no less. An extremely distinguished man. A little eccentric, maybe, but he has a brilliant mind.'

Whelmed with admiration, he clasped his hands to his chest, looked to the heavens and sighed. 'And what a drummer... Check out Sergeant Pepper's Lonely Hearts Club Band. His timekeeping is awesome. If you ask me, the Fab Four would have been nothing without him.'

And with that bombshell, he drained his glass, wiped his mouth on a sleeve and swaggered out of the door singing, 'I get by with a little help from my friends,' leaving me to scratch my head... baffled, befuddled and bemused.

Glacial

by Elaine Graham-Leigh

It's 2am and the guy next door is going to the ice machine. I turn over stickily and listen to the scrape of his front door over the carpet, the footsteps padding along the hall and the mutter of the processor as it reads his card. In my mind's eye I watch him, unshaven in a singlet and once-white shorts, a dressing gown slung over his shoulders for the sake of a propriety he only dimly feels. His eyes are fogged with lack of sleep; forgetting the surveillance, as he waits he scratches his balls.

When they first put the cameras in, I remember how angry everyone was, thinking of how they would rub themselves, squeeze their spots or pick their noses in the late-night corridors when no one was around. They imagined the security guards laughing at them, seeing them the next morning with a mocking glint in their eye. It was almost a campaign, but it's so quick, how everyone forgets.

The ice comes with a rattle, shocking him awake, and I wonder why I'm so unfair about someone I've never even seen. He slides the plastic tray out and back and shuffles past my door to his flat.

When I was young I didn't understand ice machines: only Americans had them. Ice cubes to me came in plastic trays that you filled from the tap and put in the freezer shelf in the top of the fridge. I never understood why you needed a machine to do it. On the summer afternoons that seemed hot then, I would fill a pint glass with the cubes and stick my face into it, breathing in the coolness that was more than I could stand. Sometimes they wouldn't come out however much you bent the tray and you had to resort to the hot tap on the base and swearing.

My mother had the knack, but of ice cubes she was an acolyte. She used to eat them every evening, sitting curled up over the tea towel with the tray and her novel on the kitchen counter, crunching, and I knew that no one could disturb her, not even me. Watching her, quiet and serious, flicking the cubes out with the ease of long practice, I suppose I thought that Americans had no patience to learn such skills. Not for them the hard path, the study and the mastery, not for they who had the money to do otherwise. When I was very young I even admired their thoughtless ease, their carelessness, as the machines whirred and sighed their fumes into the warming air.

Even with the air conditioning it's too hot to sleep. I turn onto my back and watch the colours of the adverts on the tower opposite reflected onto the wall above my bed. The soundtrack is loud enough that even through quintuple glazing I can feel it, the base reverberating through my spine like the treatments the carers nag me to buy.

Very faintly sometimes I think I can hear voices, and though I don't know if they're part of the soundtrack, I like to think they're the crowd. I know there are crowds down there, even though all I can see are the lights from the other towers and the orange sky. When I first moved here I used to try to watch them, but on the twenty-first floor, you're just too high up. I can't walk far these days, but if I have to, I can make the stairs in forty minutes so my insurers said it was alright. 'Risk adverse', it says on my file. That always makes me laugh.

There was a time when they said more about me than that.

There was a time when my file was pages thick, when they tapped my phone and read my mail and even, for a glimmer of a moment, thought me important. In the days when I was young, then middle aged, and spoke from platforms about the power of the people, done up in scarves against the winter that was not quite cold enough, even then. I spoke and they cheered, I worked and they responded, and somehow in a way I still don't quite understand the watched pot never boiled, and now here I am, aged in the dimness with the crowd far away from me, spending money behind their masks in the poisonous night.

There's a wasp in here, somewhere, I don't know how they get in when I haven't opened the door for days, but they always do. I can hear it buzzing against the window, knocking itself out in its desperation to get at the screens and the lights it thinks are flowers. A documentary I saw said they live off the dregs in Coke cans. I suppose they think they're flowers, too. It swoops low around the room, and despite the heat I pull the damp sheet over my ear.

My wallscreen flicks on for the hourly news. Someone (not my son, surely, he would have thought it unwise to encourage me) helpfully set it for current events when I moved in, and I've never worked out how to change it. They're talking about the Gulf Stream again, trying to reassure their viewers that something will be done in time. It won't turn off, we'll find a way, it will be alright. Maybe they believe it, those newscasters with nothing behind their eyes. Sometimes I believe them, and sometimes I don't, and sometimes all I think of is snow.

I'm not really old enough to have known snow, but I dream of it. The crisp white blanket, freezing, the air so cold your words come out like icicles. The sky hard as jet, the rivers still, the trees silhouetted stark against the sky. The sun goes down pink and red in fire and on the black background the white snow comes whirling; whirling, whirling, drifting down like judgement on a frozen world. I remember how people used to talk of the quietness, of waking in the morning with everything muffled and only a bird cheeping on the windowsill to show it had not all ended in the night. And I remember that now there are no birds.

It's getting light outside, behind the haze. The room is filled with the wallscreen burble, the swish of the traffic flying past outside and the shrill cries of the adverts. I won't sleep, but I close my eyes anyway, like the carers tell me to. I close my eyes against all of it, and I wait for the ice to come.

So Beautiful

by Susie Helme

You may recall the name Barton Mayfield. The story overshadowed the jollity that Christmas in the bourgeois suburb of Belleview. A shock-horror story can fill the column inches to satisfaction; but the media never tell you the story behind the story. That's because the families are not just aggrieved, they're ashamed.

Never again can they enjoy Yuletide festivities. Santa brings presents no more, just bad memories and tears. So it was for us. I still fill the kids' stockings, but no more parties, no more tinsel and jingle bells, no more family get-togethers, no more turkey and pumpkin pie.

To tell that story, I must go back to a time when we didn't think that anything was wrong. Barton had been a big soccer star at school, handsome, and the girls adored him. I went to all his games, his little brother, his biggest fan. I waved the pennant, held up one of those big styrofoam hands with 'Go Barton' on it. I worshipped him, then.

Then something happened that changed everything. After university, Bart started taking flying lessons and would go flying every weekend. On his first solo flight, he crashed the plane into a tree, killing his co-pilot Billy McGuire, and he himself was maimed. A broken leg left him with a persistent limp and his handsome face was all cut up. His back was crooked, throwing his chest forward on the right side.

Though of course there was an investigation, we didn't suspect pilot error; we bought his version of events. His explanation was that 'the damned anti-ice malfunctioned'. In the trauma of the surgery and the hospital stay and Billy's funeral, we accepted his story.

He never mourned Billy. Whenever anyone mentioned the boy, he just repeated his narrative of the crash. The story evolved, too, changed over time. He added bits to it, left out bits that people didn't seem to like. 'I told Billy to check the airspeed indicator, but the pitot tube was blocked. We were losing static pressure as we climbed out of the cloud.' We didn't know what the jargon meant; we just had a vague feeling that he'd decided to try to blame the accident on his co-pilot.

I only pieced the story together years later after talking to his therapist. As it turned out, I needed therapy myself.

'First off, after such a traumatic event, why did his story keep changing?' I asked the therapist. 'Wouldn't you remember every frightening detail? Wouldn't you ask yourself—Was it this? Was it that? Did I do anything wrong? And then, when questioned about the mashed-up body next to you, wouldn't you say something like, 'I'm so sorry. Poor Billy'?

'All he talked about was his own skill at piloting the plane though the icy storm,' I said. 'You know, he always referred to the accident as 'non-fatal'.' Although it had most certainly been fatal for Billy.

When the civil aviation people investigated the wreckage, they found nothing wrong with the anti-ice system nor the airspeed indicator. Nevertheless, they deemed the accident to have been caused by 'severe weather', encountered when the plane had veered from its flightpath.

The investigation revealed something else. We found this out during the insurance process. Replaying the cockpit voice recorder, they discovered that during take-off, Barton had decided to give Billy a Question and Training session, and, when not receiving the answers he wanted, gave the boy 'a right bollocking', after which the boy was virtually tongue-tied for the rest of the flight. Bart had not mentioned that. I got up the nerve to ask him about it, and he said, 'Billy was too green for solo flight.'

Now on reflection, I can see that the problem dated back earlier. He was always the big jock, the big star, I was the nerd. For every soccer game he won, I got some great grade on some exam. But he always made sure that his achievements were made the bigger deal. He directed talk at the dinner table to discussion of physical feats, eschewing intellectual topics. I didn't really mind because studying came easily to me, but he insisted on making it into a competition. If ever Mama or Daddy congratulated me on some academic achievement, he would immediately turn the conversation to his latest soccer game.

After the crash, Bart really changed. I mean, who wouldn't? How awful to go from being a handsome star to a misshapen cripple! But Bart carried it too far, becoming aggressive, as if challenging everyone to still love him despite his scars. We knocked ourselves out, still loving him, fell over ourselves trying to help him, make him feel better, convince him that life was still worth living even if you were no longer a handsome soccer star.

All those girls who'd adored him, he went back to them one by one. They sometimes gave him a date or two, but sooner or later, his behaviour would surface, and they'd break it off. At this point, he'd yell and scream at them about how they were prejudiced against him for being 'ugly' and being 'a cripple'. He'd claim to me or anyone else that the girl was 'a slut', 'a bitch', 'always mooning over jocks'. It really had nothing to do with that, though. By and large, women are not that superficial. They just couldn't indulge the passive-aggressive game he was pitching.

One girl, Betsy, later told me, 'He's charming and witty, but if you ever disagree with him, he just flips. On our first date, he got drunk at the restaurant, and kept noisily throwing his crippled leg around, as if daring me to trip over it.'

I noticed this was going on, and I tried to talk to him about it. After one date, I tried gently asking him how it went.

'She's a whore,' he pronounced. 'Told me she thinks that tosser Ben is cute.'

'What's wrong with that?' I said. 'Girls don't just go for looks.'

'Lucky for you,' he practically spat in my face. 'Goodness knows, I'm still better looking than you, even though you still have your face.'

The insurance kicked in, and we got him some expensive psychotherapy, but he didn't improve, even after four months of weekly sessions. Dr Parsons finally discontinued the treatment. At the time, we heard from Bart that the therapist's degree was 'from some podunk med school'. That story, too, evolved over time. He added that the doctor was 'an idiot, doesn't know what the hell he's talking about'; he was 'obsessed with the crash'.

Of course, that was not the story I got from Dr Parsons, years later when he no longer had to respect patient confidentiality. He told me, 'Barton simply refused to do the work. All his effort was spent trying to manipulate me.'

Manipulate. That was what it was. Bart was always manipulating people, even before the crash. He'd tell one person one thing and another person another, and when we compared notes and called him out on it, he'd get abusive. He lied about everything, even when the truth would have served him better.

Everything he did was the best. As well as constantly

rehearsing his past physical glories, sometimes he complained about his ailments, at other times, he was in denial about them. 'I'm still strong as an ox,' he'd say. 'I still manage to do all my own housework. I can build fences, fix cars. You name it.'

This was a complete fantasy. His apartment was a mess. Mama went over there once a week to clean up, and she had to contrive to do it when he wasn't home. If he were there, he'd find some reason to yell at her. And he never, never thanked her.

She and Daddy would have given him money any time he wanted, but instead of asking, he stole. And when challenged, he denied it. He'd make up some crazy, unbelievable excuse. My favourite was when he was caught red-handed with his hand inside Mama's handbag, 'I thought I'd spilled something in here, but nope, it's all clean.' Once, when Mama complained that her purse was missing, we discovered Bart had hidden it under a chest of drawers.

Whatever he was interested in was what everyone had to talk about. He loved TV sports. So, we had to hear every in and out and every score of every game.

Now, I found myself a beautiful wife, very beautiful. Mind you, I loved her for herself, but honestly, Angie was gorgeous. When people met her for the first time, they just couldn't stop themselves from remarking upon her looks. I sometimes even caught people trying to touch her long, silky black hair. I was so in love with her, and she loved me, too. But the first thought in anyone's head about Angie was—'Isn't she beautiful?'

The first time I brought Angie to Christmas in Belleview, Bart was simply disgusting. She'd been just as sweet as she could be to him—she loved being the congenial sister-in-law, and she listened with unfeigned sympathy to his story about the crash. She even made the effort to talk about sports.

The family were all happy for me to have married so well, and everyone was looking at me and Angie. The turkey was carved, the mashed yams glopped onto plates, big pats of butter slapped inside steaming rolls, and everyone was tucking into the eggnog quite merrily. Nobody noticed that for the space of about 20 minutes, no one had said anything to or even looked at Barton. During this period, he had put away glass after glass of Jack Daniels.

Angie was four months pregnant, and she looked like the Madonna stepped down from heaven. After everyone had complimented Angie on her radiant health, Mama made the mistake of turning to Bart and saying, 'Isn't she beautiful? So beautiful.'

He flew into a rage, throwing his glass down onto Mama's Mexican tile floor, where it shattered into pieces. He was yelling and screaming about how 'nobody cared about what he'd been through' and how his life was 'nothing but constant pain'. Meanwhile, one of the shards of glass had cut our cousin Jamie on the leg, staining her pretty little ruffled white sock red and provoking a shriek of shock and pain. Everyone leapt up to deal with Jamie, but Bart kept on ranting and raving about himself.

While everyone else spent the rest of Christmas Day at the hospital tending little Jamie, Barton walked—there are no cabs on Christmas Day—hobbled, back to his own apartment, and refused to speak to any of us for the rest of the holidays. Mama was so mortified she stayed in her room all of Boxing Day.

Later, she asked him straight to his face to apologise to Jamie—Mama was always clueless about Bart—and he said, 'Why? It was just a little cut on the leg where it doesn't matter,' and yelled, 'Look what I got, on my face,' pointing to his scars.

I dared to bring Angie to Christmas at Belleview the following year—you can't miss family Christmas, can you? By this time, she'd had the baby. So, naturally, all the attention was on the adorable seven-month-old. I kept looking over at Bart, though, because I could see it coming. I whispered to Angie, 'Why don't you see if you can put Winnie down early? Just to take the pressure off.' I raised my eyebrows in the direction of Bart, and she got the hint.

Before dinner, we all made a point of paying attention to Bart, listening politely to the news of the latest games on TV, asking about his health and his activities. It seemed that over the past year he had developed a problem with his right wrist, a problem that had not been there before. We'd thought it was the facial scars, kinked back and limping leg, but no, apparently, there was now the wrist, too.

Now, we have a Christmas Eve tradition. Every year Grandmother reads 'The Night Before Christmas' and the nativity story from the Gospel of Luke before we come to the table. But this year Grandmother said she was 'feeling poorly' and wanted us to do the reading. So, we decided to each take a turn reading four lines, going around in a circle. We tried to be as solemn as we could with Winnie bouncing around.

Mama started, 'Twas the night before Christmas...' followed by Daddy, Auntie Sue, me. It was up to Bart to read the most beautiful lines in the whole poem, 'As leaves that before the wild hurricane fly...' Instead, completely incongruously, he blurts out, 'See how Barton's laundry's piling up, since he only has one good hand.'

After dinner we planned to exchange gifts, but he insisted that he couldn't wrap presents 'in his condition'. Just give them unwrapped, then, we urged, but he wasn't having that. He made the cousins help him wrap his presents, and it took hours because he kept insisting on this or that, making everyone late to dinner. Daddy got hungry and ordered a pizza, and Mama started crying 'after all the work she'd done'. And the ruckus woke Winnie.

After that experience, we made our excuses, deciding to spend our Christmases with Angie's less volatile family, and over the years we had another girl, Melinda.

So, now we come to That Christmas. That Christmas, we couldn't avoid going to Belleview. Jamie had just started university at Harvard, and she would be home for the holidays, so naturally, there would be a celebration.

By this time, I could see it coming. Or at least, that's how I remember it, looking back. Angie and I tried our hardest to be nice to Bart, and that was quite a chore, not just because he could be such a pill, but because we had two little kids at our feet, who more legitimately demanded attention.

It was freezing cold, expecting snow, so I went out back for some more logs for the fire. On the horizon, headed our way, was one enormous, menacing reddish-black cloud. It seemed to get bigger by the minute, sucking up all the energy in the sky, as if gathering every drop of its fury into a great ball ready to throw at us. Each step I took, my boots felt heavier, as if growing sodden with the promise of a blizzard.

I came in with my load through the kitchen, and Mama said, 'Thanks, honey. You're a star.' Unfortunately, Bart was on the other side of the door within earshot.

Over and over, I'd tried to talk to Mama about Bart's behaviour, but she would just end up crying about how much he'd suffered. I'd emailed her clips from YouTube about personality disorders, and she didn't even open them.

She and Daddy were getting on a bit, and of course, Bart was her baby, her first. Angie was like that about Winnie, wouldn't hear a word of criticism. I'd really tried to prepare Mama for the ordeal of family Christmas with Bart, instructing her ahead of time to make sure she paid him attention, praised him for things, talked about sports.

At one point, sitting around the living room congratulating Jamie, Mama started telling Angie what a great student I'd been, how I'd graduated *summa cum laude*. 'I guess it runs in the family,' she said, smiling at Jamie.

Out of the blue, Bart says, 'I've started physiotherapy for my wrist.' We tried to indicate our approval, but the change of subject was so abrupt, I'm afraid Mama spluttered a bit, 'Oh... well... that's wonderful.'

I grimaced and rolled my eyes at Angie, which Bart unfortunately caught, remarking, 'well, now all the *stars* are here.'

Just before we were to go in to dinner, Jamie crossed her legs, revealing through her stockings the old scar from that shattered Jack Daniels glass, from that first of our fateful Belleview Christmases. Because all eyes were on her at that moment—she'd just been talking about what classes she was taking and who her roommates were—our gaze couldn't help following downward to the scar.

Clueless, clueless, Mama ventured to suggest to Bart, 'You really should apologise to Jamie, dear.'

He got up so suddenly that his bum leg bumped against Jamie's crossed leg, knocking it to the floor. He yelled, 'Apologise? Apologise? Who ever apologised to me for this?' pointing to his scarred face. Jamie just sat there with her eyes agoggle, and Winnie and Melinda started squealing.

As we were all drinking ourselves silly after dinner, Angie took the girls up to the guest bedroom to put them down. You may be surprised to hear that Bart followed her upstairs and made an awkward, stroppy, pass, attempting to grope her breast while she nursed Melinda. He apparently suggested to her that she'd 'married the wrong brother'. I wasn't surprised; I was just sorry Angie had to endure that. I honestly didn't even get angry. I was still so irritated by Bart's 'stars' rant. I certainly wish I had.

We all got too drunk, except for Angie. She knew she had to be up early to look after the little ones. The blizzard hit us during the night, the wind threw branches against the windows and rattled the doors in their frames, mercilessly buffeting the house as we bumbled our way up to bedrooms. We all slept like logs.

In the morning, I woke up to Melinda crying. I still hear it in my nightmares. Where was Angie? Never once had one of our babies cried when Angie wasn't right there, right away.

I came downstairs, my squealing baby in my arms, and her distress seemed to escalate with each step, as she sensed my apprehension.

There under the tree was the worst imaginable present Santa had ever delivered. There was my darling, the mother of my two young daughters, a mass of red under the green Christmas tree, her long black hair sprawled across broken boxes and stained wrapping paper, her limbs frozen in unnatural positions.

In from the kitchen sauntered Bart, his shirt and trousers bloody, calmly fingering a mug of coffee. He hadn't even bothered to hide the knife.

He just stood there in the doorway, saying, 'Isn't she beautiful? So beautiful.'

II Snows of Yesteryear

When Our Boys Come Home

by Susie Helme

They come in with a troop of boys we took in, a man and a woman, both dressed head to toe in black. Although that wasn't nothing unusual. Most ever'one south of Mason-Dixon had lost someone. Millie and I'd cast off our weeds jest a few weeks before.

They were gussied up all formal-like; the woman's dress had neither a tear nor a hole, nor even dust stains at the hem. He, likewise, his clothes were in immaculate condition for one who had survived the road as well as the war, a right contrast to our ragged veterans.

Behind them they drug a little sledge made of wooden planks carrying on it a dog, a huge ugly varmint all trussed up and muzzled and a-strugglin' and a-snarlin' fit to raise Cain.

Captain Munroe said, 'If your hospitality could stretch jest a bit further, ma'am. We ran into these two yest'day, and I reckoned the road ain't no place for a lady with just a man and a dog…'

I accepted, of course. The man and woman, surely. We took in whomever we could, just thankful they weren't Yankees. But the dog had me plumb vexed.

Millie rolled her eyes at me, as eleven men, dusty, bleeding and half-starved, settled in our drawing room forming puddles of pain on my mother's Chinese rug. 'Now, Millie,' I said, 'you know every group we take in might…'

'Ah knows, ah knows, Miz Suzanne. You is waitin' fo' Mast' Fayt.'

'He's all I've got left, Millie.'

'Ah knows it. Ain't ah done buried wid mah own two hands Massa Gerard an' Mast' Pierre, and little Miss Cherie?'

'And Betsey and Caesar, too,' I said.

'Lawd, if ah ain't cried enough tears ta drownd all o' Dixie,' she said.

I linked arms with her and put my face up against her smooth cool cheek, and we set there, united in our grief.

Millie was all I had left, besides the hope that someday my boy Lafayette would come a-walking down that road, dusty and maybe wounded. Maybe my Fayt was in some other lady's drawing room; some Yankee lady, even, was feeding my boy tonight.

I tended to what wounds I could with only soap and water and began tearing up yet another of my mother's petticoats for bandages, while Millie came in with cups and a pot of hot water—we had no more tea, of course—and some of the less wounded men began serving them around.

Then my sister Caroline scratched at the screen door. She'd married the younger son of Colonel Watkins from the plantation adjoining ours. She was carrying her baby Bobby in one arm and a big watermelon under t'other. 'I saw you had comp'ny,' she said. 'I left Jerome with Father. 'Spec they'll be awright for a while.'

I 'llowed as how the Colonel could probably fend off any number of marauding Yankees 'single-handed, even with only one leg', and she laughed.

I gave the soldiers a big plate and they commenced greedily to slurping the seeds all over my mother's rug. Millie flapped her apron in protest, but I said, 'It'll wash, honey; we've still got soap.'

Bobby was soon giggling and gurgling away on the rug, relishing the male attention, with seven or eight soldiers circled around playing with him, while Caroline went out back to see what she could find for Millie. Our cotton had all died, of course, with no one to tend it, and our corn and wheat and indigo. But Millie and I had planted a little vegetable patch behind the kitchen, which was, thank the Lord, thriving.

'Carrots and beans,' Caroline reported, 'and a whole passel o' potatoes. I set aside some of the small ones for seed.'

'Thanks, chère,' I said.

Millie came in with a plateful of hot biscuits, and the soldiers looked like they done died and gone to Heaven.

'I tuk some dough fum da mawnin' braid,' she said.

'Thanks, Millie. Now, Miss Caroline's fetched some vegetables. Go butcher one of the hens and rustle us up some chicken stew.'

'Yes, Ma'am,' she said.

Their hunger sated for the moment with watermelon and biscuits, the men occupied themselves playing with Bobby, while I finished administering bandages.

'You sho' are brave, ma'am,' Captain Munroe said to me, 'all on your lonesome with only one nigger to hand.'

I looked at him cattywompus to make sure he warnt getting no ideas. He hadn't noticed that the right side of my skirt swished less freely than the left. That was where I carried, during every waking moment—and loaded it was, too—my father's Lefaucheux revolver.

'Thank you, Cap'n. It's bad times, now, bad times. I lost my husband and older son. My field hands done run off North, and my house slaves went down with the flu along with my pretty baby. But any day now, my younger son might come home; maybe he'll be with some soldiers like your men here.'

'Hope he comes home to ya' real soon, ma'am,' he said respectfully.

The two in black had settled themselves into the Blue Room, away from the soldiers, and I asked them what I should do with their dog.

'Could you spare a few kitchen scraps?' said the woman.

I didn't ask Millie for her opinion on the matter. As far as she was concerned, a dog was supposed to BE food, not to be given food. We'd cooked our own house dog in the latter months of the war.

Two of the soldiers helped me drag the dog out back, and danged if the mutt didn't stop snarling and squirming the minute we turned the corner.

'I reckon your dog didn't take kindly to being all tied up,' I ventured, as I served the couple in the Blue Room, but they just set there sipping their 'tea'.

Her name was Mrs Bridges and his was Mr Fallon. Now, my mother taught me not to be ugly to guests, so I didn't raise an eyebrow at a woman travelling with a man who was not her husband, but Millie was another story entirely.

She cornered me in the kitchen. 'Chile, you gon' have dat Jezebel drinkin' fum Miz Mathilde fine china? T'ain't fittin. T'ain't fittin',' she stated and flat out refused to serve them.

I knew I was in for a scolding when Millie, all of maybe three years older than me, called me 'chile'.

'It's for God to judge, Millie, not us,' I said. 'Remember what Lord Jesus said about casting the first stone.'

By the time I brought out whatever kitchen scraps we had, the dog was so peaceful-like, I untrussed it, making instead a little rope collar and tying it to the water pump, where it proceeded to gratefully eat up the scraps and drink from the puddle of water that pooled there.

The dog was eventually so happy and gentle I untied it and

let it wander around the house. It was especially drawn to baby Bobby, and the feeling was mutual.

Bobby giggled with joy as the dog jumped here and there, barking happily and licking him all over. The soldiers prevented it from licking his mouth, but as it licked his feet, Bobby giggled with ticklish rapture. As he flailed his baby limbs, he even gave the animal a few unfortunate kicks in the jaw, but it kept coming back for more, loving every minute.

The soldiers loved it, too. I heard one say to Caroline, 'Ma'am, I reckon your little boy's done as much for us as Miss Suzanne's hospitality and Millie's good cookin'.' They'd seen so much death; it was good for them to see life.

But for the rest of the afternoon, neither the dog nor Millie would set foot in the Blue Room.

By the time the stew was ready, Bobby had started to fuss, and Caroline nursed him and lay him down to nap in the nursery, Cherie's room.

Mrs Bridges gave me a hand serving the men, ladling stew into our crockery bowls, but any time she got within four arms' lengths of the dog, it snarled and growled. When she tried to approach it, it became so vicious, I wondered if we would have to tether it again.

'It just ain't gon' let you off lightly, ma'am,' I said, trying to joke, but I couldn't raise a smile out of her.

We left them to their supper, but when we came in to clear away the bowls and were fixin' to bring in blankets for the men to sleep, who would have thought it? The dog was in the Blue Room, curled up next to Mr Fallon, happy as a dead pig in sunshine.

Caroline nodded her head in their direction and said, '*Tout pardonné* (all forgiven).'

We were in the kitchen clearing away the last of the bowls, when we heard. First, the barking—and it was not happy barking. My head was liketa stuck in molasses; I was slow. A second later, the baby's scream. In a heartbeat, I realised what those two creatures in the Blue Room were.

Caroline shrieked and dropped the bowls she was carrying onto the kitchen tiles, where they shattered, and I felt my face turn white. Millie leapt across the kitchen in great muscular bounds, her massive belly bouncing heavily here and there, shoving us aside, and her foot trod on one of the crockery shards, sending it flying up to where it cut her on the shin.

The three of us raced up the stairs lickedy-split, Millie's leg dripping blood all the way to the nursery.

The last time I'd entered this room, it had been to discover a dead baby. My heart was beatin' so fast I might could vomit.

There, our dread was answered. The beast had gone for him; but Bobby, our brave little Confederate soldier, had fought back, and where he might have taken it in the neck, had deflected the bite onto his sweet little arm. Caroline reached desperately for her baby, and a few soldiers, who had by now joined us, rushed to help her staunch the wound. I yanked at the dog's legs, and Millie had her huge brown hands wrapped all the way round its throat.

I have never seen such strength in a woman. She liketa strangle that dog to death with her bare hands. All the hardship and rage, illness and grief from five years of war poured into those big brown hands. The skirt she'd ruined digging a hole for the box sent home to us by Colonel Ashby, and the smaller hole next to it. The two white children she'd fed and rocked and sung to sleep. Pierre, for whom she'd wept tears of pride when he marched off in his grey uniform to defend our Southland. Cherie, whose christening dress she'd sewn from silk batiste and embroidered pink roses around the hem, which had become her burial gown. Her master Gerard, whom himself had been fed and rocked and sung to sleep by her own mother. Betsey, who was her daughter, and Caesar, who was her husband. I declare the woman could've strangled God A'mighty if she'd a' had him by the neck.

Hearing the ruckus, other men had now reached the nursery, and there were about twelve hands on the brute as we carried it growling and snarling outside to the water pump.

'Stand back, gentlemen,' I said. 'This job is mine.'

I tuk out my Lefaucheux, put the nozzle in the mouth of that hellhound and, though I was shaking, was sure-handed enough to blast that evil head to smithereens.

'And I do believe I have at least two more bullets,' I said, marching back inside and straight into the Blue Room.

I pointed my revolver right at the wicked couple and yelled, 'Out a' my house and off a' my land. Right now.' God as my witness if that witch weren't smiling.

Millie, her leg still bleeding, held open the door with one hand, while with the other she brandished her wooden crucifix before her face, screaming, 'Get out. Get out.' Her fat cheeks wobbling with fury, she let fly a stream of cussin' which sounded like voodoo spells in some African language. Occasionally there were a few phrases I could understand, 'Miz Mathilde fine china', 'Miz Car'leen precious chile', 'de Lawd an' da divil done tek away all o' my chirren'.

She was still shaking with rage, aiming her crucifix at them like a firearm, while I stood on the porch steps training my revolver on the cursed couple as they made their way back up to the road. Millie's invective dying down to silent, all-consuming grief as the spectres of evil retreated.

We stood on that there porch for nigh on twenty minutes, Millie and I, two women of a similar age, keeping guard against every horror sent to try our souls, from Heaven or from Hell.

The Lost Battlefield

by Elaine Graham-Leigh

This is where our battle was, here, in the top field. Eadwig said the King put his shield wall over there, where we planted the hawthorns last year, a line of great thegns with their helmets all gold and their swords flashing in the sun as they raised their war-yell. The Danes were yonder with the scarp at their backs above the river, and they were fearsome and mighty as well. Or so said Eadwig.

Eadwig should not have been there, but he was twelve that summer, old enough to think himself grown but not old enough to have grown into sense. To be fair to him, he did help us drive the cattle down to the church when Da came shouting that there were fighters coming up the valley. It was only later that he slipped out after the men.

I sat in the nave with the other women from the cotts around. We didn't talk much. Some of us were spinning, even though it was too dim to see. All my memories of that long day are shot through with the scratch of the thread against my fingers, the whirr and thunk of the spindle in the dark. I kept thinking I could hear the fighting, that every call of a bird outside was some man's death-cry.

Through the gaps between the planks of the nave wall came a low roaring, as if a killing wind were thrashing the trees. Da and some of the other men came back just before the sun set to tell us it was over. I was worried about what we might find at home, but

Da said all the fighters had moved off north-westwards, so there'd been no one passing to fire our thatch in revenge or celebration. In the morning, Da gave Eadwig a leather jerkin, good enough for a thegn and hardly bloodstained. He's worn it every winter since.

We had to leave the field all that summer for the crows and the worms to do their work. Luckily it was a good growing year, and the men cleared the copse on the other side of the stream for late hay. The next spring the field was full of red flowers. Ulf picked me a posy of them when we came up here, courting.

I've never heard who won our battle. We did hear, sometime after, that there was a new King down there in London, but how that happened, I've never known. You can still see the hillocks where the bones are, under the turf, but they're flatter every year as the earth claims them. It's a long time now since we've turned up a spear head in the ploughing. Soon there will be nothing to show that there was ever a battle here at all.

Historical note:

In 1016, Canute King of Denmark invaded England. There were a number of battles between him and the English before he made himself King of England at the end of the year. One of these was a skirmish at a place called Clayhanger. We know that this was somewhere just north of London, but there are various theories about precisely where it was. This is a reflection on what it might have been like at the time, and how the battlefield could have been lost.

Piano Lessons

by Kay Towers

When I was young, I lived in an old house in South London. It stood back from the street with a short flight of steps leading up to the hall door and a few stone steps which led down to the semi-basement door. A few rather dusty shrubs and bushes grew in the little front garden. A brass plate on the railings announced the fact that I gave piano lessons. On Saturday morning a girl of about fourteen years of age would knock at the door and ask to be allowed to scrub the steps for a small consideration.

One day, I opened the door to an elderly lady dressed very neatly in navy blue. She seemed rather nervous and said that she had called to enquire about piano lessons. I invited her inside, and she said, rather timidly, 'Would you take me as a pupil?'

When I replied, 'Yes, certainly', she breathed a sigh of relief.

'You see I saw a card about piano lessons in a shop window down the road and I went inside to see if I could have piano lessons. The woman in the shop called her daughter who was the piano teacher, and as soon as she saw me, she said rather haughtily, 'Oh, no, I only take serious students.'

'Well, this upset me very much and I walked away feeling very downcast. After all, I thought, why shouldn't I have piano lessons? I know I am not young, but I should like to be able to play the piano just a little to amuse myself.'

'As I walked along, I passed a sweet shop and I thought I would buy some sweets to cheer myself up. The girl behind the counter was smiling and cheerful and I soon found myself telling her my woes. She agreed that I should have lessons if I wanted them. You go along to Miss Sale who lives in one of those houses past the station. I am sure she won't refuse you.'

And so I arranged to give Miss Morley a lesson every Tuesday evening, and she used to come along so cheerfully and it was evident that she enjoyed her visits. In fact, she said that Tuesday was the best day in the week for her because all day she was thinking, 'Now, tonight, I shall go for my piano lesson,' and, she said, 'I look forward to it so much.'

It appeared that she had a little shop where she sold general drapery and haberdashery. One day she said that as she enjoyed her lessons so much, would I let her come two nights a week and so it was arranged that she should come on Friday evening also.

Poor Miss Morley, she seemed to lead a rather dull life. The first world war had started and she told me how the young girls would come into her shop to buy pillowcases and other items for their marriage to the soldier lad who would come home from the war.

She said that she had served her apprenticeship to the drapery trade when a girl—a hard life it must have been, for the shops kept open very late in those days. Many a long summer evening had she stood behind the counter watching through the open door the young girls in their summer frocks, strolling by, laughing happily with their young men.

She made some progress in her music and was now able to play one or two tuneful pieces, much to her delight.

One evening she said, 'Now, give me only a very short lesson tonight because I saw a young soldier running down your basement steps and I wouldn't like to think I was keeping you from him.'

Dear Miss Morley! Could you know how wildly my heart was beating? It must be that soldier boy with that beautiful tenor voice. I was very glad that she only wanted a short lesson.

Well, the war dragged on and our boys were sent over the water to France and many never returned.

Then came the Zeppelin raids and one night Miss Morley's little shop was demolished. As it was a lock up shop, she was not on the premises and so escaped unharmed, but she told me that she had decided to go and live with some relatives in Birmingham until the war was over.

She was very reluctant to give up her beloved piano lessons, but she said that she would start again when the war was over. 'Don't forget', she said, 'I shall most certainly come back'.

Now, at last, the war was over, and I was one of the lucky ones whose boy returned from the war. In due course we were married and set up our home together in the old house. I still gave a few piano lessons, partly because I liked teaching and partly because the extra money was useful.

I arranged to leave my evenings free to spend with my husband. One late afternoon I was saying goodbye to my last pupil—a pretty child with fair hair.

Just as she was going she turned suddenly and said, 'Oh! I nearly forgot to tell you. I was asked to give you a message by a lady who was standing just inside your gate when I came for my lesson. I could not see her very well as it was getting dark, but I think she was a small elderly lady. She said, please tell Miss Sale that I am so sorry that I cannot come for any more lessons. I think she said that she was Miss Morgan.'

I said, 'Thank you, Pamela,' and as I walked downstairs I thought it must have been Miss Morley, but why did she not call and tell me herself?

When I entered the dining room Reg was already home. 'Hullo', I said. 'You're early tonight'.

'Yes,' he said. 'I got away earlier than usual. By the way, who was your last pupil?'

'That was Pamela,' I said. 'Isn't she sweet?'

'Well', he said, 'she is rather a strange child. I came along just behind her and she was standing by the bushes talking to herself.'

'Talking to herself!' I said.

'Yes', he said, 'She must have been, because there was no one there.'

Die, Die, Die

by Susie Helme

The length of Watling Street is rubble, stained red with blood. My queen lies butchered, stabbed a hundred times by Roman javelins, her head ripped off at the neck, flies buzzing around the red-brown blood staining the blue stripes on her once-brave face, unwashed for so long that they are caked into hexagons like a tortoise's back.

I am beside her, not a place on my body that is not bleeding.

I had heard the whispers among the Trinovantes. Though all the kings in Albion bow to the oppressors, though all the tribes in Britannia pay tribute, she would not. She would ride to avenge us. She would not submit.

I am not of the Iceni. A Brigante, I ran away after the treachery of the coward queen. The Catuvellauni king, he stood up to them. He fought back. Then he sought sanctuary. How could she give him up to the invaders? That queen no longer has my allegiance.

The Iceni queen, they brought me to her after her virgin daughters were raped. This we shared.

It was cold. Her warriors had wrapped her in a sheepskin. She looked almost small in it. She had put away her toga; no longer would she dress to fit their fashion. She wore a blue-green checkered tunic woven of wool. Blue stripes of woad down each side of her face.

Stranger that I am, accept me, my eyes said, accept me as your daughter.

Die, Die, Die

They told her I would be her serving girl, but she did not ask of me food nor drink. She wanted to see my shooting arm.

I am a servant, not an archer. I shot badly, missing the inner circle by a palmswidth, but as I released the bowstring, I cried, 'Die, die, die.'

She liked that. I wanted blood; she wanted blood. She patted the furs upon which her eldest had lain.

Trinovantes, Cantiaci and Catuvellauni joined our enraged march. We have wiped Camulodunum from this earth, the Trinovantes' revenge. Cerialis and the Legio IX Hispana extinct, the Temple of Claudius razed, the city torched, Catus Decianus fled to Gaul. Not a man, woman or child is left living, not a brick left upon its foundation. Only the Balkerne Gate stands. We saw the smoke still rising all the way from Londinium.

That town, too, felt our wrath. Londinium is ash. Verulamium, who had collaborated with the foes, is sacked, in ruins. We cut off the breasts of the noblewomen and sewed them to their mouths. The men, we impaled vertically upon spikes while still alive. The children, we cracked open their little skulls like gourds with our battle axes, our queen exhorting vengeance for her daughters' outraged chastity.

Their celebrated discipline, their order, their ranks of men in neat formation. Did they think that would affright us? Our warriors did not stand in pretty rows. We were too furious. We were instead like an angry knot, the fiercest elements in the centre front, weaker ones on the flanks.

Out of the mist they emerged, first the shiny metal casques, then the 10,000 clanking armoured torsos. Two legions, fresh from devastating Mona—may holy Brigit burn their eyeballs until they pop. Last to enter our eyes and ears were the feet, marching, marching, boots marching, drums beating the rhythm.

I have given my life for her, and I am willing. The seed of the vile legionary growing in my belly, too, will die.

The golden torc of her royalty lies dirtied and defeated upon the ground. They will melt it into aureus coins, and spend them on drinking our ale, debauching our women.

They created a desolation. But it is not over. It is not over until Britannia is free. Until Caesar is in chains and his vitals boil in our soup. Until their mercenaries desert to follow our banners, and barbarians like me and my queen sack their great city. Until every marble statue is smashed into pieces, every temple ground to dust. Until every Roman dies screaming, every Roman head is on a spike, and they lie bleeding with their intestines spilt upon the grass.

Their glorious Rome will be a desolation. From the Otherworld I will watch the smoke rising from the ruins, and I will curse the robbers of the world. I will turn back and watch them all die, die, die.

The Round Up

by Rajes Bala (Rajeswary Balasubramaniam)

April 1985, village of Batticaloa, Eastern Sri Lanka

The ferocity of the simmering heat of the April sun was evident even as early as 9 o'clock in the morning. Our bitch Daisy, with its pups, was searching for shade in the banana garden. The white hen with its multicoloured chickens, which had hatched last week, was dutifully searching for food. Our cat, tired of searching for fried fish in neighbouring kitchens, was curled up in a corner of the cement veranda.

The cuckoo was cooing from our mango tree. My younger brothers were imitating the cooing sound of the cuckoo, irritating my grandmother in the process. Father was bathing in the well. Mother was making *pittu* (rice flour and coconut) in the kitchen.

My elder brother was reading something in the front hall. He was always reading something.

Under the shade of the guava tree, my two little sisters were playing the mango-seed game on the squares drawn on the ground. They were ten and eight years of age, worldly innocent.

Grandfather was praying in the prayer room. Words from religious hymns were emanating with feeling from his toothless mouth. The familiar words of the *Suprabatham*, blending with the breeze that came past our jasmine plants from next door Parvathi Aunty's house, soothed my ears. I was grinding *chilli sambol* for the *pittu* on the grinding-stone.

What a beautiful morning it was. This morning, the turning point in my life.

Through the gaps in our barbed wire fences, the river Thillai (Thillai Aru) could be seen winding like a snake. The golden rays of the morning sun glittered on the water. The Thillai was dry and looked like a canal. The beauty of the sun's rays, clinging onto the body of the river like a dress, always enthralled me.

Engrossed in the serenity of the morning, my thoughts were disrupted by the howling of dogs in the distance. Their ferocious barking signalled opposition. A sickening feeling was beginning to grip my stomach from its very pit.

In those days the villagers believed that if there was a fox howling on the outskirts of the village, a death was impending. Today, a barking of dogs on the outskirts meant that a Round-Up was on the way.

Mother came running out, leaving the cooking unfinished. Father, with unwashed soap still on his body, was looking in the direction of the road. Grandfather, who had been so fervently reciting religious hymns, appeared on the veranda, his face distraught.

The howling of military tanks could be heard in the distance. Hundreds of soldiers in military vehicles and on foot were surrounding the village with menacing machine guns and emotionless eyes, like messengers of death. With a burning sensation from grinding the chilli sambol, my soul stirred. Helplessly, everybody in the house looked anxiously at one another.

'My mahane (son), run away somewhere,' our mother begged my elder brother. In neighbouring compounds, some youths were running through the fences. The hunt had begun. They were clearing the forest. They were hunting the Tamil 'terrorists'!

In the last Round-Up, the Sri Lankan army had destroyed all

The Round Up

the fences and cut down all the big trees. Because Tamil militants would attack them from hiding behind them, it seems. Not only that, they also did not want these fences and gates to deter them from moving about freely as they invaded Tamil homes.

The enemy's guns have dented the swollen pride of the Tamil community, already torn asunder by its own divisions of caste and creed and petty bickering.

While the young were running, the old hiding, mothers wailing, forlorn and helpless grandmothers screaming and young girls disappearing, the dogs and the fowl were making a hue and cry. The *Suprabatham* from neighbouring Parvathy Aunty's could still be heard, the music missing the beat, interrupted by bursts of gunfire.

The army was closing in. Dust rose up from lanes unused to large vehicles. Bullets riddled the bodies of those who ran. They fell like trees cut down by winds of cyclonic velocity and power.

Mother Earth shook, unable to bear the wounded wailing of mothers. The army was advancing all around the village.

There was perspiration on our mother's face and rivulets of tears pouring down from her eyes. Father's face was pale and livid.

I could visualise Yama (the demon of Death) and his legendary rope of death in the eyes of my little sisters. My elder brother found himself trapped in our own home. He couldn't run anywhere.

The soldiers have surrounded the house. My younger brothers have lowered themselves into our well, the water level fortunately remaining just below their noses, in the hope the soldiers would not be intelligent enough to look down into the well.

My two little sisters hid in a corner, along with the hen, hiding its chicks under its wings.

Our grandmother beat herself on her head and mouth, looking at me.

Though I have not become a 'big girl' yet, the men in uniform casting their eyes on me are not likely to bother about that.

My grandmother, in unspoken apprehension, seemed to be imagining that my elder brother and I would become prey to the advancing military vultures.

I closed my eyes tightly. I wanted to imagine that all that was happening around me was just imagination, a frightening dream. Would imagination become true? Would dreams turn real? Mother dragged me across the floor and pushed me behind the sacks of paddy rice.

Only God can save me, I thought.

The soldiers thundered down our lane. Our gateways became platforms for their big boots. Death and destruction were masquerading under the name of the State.

In the streets, youths caught by the army were being bundled into trucks. Those youths who had been shot were being dragged along, their blood painting our streets red.

Is this generation heir to the heroic heritage of the Tamil kings, who had hoisted their flag from Kanyakumari to the Himalayas?

Hidden behind the paddy sacks, I surveyed the world through the window.

Oh! That the earth should split asunder and swallow us all up? What sins have the Tamils committed to deserve such terrible suffering? Is this a just punishment for demanding to speak our own language, which we have spoken for aeons, in the land in which we had crawled as children?

Mother was begging with folded hands.

The soldiers were beating up my elder brother.

My dearest mother was crying, spasms convulsing her abdomen, which had conceived and brought forth my brother into this

The Round Up

world. 'You look young, the same age as my son. How would your mother feel if you were beaten up in front of her eyes in the way you and your friends are doing to my son?' My mother would have wanted to ask the soldier, but she didn't, out of fear.

My father, who went to the rescue of my brother, was hit on the head. Blood gushed forth.

My little sisters screamed.

When Grandmother tried to intervene, she was stamped upon like a worm by a booted soldier.

The screams of my brother pierced my heart. His body was now the property of the soldiers who had come down our lane. They beat him and kicked him. Accusing him of being a terrorist, they pierced his chest and stomach with their bayonets.

The cries of my brother, who had once taken me in his lap, deafened my ears. Nothing came out of his mouth except the words, '*Ammah, Ammah*' (Mother, Mother). His screaming grew less and less audible.

Where has fled Lord Shiva, to whom our grandfather has been singing with his earnest prayer? To a strange and distant place where some of his so-called human creations do not commit such acts of barbarity upon his other creations?

Mother had fainted.

She was not able to see the half dead body of my brother being dragged along the street. Father's face looked horrible, with the blood dripping down from his head.

One soldier dragged me out from my hiding place. Grandmother held onto me tight. There was fire in her eyes. Wouldn't the world explode in flames? What a tight hold it was, even in her withering age.

Grandfather, who only a little while ago had been holding on tightly to the feet of sacred Shiva, was now holding tightly the dusty booted feet of the soldier, imploring him, 'Leave my granddaughter alone.'

Tamil womanhood was being bargained for in a frenzy of communal hatred.

The army Captain looked at me from head to foot.

Did the budding beauty, only fourteen years old, mesmerise his jaundiced eyes? His gaze was going far beyond my body. Such a look it was. I did not cry. My senses had become benumbed.

In one such previous Round-Up, many Tamil women had become prey to their lust. Whether they were eight or ten or twelve was not a problem. If they thought that they could satisfy their depravity, it was all right.

They are animals. With cannibalistic hunger. They search for Tamil militants; and we are the sacrificial lambs.

One soldier was moving his hand slowly down my long hair.

Grandmother spat at him. Grandfather banged his head on the soldier's feet he had been holding.

Father, with blood drying on his head and face, brother lying half dead, senseless mother, wailing grandmother, pityingly imploring grandfather—what can Tamil womanhood do?

Won't you, Lord Shiva, perform your cosmic dance of destruction?

Krishna was there for Thraupathy in *Maha-bharatham*, Hanuman for Sita in Ramayana, but who is there to help the Tamil woman in the Sinhala-Tamil war? Closing my eyes and biting my lips, I prayed.

The army Captain stared at me. Maybe he had a daughter like me. Or a sister? Or even a niece? God knows what went through his mind.

At his signal, the soldier holding me slackened his grip.

Mother Goddess Kali, who destroys the men of evil, why have

you run away from Sri Lanka? Come running... come running... come running back and save us! I thought like a mad woman.

The Sinhalese Army, the *asuras* (devils) have started moving to Round-Up our village. Wouldn't Krishna be reborn to destroy them? Should the destruction of the Kali yuga descend only upon the undeserving Tamils?

That day, in our village and adjoining villages, more than two hundred Tamils were arrested. Countless numbers were attacked in their own homes. While hawks and ravens flew unimpeded in the sky, innocent Tamils were shot down like birds on earth.

Our land, spread like a green *saree*, was dotted red with Tamil blood. The wailing of mothers shamed the soft winds.

When you pass the sandy plateau of the River Thillai, which flows between the sea and our village, you come to the belly of the Bay of Bengal, from where ships travel to all parts of the globe. On that sandy plateau constructed by God, dividing river and sea, we played as children, catching crabs. We imprinted our little footsteps, touching and running along with the oncoming waves.

The sandy plateau has today become a crematorium. There, our village youths were taken. Would the soldiers have said with scorn, 'The Tamils are good at mathematics?' or 'Hey, Tamil dog! Dig a hole six feet long and three feet deep.'?

Upon that crisp order, our youths dug their own graves. Forty-four of our youngsters, many of them still alive, were buried that day. The half dead body of my elder brother and another forty-three bodies were heaped together.

That evening hour, when the sky was painted bloody red, the black smoke rising from the bodies burnt with tyres heaped on them, signalled to the world the cruelty of humanity. Past the river, our mothers cried out for their sons' lives dissolving into black smoke.

My ageing father and my grandfather, who were arrested, returned home in a few days after being tortured.

On that day alone, one hundred and twenty-five Tamil women in our village were made widows.

In the ten years since the Round-Up, how many widows has our village seen? Is there any accounting of the women who were horribly raped?

Nowadays, Round-Ups are of a different type. Along with the ruthless military wing of the security forces, named the Special Task Force, extremist Muslim fanatics, too, would besiege our village. Then came the Indian Peace Keeping Force (IPKF). It was like an earthquake surpassing the thunder.

Today, in our village, yesterday's relatives inform on militant groups known to them and incite internecine killings, citing present day squabbles. Private scores are settled by the AK 47.

Women like us are desperate about our future, not knowing what it will be. My grandmother would hug me and cry. It pains me to hear her say in anguish, 'There is no elder brother to do well for you.' There are many sisters without elder brothers, widows without husbands.

Thousands of Tamils have escaped and gone to distant lands on the pretext of 'the Tamil problem' in Sri Lanka. What can we say for the Batticaloa Tamils?

It is said that the much acclaimed Sinhalese king of ancient days, Dutugemunu, who killed the Tamil king Ellala when he was a young prince, had lamented that he could not sleep, besieged on the one side by Tamils and on the other by the Indian Ocean. Surrounded on all sides—with the Sinhalese on one side, the sea on the other, the Muslims on the north, the Thillai River on the south—where could the villagers of Batticaloa escape for their lives?

Small boys, who had just given up drinking their mothers' milk, have joined the armed struggle, vowing to fight for their mother tongue and motherland rather than die at the hands of the enemy. The children of my village are dying on the seas and on the battlegrounds for the freedom of Tamils.

We have had enough of the sufferings. We need peace. Even now, I stare at the sandy mound on which my elder brother was buried and burnt.

Based on actual events in 1985 in the eastern province of Sri Lanka.

El Dorado and the Potato Curse

by Susie Helme

The room was lonely, but it wasn't cold. The poor soul put another log on the coals and lit a taper for his pipe. The gaoler had allowed that luxury, as well. He sat down to the large wooden table and put the flame first to a candle then to the pungent dried leaves called by the Taino *tabaco*. On the morrow, he expected a visit from someone who had agreed to convey for him a letter. He couldn't have asked a family member; they would have been searched.

To the Right Honourable my good Lord and kinsman Sir Charles Howard, he began.

When all else had deserted him, Lord Howard had still given his support, although yet again he had provided him no return on his investment. For the second time he had failed to find the fabled city of El Dorado which the natives called Manoa, and for the second time had returned without the gold with which he had promised to enrich His Majesty's realm.

Alone in the Tower, awaiting His Majesty's justice, this letter would be his final confession. Here, he would divulge what he could not communicate to the Privy Council, what he had as yet disclosed to no living soul, the true and full account of his second voyage to Guiana.

I have no son to whom I can relate the tale, he wrote, *him to my great grief I left buried on the shores of the Orenque River.*

He assured his kinsman that he sought not release from his bounds nor reprieve from his sentence. The account is *writ neither to conceal nor to confess*, he wrote. He wished merely to recount the horrors, to stand in the sight of Providence as witness.

From the outset Raleigh's enterprise seemed doomed to calamity. His 14 ships and barge were forced by ill winds to port in Ireland from where, when they set sail for the Canarias to reprovision, they were taken for pirates by the Spanish who killed 15 of his men. Beset by dysentery on the crossing, it was past Trinidad upon entering the Bay of Paria when the first *atrocity*, as he deemed it, occurred.

Inexplicably, one of the men on the barge was found dead, and when the body was searched for clues as to the reason for his demise, the men found inside the mouth of the corpse a liquid black substance, which by its smell was determined to be decayed mashed potato root. His men supposed that the dead man had eaten some of the green bits and thus died of strychnos poisoning.

Raleigh wrote:

> *By the sight I had membrance to my plantations in County Cork which by the love and generosity of Her Majesty I had been enriched, and where I had planted the Solanum root from St. Iago which the Spaniards call patata and the Mapuche call poñis, and it had heartily increased. Your lordship may recall that I found there such an abundance of these truffle-like roots that all the ships of the world may be therewith laden from thence.*
> *This fruit did originate from Peru and is akin to the openawk of Virginia and to the Black Nightshade identified by Pliny as strychnos, but*

though the green parts are toxic, humans may eat of the ripened roots, and supplemented by only milk or butter may obtain all the nourishment required for their sustenance.

To the Mapuche naturals of those shores it was the staple of their diet, their only other cultivated crop being corn, so that they set little value thereupon. So where Francisco Pizarro's men had bargained in Peru with Spanish ducats for the produce, I bade my men simply dig them up and load them into the hold of the galley. The naturals might have protested, but we had arquebuses where they had only spears.

A sorceress, which they call machi, ran among the dug-over mounds shouting, but as we had no interpreter with us at this time, I had no understanding of what she spake, doubtless having something or other to do with dislike of our taking her country's produce.

Raleigh's botanist had been much interested by these underground fruits, though he had not been able to interest the English in their digestion.

The various natives of the Orinoco also grew a starchy tuber which in its unripe stages was poisonous. The mystery was that the substance in the man's mouth was not from this tropical tuber, but instead from the mountainous Andean variety. The fabled Guianaian root called by the natives *cushcush* was nothing like it. Some considered it to be an entirely different crop. It was sweet and orange in colour and its flesh was moist; the decayed mash would have been browner with a nutty smell.

He continued:

The potato which caused the demise of my man came, by any chart, from at least a thousand leagues distance, a perilous undertaking, nigh impossible if overland, if by sea, a journey of six or seven months requiring navigation around the Horn. Who, from this other world, could have introduced their presence upon our barge? And who from this world would have wished to do so? And how?

The second strange occurrence was at the mouth of the Amana after a prolonged period without revictualing. In the hot jungle, the men sweated abysmally, and the stench of the company, compounded by the desire for fresh meat and wine, drove the men to distraction.

Encamped on the shore to search for food, the silence of the forest surrounded them all around, alert, watchful. The shadows of leaves flickered across their bedrolls, and they flinched at every movement, ever expecting the soft pad of a jaguar's paw, the darting of a blood-sucking bat, the slither of a giant anaconda. Those waters, hellish for lightning and storms, contained the ugly serpents *lagartos* (alligators) which could in a moment drag a man down to the depths. The trees concealed the fierce negro Djukas, who had hitherto proven hostile, or perhaps cannibals from the Guanipa and Berbesse. In their sleep the men experienced nightmares that awakened them screaming.

Raleigh had rested aboard the flagship *Ark Raleigh* but was summoned to the camp by shouting. Rowing ashore across the dark serpent-infested waters, he learned that the reason for the commotion was an intermittent sound of drumming from the forest. It came first from the north, and then from the west; they had the impression that they were surrounded by ill-wishing drummers. As he listened to their accounts, Raleigh too heard the drumming, this time from the east.

We were encircled, it seemed, by drums beating the heartbeat of the jungle, calling forth wild spirits from the shadowed canopy.

The men clamoured to decamp back to the ships, but he commanded that they instead form a posse to seek out the drummers, which he himself led. They chased the sound hither and thither among the dense foliage, and only the smoke from their campfire kept them from losing orientation. Finally they managed to seize the drummer or one of the drummers. It was a woman, of Indian colouring.

He shone his lantern upon her, and his breath stopped. Her face had no features. In terror at the sight, he dropped the lantern and had to take another one from one of the men.

There are tales, and I cannot avow on my credit what I have heard, of people in these lands with eyes in their shoulders and mouths in their chest. Was this such a creature? Yet upon the second shining, we could see that the effect was due to her wearing a dark hooded cape pulled fully down. I bade one of the men pull it back, and gasped again in wonder, for although she did have a face, her eye sockets were sewn shut as if the eyes had been surgically removed.

Who knew what the woman was doing in the forest at night, drumming, completely blind? Still, she seemed to bear the camp no ill, so Raleigh ordered everyone back to their bedrolls. Revictualed or no, they departed in the morning.

In Chile, the Mapuche had told him through an interpreter that after death, the soul travels to a blessed isle in the east to subsist without work feeding upon 'black potatoes'. It was their belief that an evil spirit or *kalku* can seize a person's spirit and turn it into a *wekufe* or force of evil. The evil *wekufe* can take a number of forms, either a giant bird with the head of a *kalku*, or a large shape-shifting beast called a *waillepen*, or a human-formed, blood-sucking ghost called *witranalwe* if it was on horseback and *anchimallen* if it was on foot.

Raleigh and his lieutenants had witnessed a fertility ceremony performed to ward off *kalku* and invoke the blessings of their gods upon the harvest; this one was to bless the potato crop. This occurred before they had dug up the roots and loaded the stolen produce into their hold. The ceremony consisted of a dance, the principal performer being the machi sorceress.

He wrote:

> *This sorceress is painted in blue and yellow and wears a hooded cape exactly like unto that worn by our midnight drummer. She conducteth this dance in the light of a full moon while beating incessantly upon a drum, until, having imbibed of chicha, their corn liquor, or of a liquor they make from poñis (potatoes), she falleth into an ecstasy, all this time with her eyes closed.*
>
> *Now, I must invite your lordship's recall that the potato steppes of the Mapuche look out over an entirely different ocean, the South Pacific. We were on the other side of Panama, on the Orenque, which poureth into the Atlantic. Yet twice now I had had strange membrance of my voyaging in Chile. Yet again, the sense of someone following me from that other world was inescapable.*

> *What shadows dost Providence cast upon those it would punish? Who but the Almighty might breathe life into such unnatural creatures and portents to hound a man in the twilight of his sins?*

These were the first two occurrences. The third occurrence happened while the men camped on the island of Assapano, fearing to remain with the anchored ships due to a terrible storm. There they feasted on a beast called *armadillo*.

They awoke at dawn to the sound of mosquitoes buzzing, finding that though the billows had subsided, insects covered their nets so thickly they couldn't see from thence. Two men were sent into the forest, taking some netting with them as protection, in search of dry firewood with which to smoke out the insects and dry the netting, but after several hours they had not returned.

Presently they set out in search of the men and found to their chagrin that not far from camp they lay dead. Feeding upon the dead men, their muzzles dripping red with blood, and all entangled in ripped pieces of the mosquito netting, were three of the most horrifying creatures they had ever seen.

The men had been shot by arrow, the perpetrators evidently having fled in terror at the sight of these beasts. They looked like dogs, but were bald, too tall to be dogs and too hairless to be wolves, and as they reared on their hind legs to tear great bloody chunks out of the necks of the corpses, they seemed almost simian. Had they been in Africa and not America, Raleigh would have said they were oversized monkeys.

By now, they had thoroughly examined all the beasts of these parts, and it being his second journey, he had thought himself familiar with anything that might cross his path. He fired a shot into the air and the animals took off. The men with him were either crossing themselves or running away back toward camp, when across their path fell a maroon centipede as long as a man's forearm with a profusion of yellow legs that started wiggling the moment it hit the earth, swiftly propelling the horrific arthropod toward them. They shrieked and shot at the creature with their arquebuses.

He wrote:

> *We had seen centipedes, though perhaps not as long as this one, in the Andes as well.*
> *As to the fiendish beasts, I had membrance to divers designs on the crockery of the Mapuche, where potatoes were painted with disfigured human features or morphed into human faces. There was one pot I recall where the potato was transformed into a hairless dog.*

Was the dog-like creature in the forest large enough to be a shape-shifting waillepen?

It did seem to me then as if even the beasts of the South Pacific were following me into the Orenque jungle.

We faced a land of apparitions, where shadows were fearless and spirits flitted in ways unnatural, the price of a man's arrogance before the unknown.

At Cumana Raleigh remained with the main fleet anchored, sending his lieutenant Lawrence Keymis upriver to scout out tributaries, and during their absence another adventure occurred.

Throughout the entire voyage, Raleigh and his men had not yet seen one ounce of gold, so when he learned from their Orenoqueponi pilot, who had been christened Ferdinand, that there was a people called the Tivitivas who dwelt in trees and traded *canoas* to the Inga for gold, he was all agog, hoping that at last, this connection might provide him with information as to the route to the shining city. They inhabited, Ferdinand discovered, a region along the Macuri River near the islands of Pallamos. There they were comprised of two rival castes, the Ciawani and the Waraweeti, who were at constant war with one another, and they had a *cacique* (chief) named Putyma.

So, taking an expeditionary force, they made their way there to the tree settlements of the Tivitivas, enquiring through Ferdinand as to the whereabouts of the chief Putyma's abode.

Coming to the tree-top house, Raleigh and his men mounted the ladder to enter and were astounded to find no one there. Instead there was the skeleton of a man sitting upright, assumably the chief having died. His skull was decked all around with colourful feathers, and gold plates such as those Raleigh believed were manufactured in El Dorado hung about the bones of his arms, legs and thighs.

All that time we had come not to any gold, nor silver, nor any other certain manufacture of the city of Manoa, and such was the lust for gold in which the men, myself included, had been bred that we fell upon the carcase with great recklessness, extracting the gold plates from where they had been fastened, so much that the bones of the carcase were thrown hither and thither and the feathers flew all about the room, and the rest of the skeleton, having no structure to uphold it, fell in a loose clump upon the ground.

At that point, a band of warriors burst in, which I vouchsafe must have been the cacique's kin, who were all aflame at the treatment their leader's corpse had received by our hands, whereby we had aggrieved them in their religion. It was verily

El Dorado and the Potato Curse

surmised that Ferdinand had obtained his information from whichsoever caste of which Putyma was not a party, and that they had practised to deceive him so as we should fall victim of some drollery.

Whether it be Ciawani or Waraweeti, they pursued us, on horseback, back to our boats. One of them came so near to mine own mount that that it shied, almost throwing me to certain massacre by these savages. His face was painted white like a great ghost.

Was this a human-formed, blood-sucking witranalwe, again some creature following me from the Chilean world?

During this time Captain Keymis had inescapably come into conflict with the Spanish at Santo Tomé, a town that had been fortified by Don Antonio de Berreo, a former seeker of El Dorado and now governor of Guyana and Trinidad. Here Raleigh's son Watt was killed. For two months the English fought off the Spaniards and searched the environs of Santo Tomé for gold mines, without success, and in March they returned to the fleet.

Beset from all sides by attackers, the fleet set off downriver. From port, it was Berreo's Spaniards, who, after their departure had regained Santo Tomé and were bent on revenge. From starboard, it was the Tivitivas, whichever of the castes was incensed by the treatment of their chief's skeleton, shooting arrows from their *canoas*. But as the waters of the Capuri grew deeper, the ships were able to outrun them.

In my report to His Majesty's councillors 'twas writ that after we exchanged harsh words, Captain Keymis committed suicide. Alas, to my great shame and guilt, which I shall ever acknowledge to your lordship's ear alone, this is untrue. For in my anguish at the loss of mine own son's life, and in my anger against Captain Keymis' engagement of the Spaniards, which *was both in contravention of His Majesty's order and was to beset us with enemies for the rest of our journey, I did myself shoot him.*

This act being witnessed by the men lost me whatsoever shred of respect still clung to mine authority as commander of the expedition, and from that point the ships began to desert me.

After the voyage up the Capuri, we hasted away toward our purposed discovery and came at last to a great expanse of salt water. In one last resolve of faith, methought we hath good hap to come upon the lake upon which standeth the city of Inga, a salt lake 200 leagues long which the Jaos call Roponowini. But it was not so. We had instead arrived at Serpent's Mouth, and the isle of Trinidad was visible in the distance. It was the Atlantic Ocean. I was stricken into a great melancholy.

Abandoning all hope of El Dorado, Raleigh set sail for England. En route, all his other ships turned pirate, deserting the fleet, and he limped home, failed and goldless, to face the King's wrath with only one ship.

My dear son lying under foreign soil on the banks of the Orenque, unblessed of a Christian burial, I have no more desire for mine own life. It pleaseth His Majesty, to satisfy the Spaniards and in justifiable displeasure at my lack of booty, again to place me in irons.

I remain possessed with the notion that a Mapuche kalku hath seized my soul, and I doubt not the verity of this fear. Lacking in interpreter I had comprehended not the utterances of the machi sorceress as we stale her country's potatoes, these fruits which hath enjoyed their fertility by the blessings of the ceremony we observed, but I doubt not that she was desirous to put a curse upon my spirit.

Her curse hath visited upon me death by potato of one of my men; devouring of two others by horrible, ravenous hairless beasts who may have been the demoniacal metamorphoses of potatoes; bewitching of our encampment by an eyeless, caped drummer-woman mayhap under the ecstasy of potato liquor; and mine own near demise at the hands of a human-formed blood-sucking ghost on horseback who was very far from abiding a peaceful afterlife eating black potatoes.

I beg your lordship to consider, thenceforth whensoever shall the English go forth into foreign parts, that we should pay the just and fair price for whatsoever we shall take.

By my hand and my folly, I bequeath to you these dark memories, that by your mercy, they may find rest where my bones will not.

I pray that the good Lord receiveth my soul.

Written from the Tower, on this Saint Crispin's Day, in the year of our Lord sixteen hundred eighteen.

Raleigh's tobacco pouch lay beside the completed letter on the table. He took up the pen from his quill and, using it as a blade, carved upon the leather, *Comes meus fuit in ill miserriumo tempore* (it was my companion at that most miserable time).

Historical note:

The story of Raleigh first bring the potato to Ireland may be apocryphal. See Salaman (2000) p. 149 and Safford, The Potato of Romance and Reality. Botanical historians say the potatoes first grown in Ireland came from Spain. See the 1750 Cáth Bearna Chroise Brighde. His botanist Thomas Hariot brought back tobacco and 'openawk' plants from 'Virginia'. But if Raleigh had been involved in the introduction of the potato to Ireland, he would either have obtained them from Chile or from Cartagena

(Columbia) via Francis Drake, who docked there after rescuing his starving Roanoak colonists.

Raleigh's failed colony of Roanoak was in what is today North Carolina. The entirety of the land claimed by England was called by Raleigh 'Virginia'.

Raleigh's men stealing the potatoes is my invention. Actually, Raleigh believed the best way to establish dominion over the natives was to instigate friendly relations, and he insisted that his men pay for everything they obtained from them.

I've used some of the placenames (e.g. Assapano) and incidents from his first expedition.

The crockery with disfigured human features was actually more characteristic of the Moche pottery of Peru.

Putyma was actually the name of the lord of another region, Aromaia.

Raleigh's shooting of Captain Keymis is my invention, but it could have happened.

The Jews' Garden

by Elaine Graham-Leigh

The garden was out of sight of the Bena house, hidden by the slope of the hill. Only the branches of the fruit trees appeared above its walls, waving dark against the morning sun. The gate in the corner of the kitchen yard led to the alley between, but the Bena family seldom went that way. They faced forward, down to the workshop and the river and the new lower town beyond the bridge, away from the garden and its ancient stones. Except in the spring, when the blossom swirled over the wall like snow and Matheline's father growled, 'that garden should be ours.'

Matheline's mother told her that it had belonged to them once, until grandfather Raimond sold it to Creschas of Orange for fifty *livres*. That money had paid for extending the workshop and had bought besides the half-share in the carding shed over at Limoux which would be in Matheline's dowry when she married Aymeric Canet. It had been a good bargain, too good to be without a cost attached. Land here in the *cité* of Carcassonne was expensive, but fifty *livres* was still a high price for a garden. They had been tempted and now they regretted it. It went to show, her mother said, that you could never trust a Jew.

Matheline thought she remembered, from when she was very young, her grandfather sitting over wine with a man who had a long, grey beard and curling ringlets on each side of his face. They were talking, and laughing, and then her grandfather slapped his arm round the other man's shoulders, as if he was a friend. People said that long ago, here in the south, Jews had lived just like everybody else. The Jews' house was only up the street. It had a tower so old it could have come from the time of the Saracens. Matheline had played with Sarah and Isaac, Creschas' grandchildren, sometimes, until the family stopped coming to Carcassonne. Gui Peire came up from the lower town to check on the house and the garden, once in every new moon, but otherwise the house and the garden were empty.

When Matheline was sixteen, she broke into the garden. It was one morning after Easter and she had been taking cuttings from the herbs in the kitchen yard. It had been a dry, cold winter and the plants that hadn't died were thin and withered. There was hardly enough to cut; she would have to send Anna out to buy in the market. A breeze had blown in from the east, over the wall from the garden, bringing with it the scents of all the things growing in that good soil, thyme and rosemary and the fruit trees flowering.

It had been like a breath of a wider world and she had been suddenly angry. Why should the Jews have all that richness and beauty, while she knelt in the dust? Why shouldn't she take some of it back?

She hooked her empty basket into the crook of her arm and marched out of the yard. Across the alley was the gate to the garden, half-hidden in flowering creeper. She pushed the tendrils aside and tried the handle. It was locked, but the wood around it was old and rotten. She wrenched at the ring of the handle, once, twice, and then the third time, there was a great crack and the gate juddered open. She froze for a moment, sure that someone would come to investigate the noise, but no one did. She shoved around the edge of the gate and into the garden.

The rosemary bushes were everywhere, decked with mauve

flowers. She cut bunch after bunch of the stalks, pulled handful after handful of thyme, even chopped sprigs of lavender with the flowers still tight and pale, just because she could, just for the sake of taking it, hacking at them so roughly that she was pulling some of them up by the roots. There was so much it wouldn't all fit in her basket, she had to leave some of it piled by the side of the overgrown path, throwing it out, breathing heavily as if she had been running, or fighting.

The gate wouldn't lock again. She managed to pull it so that it at least looked closed. She wondered if Gui Peire would have trouble because of it.

'It serves him his deserts, a Christian working for Jews,' she told herself. She wasn't sure if she believed it. She crossed back over the yard and went in at the kitchen door. Anna turned from where she was tending the cassoulet over the hearth.

'God's bones, where did you get all that?'

Matheline tipped her chin up, ignoring the question. Anna might forget that she was a woman grown now, but she didn't.

'I'll leave them here for you to see to the drying,' she said.

Anna gave her a long, level look, holding her eyes until Matheline turned away.

'Yes, Mistress,' Anna said to her back.

She weighted the title like a blow, and Matheline couldn't stop herself from flinching. Anna could not have known where she had been, what she had done, but it seemed as if she did, and that she judged her.

Lying sleepless that night beside her sisters, Matheline turned it over in her mind. Was stealing from Jews a sin? Was it wrong, to take from the garden? She didn't know what a priest would say, but it felt to her now like theft, and worse, destruction. She remembered that frenzy of cutting with a shudder, how she'd wrenched the lavender from its home and left it uprooted and dying. She didn't want to do that, ever again.

She vowed also that in penance she would never go to the garden again, but as the weeks passed and Gui Peire came and went without any enquiries or repairs to the broken lock, it began to seem as if never was quite a long time. There was no harm in just looking, she thought. She would not be stealing anything. So, all that year, whenever she could get free unobserved from her household duties, she slipped away to the garden.

One day, in the following spring, she was sitting up at the far end, out of the sun, where the chicory and the bellflowers bloomed among the rocks at the foot of the east wall. She had a bit of stitching in her lap, but she wasn't working on it, she was simply watching the tree branches swaying over the blue sky.

The scrape of the gate against the stone lintel was so unexpected that for a long moment, she couldn't understand what it was. Then she realised.

She jumped up, shedding cloth, needle and thread, trying to straighten her skirts and tidy her hair. She had let her headcloth fall back into the undergrowth behind the stone she had been sitting on. She couldn't see where it had gone. Where was it?

Leaning over, she spotted a corner of the cloth, but it was caught on a twig and wouldn't come to her hand. She pulled it hard and heard it tear.

'Oh, by God's b****cks!' she cried.

'Now, now, is that any sort of language for a young lady?'

It was a man's voice, but with a laugh in it. She turned round and saw him on the overgrown path, grinning up at her.

He did not look like a servant. She noted the bands of Italian brocade edging his tunic and the little, silvered feathers on his cap. He looked like a successful merchant, albeit a young one, only a little older than her. He took off his cap, revealing blond curls, and bowed to her.

'I know who you are, don't I?' he said. 'You're Matheline, Arnaud Bena's daughter.'

He said it with such an air of triumph that she couldn't help smiling back at him.

'And I know who you are. You're Joshua of Orange's son Isaac.'

She held out her hand and he took it as she stepped down to the path. She stopped in front of him.

He wasn't tall, his chin was barely higher than hers, but his eyes were deep blue-grey, narrowed against the sun. He went on holding her hand.

'Good day, then, Matheline,' he said. His hand was smooth and cool on hers.

'Good day to you,' she said. 'Good day.'

All that spring and summer, it seemed to Matheline that no time was real except for the time she spent secretly with Isaac, in the garden. She drifted through her days as if nothing could touch her, not her sisters' squabbling, nor her mother's talk of gowns and the Canet family's expectations; not even her father's complaining that the Jews could charge much more interest than he could on their loans. She did wonder in passing if he had always said such things about them, or if she was only now noticing it.

None of it mattered, though. None of it was really there, only Isaac. Only him.

When the air was heavy with sun and thyme and the bees buzzing in the lavender, drowsy with heat and kissing they would lie on his cloak under the apple trees and talk.

He had been sent now to oversee his family's Carcassonne business, but he had travelled all over. He told her of Pisa and Genoa and Avignon of the Popes, and she caught him up on ten years of Carcassonne gossip. They talked about the world, about his life and hers, and he said that in all his journeying, he had never seen anyone as beautiful as she.

One afternoon, watching the clouds scudding through the branches, she said, transported, 'I think we have found the way into the Garden of Eden.'

He propped himself up on one elbow to look at her and she was suddenly afraid that she had blundered.

'I'm sorry, should I not...? I didn't think...'

He took her hand, where it lay on the cloak between them, and kissed it, then her lips.

'You could never say anything wrong, love. Anyway, don't you know that Adam and Eve are in our holy book?'

'No!' she laughed, half-shocked, 'Really?'

'We are not as different as you think,' he said, and he kissed her again.

Then, on a day in the middle of July, he was late. It was hot, so hot and close she longed to fling open a window even though she was outside. She waited on the path, feeling herself wilting like the flowers. He had never been late before. What could be wrong?

When at last she heard his step in the alley it should have been a relief, but as he slipped through the gate, she saw he was wearing no tunic over his shirt, that he had on old shoes and a plain hood over his hair. He was usually so careful of his clothes, so happily proud of the money it had cost for him to have them, but now he could have been anybody. Fear gripped her like a fist around her heart.

He pushed the gate shut behind him and stopped.

She asked, 'what is it? Oh, love, what is it?'

He was staring down at his feet in their stained, rough shoes. 'I have had word from my father,' he said. 'I have to leave. I have

The Jews' Garden

to pack up anything I can, and leave, and not come back.'

'When?'

He looked up and she saw the chill that seized her reflected in his eyes.

'Now.'

'Now?' she echoed. 'How can you go now? How can you leave a life with so little time? And not come back? Not ever? What does he think you…? What does it mean?'

Her head was swimming. She felt herself begin to sway, gripping a rosemary bush for support, crushing the stems. He rushed to catch her.

'Let's get you into the shade,' he said.

He drew her under the trees, under their apple tree, where they used to lie. This time he had no cloak to put down. She stood, letting the trunk hold her up, and he leant next to her. The scent of crushed rosemary hung around them.

'It's not my father's fault. He had word, from Paris. It's a close secret, but he has friends in strange places, they know he has interests here, still, so they warned him. The Lord King is going to round up all the Jews in the kingdom, imprison us and take all our property. After that, if we are lucky, we may be allowed to leave. If not…'

He waved his hand, a gesture that sketched the castle, the prison, the walls and the King's fine new gibbets on the high road to Narbonne.

'So I have to leave. I have time, I think, to get out of France and into Provence before the day appointed. Before they start.'

'I see,' she said.

She did see, she knew these things were done, in other places, in the north where the sun never shone. She had just never thought…

'I can see it's not your father's fault; it's mine. My father and people like him. I'm sorry.'

She turned away, unable to look at him. He patted her on the shoulder, the first awkward gesture she had ever known him make.

'You could come with me,' he said into her hair. 'Be my wife and come away with me, it will be as if we brought the garden with us.'

She didn't move. 'And what will your father say, to your marrying a Christian?'

'You could convert. Besides,' he shrugged, 'he would come to accept it in time. And if he didn't, we could go far away. Be damned to him!'

She could hear the laugh brave in his voice. He slipped his arm round her waist, holding her close, and she rested her hand on his.

'And the laws? The laws that say no Jew may marry a Christian?'

'Then we'll go somewhere where there are no laws. We'll go to Chin, or Arabia, or the land of Prester John if we have to.'

'And build ourselves a palace of rubies and gold, with fountains and gardens at the centre like in the days of the Saracens?'

'You have it exactly,' he said.

She turned back round then, so that she could see his face. He was still smiling, but his eyes in the shade of the tree were sombre. She could tell that he knew as well as she what they had to do, and she loved him for pretending.

'When you find the land of Prester John, you can come back and fetch me,' she said.

After a while, crushed against his shoulder, she raised her head and saw how the sun had moved.

'You have to go, if you're going to be on the road before night.'

'I do.' He pushed back her hair where it had come loose from its braiding. 'Will you be all right? What will you do?'

'Oh, I'll be all right,' she said. 'I'll marry Aymeric Canet and live in their house out at Montolieu. It may even be that there will be a garden, in time, although it won't be as beautiful as this one. And you? What will you do?'

'We have the house in Orange, and my father has friends in Genoa and Padua, and maybe further than that. He has said before he thinks our future is in the east.'

He tipped her chin up with his finger, tracing the tracks of her tears.

'Don't cry, love, there's nothing to cry for. When I get to Chin, I'll send you back some silk.'

'Aymeric will like that,' she said, trying to be tart.

He smiled at her for one last time.

'I'll send him back some as well.'

After he had gone, she sat for a long time in the heat, watching the shadows creep out from the walls and the jasmine flowers open, white and sweet, until it was almost full dark. When she raised her hand to brush away her last tears, it smelled still of the rosemary. She went into the house holding it to her face.

***

When, a week later, the property of all the Jews in the kingdom was seized by the King's men, the seneschal had the garden locked and barred. It stayed that way for years, while the weeds grew and the creepers undermined the walls. When the seneschal came to sell it, Arnaud Bena said that he was too beset by the royal debt collectors, who were so much worse than the Jews had been, and by the costs of his daughters' marriages, to be able to find the price.

It went eventually to Simon of Albencon for ten *livres*. He wasn't much for flowers, he said, but he needed somewhere in the *cité* to keep his goats.

Historical note:

On Friday 22nd July 1306, King Philippe IV had the entire Jewish population of the Kingdom of France, about 100,000 people, rounded up and imprisoned. Their houses were searched, and their property seized by the Crown. They were released gradually between that August and October with little more than the clothes on their backs and forced to leave France on pain of death. It is not known how many died in prison or on the journey.

In Carcassonne, in the south of France, property seized from Jews and sold by the King's seneschal included a garden belonging to Isaac d'Orange. This is almost certainly not its story.

Chocolatl

by Susie Helme

The old crone rubbed her cold fingers against her leather apron to warm them as she arranged her utensils. Her hands were clean, her fingers gnarled with age yet spotless of any dirt, nails neatly groomed and pared. A stone jug on the table was filled with clear spring water. She poured a few drops from it into one hand and then the other and flicked the moisture into the fire. As it sizzled, her shadow loomed large against the wall.

The supplicant knelt beside her, whimpering.

'Grandmother, I cannot forget it. My spirit will not heal. He came to my door in his black hood with his face all painted blue and red. They took her from me, with their knives. She looked at me, straight into my eyes, screaming, as they wrenched her from my arms.'

'She is with the gods,' the old woman soothed.

Another stone jug held fresh llama's milk, still steaming. This the old woman poured in a slow drizzle into a cauldron of heating water hanging over the fire, and the sweet milk smell filled the hut.

The supplicant clutched at her breasts, remembering, and sobbed anew.

'My magic will heal your spirit,' the magic woman promised.

The crone took a handful of dark seeds from a sack, which she tossed onto a metal pan over the fire and roasted until they surrendered their aroma into the humid air of the hut. Then she moved the roasted seeds into a mortar with some red chili peppers and ground them with a pestle, then sprinkled the powder gently into the cauldron of heating liquid. Now and again, she added to it, a stick of spice bark, a pod of spice bean, a stalk of sugar cane. She stirred it with a wooden spoon as she spoke words in a slow drone over the fire, ancient words, words from grandmothers' fires and those of grandmothers' grandmothers, words that men have never heard.

Her words spoke of older gods, kinder gods, gods from a simpler world of beauty and love, gods, goddesses who still paid court to Toci as Queen of Heaven. The pungent brown smell made the girl's eyes water.

'Grandmother, I cannot accept it. She was born of love, the love my man bears for me, the love I bear for him.'

'From death springs new life,' she said.

'My man tells me so, but I do not want new life. I want her. She died of violence. The gods do not love this.'

'Only the gods of men love this. Tlaloc and Huitzilopochtli love this. The goddesses, Metztli and Tlalecuhtli, do not love this.'

The gods of men loved war, blood, killing, even of young babes. The priests and necromancers had their games and their sacrifices. Men's magic. The gods of women, goddesses, loved clean fingers and warm fires, fresh-ground corn flour and llama's milk, babies gurgling at young girls' breasts, beds piled to the rafters with fresh straw and soft skins. This was women's magic.

'My breasts still fill at the thought of her. I would fling myself into your fire.'

'You are not for the fire. The fire seeks another,' the magic woman said.

She whacked a cup of carved breadnutwood onto the table and next to it one just like it. She handed the girl the first cup and ladled into it some of the hot brown mixture from the cauldron.

'Drink, Daughter. *Chocolatl*, the drink of the gods,' she said.

This much will soothe the spirit and awaken the mind, the old crone thought. But this day's magic would go further.

'This cup brings life back to you. The other cup wants to take a life,' she said.

The girl sipped the silky potion obediently, the sweet steam collecting at her hairline. Her nostrils widened as the spice entered her bloodstream, and the thick sweetness filled her body. Her shoulders loosened as she felt the warmth down in her womb. She smiled for the first time in many days.

'The priest, Tlatoani. Your child is not the first innocent he has wrenched from its mother's arms.'

'Two of my cousins…'

'Yes, Daughter, and it is not only your cousins. Tlatoani says the children will speak to the gods and call upon them to give us victory in war. But that is not what the children say to the gods, is it, my dear?'

'No, they cry, they cry for their mothers.'

'And have the gods given the men their victory in war?'

'No, our fathers and brothers are killed, and our sisters and cousins are taken as slaves to foreign cities.'

The old crone walked around the fire and addressed the girl across the flames, 'My fire does not want you, Daughter. It wants him, Tlatoani.'

'So he can take no more babies up to his killing table atop the temple?'

'No more babies.'

'Yes, Grandmother, the monster should pay the price for all his killings.'

'Blood shall be the price for blood, and he shall be the one to pay it. It will be Tlatoani, not our babies, speaking to the gods asking them for victory in the men's wars. Will you serve me, Daughter?'

The old woman's magic had sated her as she drank from the wooden cup; her belly was full and the hole in her heart soothed. She no longer wished to throw herself on the fire.

'I am your servant, Grandmother, instruct me. What must I do?'

The old crone turned without answering and took a glass vial from a high shelf against the wall, and the girl understood.

'The men will demand vengeance,' she objected.

'Huitzilopochtli's knives do not seek you, my child.'

'But you, Grandmother?'

'You speak truly, for Tlatoani would not trust food nor drink from my fire. Your cousins, will they serve me?'

'Yes, Grandmother, I am certain of it.'

'Then we shall speak to them and the other mothers in grief. We shall take him all together, and thus the men cannot demand vengeance. How many daughters have been wronged?'

'Me, my cousins, and… altogether nine, since the new moon.'

'It is good. Nine is a magical number beloved of the Queen of Heaven. Each of the nine shall add a drop from this vial into this cup.'

The girl greedily grasped the other cup with one hand, as with the other she drained her own cup down to the bitter, gritty powder at the bottom.

The supplicant departed from the hut smiling.

Behold how women's magic heals, the old crone thought.

III Funnybones

The Curious Case of the Kitnapped Cat

by em.thompson

Heather Prendergast blinked as a piece of chalk whistled past her ear.

'You at the back, there,' Professor Morrisson shouted. 'Would you like to tell the rest of the class what you're thinking?'

'Is that a trick question, sir?' Prendergast asked, assuming that Morrisson had lobbed her a curveball. After all, he knew better than most that she was, as a rule, ready and willing to share her thoughts with anyone prepared to listen. The problem was that they were few and far between. Anyones, that is. She had no end of thoughts.

'In your own time, Miss Prendergast,' Morrisson said. 'I'm sure we would all like to hear what you have to say.'

Prendergast stood to attention, cleared her throat and said, 'when we have eliminated the impossible, whatever remains, however improbable, must be the truth.'

'As I thought, you weren't listening.' Morrisson looked around the classroom and gave his stubble a thoughtful scratch. 'Right then, who would like to recap for Miss Prendergast's benefit?'

Terrence 'Tiny' Bottomley put up his hand. 'You were telling us that the most important weapons in a modern detective's armoury are forensics, CCTV footage, DNA analysis, psychological profiling and artificial intelligence software. These days, policing is all about lab work, not guesswork. Rigorous scientific process is the order of the day.'

As he paused for breath, Prendergast chipped in with her twopenneth's worth. 'All well and good, but I beg to differ,' she said with a certainty of purpose that brooked no doubts. 'In my book, there is no substitute for good old-fashioned gut instinct. In the words of the greatest detective ever to have lived, you can't see the lettuce and the dressing without suspecting a salad. Ask a glorified abacus to crack a case involving a colander of tossed greens, a stick of celery, some diced cucumber, a dash of olive oil and a dribble of balsamic vinegar, and see where it gets you. I would humbly suggest, not very far.'

'Give me strength...' Morrison rolled his eyes in a show of anatomical exasperation. 'That's it. I've heard enough. And the rest of you, stop sniggering. Class dismissed. Not you, Miss Prendergast,' he said with a note of ominous intent. As the other students shuffled out chattering like natterjacks, he clasped his hands behind his back, looked Prendergast in the eye and broke into a ferocious scowl. 'If I may say, Miss Prendergast,' he said, 'it is high time you bucked up your ideas. Intuition has no place in modern policing. Hard, cold facts are the be-all and end-all. I should know. Damn it, I spent thirty years in the Met before being appointed Professor of Applied Deduction here. Had you taken the trouble to read the prospectus, you would know that I have a Master's in Administration, a Doctorate in Policing and a PhD in Social Policy.'

'Gosh, sir, your mother must be awfully proud. But with all due respect, a pen-pusher with a few diplomas from goodness knows where is hardly an ideal role model. As my aunt would say, those who can, do. Those who can't, teach.'

'I beg your pardon?' Professor Morrisson glared at Prendergast as if he had a deaf wish. 'Good grief, I have never heard the likes of it in all my born days. It's hardly surprising you are the most unpopular girl in college.'

'Oh, come on, sir. Nothing could be further from the truth. Terrence Bottomley is forever pestering me to go out with him. As if... Oik. And really—how was I to know that all my classmates would be too busy washing their hair to attend my inaugural Sherlock Holmes study group? We did roleplay, or at least I did. I had a whale of a time.'

'Oh, is that so? And does that include Tomkins?'

'Yes, sir.'

'Busy washing his head, was he? He's as bald as a coot.' Morrisson tapped his chin with the blunt end of his pencil and said, 'can't pretend I'm not worried about you, Prendergast. I've noticed that you always sit on your own at the back of class. And correct me if I'm wrong, but I don't remember seeing you at the Christmas party.'

'There was a party? Golly. No one told me.'

'Maybe it would help if you dressed... well, let's just say, a little more modestly. It might have escaped your notice, but none of your classmates buy their clothes in Paris and Milan.'

'I say, sir, that's rather elitist, wouldn't you say? It's hardly my fault they have no taste.'

'What I'm getting at, Heather, is that you need to make more of an effort to fit in. Reporting Rory Gardener for having a bald tyre on his wheelchair and demanding that Sandra Bullingham be expelled for dropping a sweet wrapper on the pavement haven't exactly endeared you to your fellow students.'

'Begging your pardon, sir, but littering is an extremely serious offence. If we can't keep our own house in order, how can we be expected to police the nation? Cripes, anarchy would break out in the streets.'

'Enough. Fact is, I asked you to stay behind to discuss your coursework.'

'Thanks awfully, sir. I've been meaning to have a word in your ear about that. One out of ten was frightfully mean. I did my best.'

'That, Miss Prendergast, is what concerns me. If I may say, you are not cut out for public service. Considered a career in hospitality? I hear McDonald's is recruiting.'

'Not likely, sir. I've had a passion for solving crime ever since I caught Brown Owl and Scout Leader up to no good in the boiler room at boarding school. It put a whole new slant on the meaning of bob a job, I can tell you. Must say, crouching in that cupboard, peeking through the keyhole all afternoon made a dreadful mess of my gym slip, but needs must as needs be, I suppose. To be fair, I must admit that paperwork isn't my strong point, but give me a case to crack, and you have my word I won't let you down. Guide's honour.'

'Hmmm. Well, maybe I'll give you one last chance. After all, your aunt paid for the new sports pavilion, not that the principal would let that cloud his judgement,' Professor Morrisson said, then muttered, 'not much it wouldn't,' under his breath. He sighed, shook his head, and sighed again 'Very well. For this week's assignment, I want you to write an essay about tracking down a missing person. And you'd better step up to the mark, young lady. Make no mistake, you are drinking at the last chance saloon.' He pressed two fingers together and held them up for her to see. 'I am that close—that close—to asking you to leave. The chance of you passing your exams is about as likely as my wife winning a beauty contest, and she's built like a sumo wrestler. Packs a punch like one too,' he said with a grim grimace.

Deep in the dumps of despair, Heather Prendergast trudged back to her digs with her shoulders hunched and her hands in her coatigan pockets. A girl of action, not words, listening to Professor Morrisson drone on about procedural persnicketies was not what she had in mind when she enrolled at Merton Police College.

How on earth, she asked herself, was she going to salvage a career that looked as if it had hit the buffers before it had even left the station? Her spirits slumped still further when she found Terrence 'Tiny' Bottomley waiting on her doorstep.

'Can't,' she said when he invited her to join him for a milkshake and a muffin at the campus coffeeteria. 'Must have a word with Cook, Missus Pratley, about the food in the dining hall. If I see another chicken curry or pasta bake, I swear I'll lose the will to live.'

'Mind if I tag along?' Tiny asked.

'Mind? I'd be mortified,' said Prendergast as diplomatically as she knew how. Feeling smaller than a gnat's mandible following her classroom humiliation, she left Tiny to mope and made her way to the college diner. After making a detour to the library to return a copy of Elementary Anatomy by Doctor John H. Watson—a ripping yarn, if a little too explicit in places and not explicit enough in others—she arrived to find the kitchen relatively cookless.

Manning the fort—in a gender neutral manner of speaking—was a job-opportunity skivvy mindlessly scrubbing congealed grease off curried saucepans and scraping baked pasta off pewter porringers.

Seeing how long in the face she looked, Prendergast asked, 'I say, young lady, are you alright?'

With a sniffle and a snuffle, the girl dabbed her eyes with a cornerflap of pinafore. 'Don't know what to do,' she mumbled. 'Been looking after gran's cat, Puffball, while she's in hospital having a new hip fitted. When I went to pet him in me tea break, he was gone. Can't have done a runner. I locked the door when I left. Anyway, his shit-tray's missing. Someone's nicked him. Must have. Gran will go mental if I don't find him. He's all she's got since me granddad ran off with his therapist. Last I heard, they were living the life of Reilly in Billericay.'

As is so often the case, a casual comment triggered a humzinger of a brainwave. Not just a penny but a mighty fifty-pence piece dropped as it struck Prendergast that if she could crack The Curious Case of the Kitnapped Cat, it would restore her credibility with Professor Morrisson, win the respect of the ghastly swots in her class and steer her career back on track. Hiving with excitement, she said, 'chin up, young lady. This might just be your lucky day. You see, I'm apprentice constable Heather Prendergast, one of the home county's foremost trainee detectives. Rest assured, you can leave the matter in my capable hands, Miss...'

'Debbie Smith,' the kitchenary assistant said. 'Me mates call me Debbs. Mind if I call you Preggers?'

'I'd rather you didn't.'

'Well, I'm going to, so like it or lump it.' Debbie cocked Prendergast a snook and stuck out her tongue.

Resisting the temptation to give the unspeakable brat a clip round the ear, Prendergast found a smile and said, 'righty-ho, Debbs. What say you we meet up after school and get cracking?'

That afternoon blinked by in the lash of an eye, figuratively speaking. As was her modus operandi, Prendergast sat at the back of the lecture hall, gazing out of the window, dreaming of an illustrious career as Prendergast of The Yard. Trying not to yawn as Professor Morrisson prattled on about this and that in a monotonous monotone, she asked herself why on God's good earth was she frittering her life away listening to a washed-up pension-pusher extol the virtues of pseudo-scientific claptrap? To her way of mind, a superannuated PC Plod with a few highfalutin study coupons was hardly qualified to lecture her—to lecture anyone—on blood spatter analysis, psychopathic amygdala or mass spectrometry forensics. Let's face it, he was hardly Hercule Poirot.

By the time her last class—Racial Profiling and Tasering—wound to a dreary close, Prendergast had confected an audacious plot of action. To say that she was a jangle of nerves would not be overegging the pudding. Fact was, she was on tenterhooks—and for good reason. Having devoted a lifetime to the study of Sherlock Holmes, Sam Spade, Frank Drebin, Philip Marlow, Lieutenant Columbo and other masters and—in the case of Miss Marple and Jessica Fletcher—mistresses of the noble art of crimebusting, she could scarcely believe that she had a real life felony to investigate.

If she cracked the case—and she had not one shadow of a doubt that she would—it could take her one step further along the yellow brick road to her destiny as Inspector Prendergast of New Scotland Yard. Having said that, it went without much saying that all would not be plain sailing. In particular, it was as clear as moonlight that Debbie Smith was no Maddie Hayes. But still, as Aunt Elizabeth never tired of reminding her, needs must as needs be in the pursuit of justice, adolescent whippersnappers notwithstanding.

Keen as mayonnaise, Prendergast hurried back to her digs, raring to go. After wolfing down a chocolate orange and a finger of fudge to equipoise her blood sugar levels, she rooted through her cloak and daggeries and applied some subterfugal makeup. Togged up to the nines, she inspected her reflection in the wardrobe mirror and, confident that not even she would recognise herself, set off for a hard night's day gumshoeing.

'Why are you dressed like an old codger?' Debbie asked, trying not to giggle when Prendergast came striding down the lane.

'I'm in disguise,' Prendergast explained as she adjusted her false beard and straightened her wig. Granted, her overalls itched like a monk's twitch, and as for her hobnail boots, clumpy was not the word. Or maybe it was. But as Aunt Elizabeth would say, one must make sacrifices in the line of plainclothes duty, bargain bootwear notwithstanding. 'I'm planning to stake out the park,' she told Debbie. 'I've a hunch that Puffball might have been snatched by a vagrant with a Dick Whittington complex.'

Barely ten minutes later, as the clock flies—give or take a tick or two—trainee police officer Heather Prendergast and her makeshift Watson, cookery assistant Debbie Smith, could be found lurking in Ducktail Park, a stone's skip from the scene of the crime—Debbie's bedsitting slum in Merton Estate. Assuming the air of a common-or-garden horticulturist, Heather took cover behind a rhododendron bush and—to use a technical term miss-learnt in Copperslang class—cased an eye over a bedraggled straggle of homelessness swigging cans of gaseous water by the ornamental pond. As her snacktime sugar-rush ebbed and her dopamine receptors flagged, she was beginning to nod off when she felt a hand on her shoulder.

'Here, what's your game, mate?' an officious voice demanded.

Prendergast pressed a finger to her lips. 'Shh... ' she whispered. 'I'm looking for pussy.'

'Oh, you are, are you?' The park keeper said. 'Well, we'll see about that. Consider yourself bang to rights, you dirty old git.'

Prendergast swallowed. She swallowed twice. She swallowed several times. She was about to move seamlessly into panic mode when parkman howled and staggered back, clutching his backside.

'Come on, Preggers—let's leg it before that jobsworth digs the trowel out of his arse and busts you for tompeepery.' Debbie grabbed Prendergast's arm and dragged her into the bushes. 'If you take off that rubbish disguise,' she said, 'he'll never recognise you.'

'But I'm not wearing anything under my overalls,' Prendergast stuttered. 'Just a bra and knickers.'

'Count yesself lucky. All I got on under me tracksuit is an electronic ankle tag,' Debbie said with a smutty smirk. 'So it's strip down to your Lady Godivas or get your collar felt. Your choice.'

Left with no sartorial alternative, Heather Prendergast did as Debbie suggested and hid her blushes in the bushes. When she was satisfied the coast was clear, she tiptoed out of the shrubbery, goosepimpled and shivery, with Debbie a tipstep behind.

'Rats,' she cussed as she rattled the park gate. 'We're locked in.' Blushing like a radish, she took a deep—a very deep—breath. 'Only one thing for it, Debbs. We're going to have to climb over the fence.'

'Piece of piss,' Debbie said. 'One of my fellas lives in a third-floor squat. I'm in and out of his bedroom window like a randy spider. Come on, follow me.' Like a will o' the wanton wisp, she clambered up the fence and jumped down on the other side.

'Lordy Lou, what a palaver,' Prendergast gulped as she gripped the fence and searched for handholds in the sheer. But minded that Prendergast of The Yard knows no fear... earwigaphobia and occasional bouts of dreadheightedness excepted... intrepid as always—reckless, it might be said, or witless—she grabbed ahold of the railings and hauled herself up, hand over fist, fist over hand, foot by foot, one yard, two yards, three... Bruised, battered and bemused—her hair was a frightful mess and her nails were scuffed beyond affordable repair—she scrabbled over the toppermost railing like a dyslexic pool vaulter and was about to leap to freedom when she was accosted by a bellow from below.

'Hello, hello, hello, and who have we here?' the policeman shouted at the top of his voice. 'This is a municipal park, not a nudist camp—more's the pity.'

With a helping hand from the long arm of the law, Prendergast clambered down the shallow side of the fence, embarrassed beyond all measure by her virtual nakedness. Before she could fabricate a plausible lie, Debbie burst out of the bushes like a pocketsprite and came haring to the rescue.

'Me mate was assaulted by a sleezy bloke with a scraggy beard and grey hair. He near as not stripped her naked and would have done me, too, if I hadn't legged it,' she said before Prendergast could plant a foot in her mouth. 'We hid in the duck-house till it were safe to scarper.'

'I see,' the policeman said in such a way as to suggest that he didn't believe a word... not a misplaced comma, not a slovenly colon, not a periodic full stop. 'You'd better accompany me to the station and give me a full description, Miss...?'

'Holmes,' Prendergast said. 'Shirley Holmes. And this is my assistant, Dot Watson.' She waved a hand at Debbie, who waved two fingers back.

It was late—very late—by the time that Heather Prendergast and Debbie Smith left Merton Police Station. Or to put it another way, it was early—very early—in the morning before Prendergast was released from the cells, having persuaded the desk sergeant that her naked swanabout was a rag week stunt. She was raising money for the Police Benevolent Fund, she claimed with a poker face. To add credence to her perfidy, she debit-carded an eye-watering swipe for the charity.

In return, she was let off with a raised finger rather than an official caution. Another hefty cardswipe sufficed to purchase a grubby ex-conman greatcoat from the lost and nicked department. Although it hid her shame, to be frank—as she went to great pains to be—it was hardly the height of cutting-edge fashion. But what really sent her hackles into orbit was the ghastly colour—olive-green clashed with her ginger hair like impetigo on a honeydew melon. Still, needs must as needs must, she reminded herself stoically, colourclash anathema notwithstanding.

When Debbie said that she looked like a dosser, she huffily pointed out that—to quote Aunt Elizabeth—beggars cannot as a rule be choosers. Anyway, she said snootily, preloved clothes were all the rage in the circles she moved in.

'So let me get this straight… you forked out two hundred squibs for a grubby raincoat with no belt and most of the buttons missing just to be trendy?' Debbie gave her head a slap to make sure she wasn't imagining things. Unconvinced, she pinched a leg and, to make quite sure, pinched the other.

'Shabby-chic doesn't come cheap, Debbs,' Prendergast said with a superior smile as they set off for the Merton Estate. 'Hang about… ' She pointed to a *something* moving in a dimlit alley on the unattached side of a semi-detached house. 'Think that could be Puffball?' She gripped Debbie's arm and, softlee-softlee-catchee-pussee, sneakerpimped into the alley. But rather than four legs, whiskers and a tail, the object of her suspicions turned out to be a flabby backside wedged in a frosted glass window.

'Excuse me, sir,' Prendergast said in her most officious voice. 'Mind telling me what you think you're doing?'

'Piss off,' came the curt reply.

'Now, now, sir. We'll have none of that language, if you please. I will have you know that I am a police officer,' Prendergast said, and almost added, 'almost,' under her breath.

A profanity or two later, the voice belonging to the bum said, 'lost my keys and tried climbing in through the toilet window but got stuck. If you give me a leg up and a push, I should be able to wriggle through.'

Prendergast glanced at Debbie, who shrugged as if to say, WTF? After a quick confab, the girls put their shoulders to windowman's bumcheeks and shoved with all their might. After a good many grunts and groans, the backside disappeared into the black of beyond.

'Thanks a million, my lovelies,' windowman whispered through the window. 'Do us a favour and keep this to yourselves. Don't want the old lady to get wind of it. Like as not, she'll put me on a goop wellness diet. Now, off you pop.'

'Right you are, sir. Mind how you go.' Prendergast said as she passed bum-man's balaclava, torch and sack through the window. Pleased as Punchinello to have discharged her civic duties with such due diligence, she bade Debbie goodnight, made her weary way home and flopped into bed like a flippertigibbet. Within seconds of her head hitting the pillow, she had drifted into default dreams of Prendergast of The Yard—the greatest detective the world would ever know.

Next morning, Prendergast burst into the classroom in somewhat of a tizz. Through no fault of her own—nothing ever was—she was a little late, but only by an hour or two. She looked around, not sure whether to be puzzled or relieved or both, to see that Professor Morrisson was nowhere to be seen. When she asked her classmates where he was, they ignored her.

Only Tiny Bottomley acknowledged her existence. 'The prof's house got burgled last night while he was asleep,' he told her. 'Forensics reckon the perp was wearing gloves, but they found two sets of dabs on a downstairs window. They think it might be Tubby Thompson's gang. The organised crime squad are checking all the security cameras in the vicinity to see if they got caught on film.'

'Jolly good show. Sounds like a result,' Prendergast said with a rub of the hands. 'It's possible I might recognise someone. Think I should offer to help with the investigation?'

'Wouldn't bother,' Tiny said. 'Like they say, too many cooks spoil the broth.'

'I wasn't suggesting I make them lunch,' Prendergast said, tongue possibly in cheek. Possibly not.

'Hey, those pink patent-leather sandals are ever so cute,' Tiny said with a glint in his eye. 'Must say, I like the dress. Spandex doesn't half suit you, and the freesia polka dots go great with your freckles.'

'What, this old thing?' Prendergast fingered her pleats with an air of casual aplomb. 'I've had it weeks. Wouldn't be surprised if it hasn't already gone out of fashion,' she scoffed with an offhand flick of a wrist.

And then she was struck by one of the most brilliantest ideas to permeate her little grey sludge all day... all month, quite possibly. 'Tiny,' she said, hardly able to precipitate her perspicacity. 'Know anything about drones?'

'Why?'

'I'm on the lookout for a kidnapped cat. It's a highly sensitive matter, so keep it under your hat. I seem to remember someone once telling me that search and rescue teams use drones to find missing persons.'

'That was Professor Morrisson. He gave us a lecture on the subject yesterday. Weren't you listening?'

'Oh, really, Tiny. Course I was. Just wanted to make sure you were, that's all. So how do they work? In practice, that is, not all that baloney Morrisson kept harping on about.'

'Let's discuss it over a milkshake and a muffin,' Tiny said. 'And call me Terry. After all, we're best mates.'

'Crikey, is that the time?' Prendergast made a pretence of checking her watch. 'Must wash my hair before I forget. Unless you can remind me what Professor Morrisson said.'

'Oh, all right,' Tiny mumbled. 'There's these new miniature spy-in-the-sky copter-drones, see. They work by remote control, like playing Grand Theft Auto.'

'Grand What What?' Prendergast gasped, shocked to the tucks of her little cotton socks. 'Terrence Bottomley, wash your mouth out with soap and water. Kindly remember where you are. We are studying to be police officers, not washerwomen... washermen... washerpeople.' She paused for thought, cleared her throat and asked, 'so, how would I go about getting my hands on one of these pie in the sky thingummies?'

'Spy, not pie. College has a bunch in the labs. They've been upgrading them with artificial intelligence. Security in the science block is pants, so you could lift one, easy, and no one would be any the wiser.'

'Hmmm... strictly speaking, that would be against the law, but don't suppose anyone would notice as long as you put it back first thing in the morning.'

'Me?' Tiny's eyes all but popped their sockets. To say that he was gobsmacked would be doing gobsmacking a disservice.

Prendergast cosied up to him and pouted her lips. 'Surely you can do me this one little favour, Terry. Pretty please?'

Caught on the thorns of a dilemma, Tiny shuffled, squirmed, squirmed and shuffled in no particular order. 'Oh, all right,' he said—with the greatest reluctance, it must be held. 'But if I do, will you come out on a date with me?'

Heather answered with a lashflutter and a smile.

'We can grab a burger at that new place on the High Street and then catch a movie. There's a double bill at the Gaumont—

Reservoir Dogs and *The Sound Of Music*.'

'Oh, goodie. That would be such fun.'

'Can we sit in the back row?'

'Why not?'

'And can I snog you rigid?'

Tiny picked himself up from the parquet floortiles and dabbed his bloody nose with the back of his hanky. 'I was joking,' he moped.

'Well, I wasn't,' Prendergast hissed through gritted teeth. 'I'll expect to see you outside the cafeteria at seven... with a drone.' She set her jaw and narrowed her eyes. 'And don't go getting any ideas, or you'll be eating breakfast through a straw.'

Prendergast was late for the rendezvous—it had taken her near enough forever to decide what to wear. Caught in several minds, she eventually settled on an everyday pair of hipster jeans with *fleur de lis* motifs on the flares and the first buttercup-lemon Muga silk blouse that came to hand. To make matters worse, it took an absolute age for her nail varnish to dry.

Unimpressed, she made a mental note not to skimp on essentials in future. Still, what can you expect for only fifty guineas, she told herself with a frugal smile. Me, oh, my... the lengths a girl must go to look presentable, she sighed as she laced up her Miu Miu platform sneakers. She was sure that dear old Sherlock never had this trouble; a tweed suit, cape, spats, brogues, a magnifying glass, a deerstalker hat, a revolver, and voila—he was dressed to kill. After a quick glance in the mirror and several much longer ones, she grabbed her shoulder bag from the baghook and dashed out of the door, keen as custard to knuckle down to sleuth.

'Sorry I'm late,' she said when she joined her crack undercover team puffing and panting like a geriatric puffin after sprinting down the lane. 'Hope you didn't get bored waiting.'

The Curious Case of the Kitnapped Cat

'No worries,' Debbie said as she zipped up her jeans and tucked in her t-shirt.

'We found stuff to do,' said Tiny as he wiped the lipstick off his pimply face, brushed the hair off his turtle-neck and belted up his bell-bottoms.

After a quick headcount to make sure that everybody was present and correct, Prendergast led the way to a humpy hillock with a panoramaed view of the rolling hills, the undulating dales, the historic village of Merton-on-Wandle, the ancient woodlands stretching far into the distance, the lazy old river awash with raw sewage and dead fish and the six-lane highway slicing through the idyllic countryside like a chainsaw massacre.

After briefing her team, she rubbed her hands, ready to spring into action like a clockwork goat. 'Jeepers, is that the drone?' she gasped when Tiny took a techniflummoxed whirlybird out of his carryall.

'Sure is. State of the art. Onboard camera with an ultra-definition telephoto lens, high-resolution microphone, miniature hard disc recorder and an infra-red sensor capable of detecting a pulse at two hundred metres. This is the remote control. Neat, eh?' Tiny showed Prendergast a small box-shaped box with three rows of buttons, an LED display and a telescopic antenna. 'If you want the drone to go left, nudge the joystick left. If you want to go right...'

'Yes, yes, I get the picture.' Prendergast wrested the remote from Tiny's hands and dismissed his protests with, 'I'm heading up the investigation so I'll take charge, thank you very much. What's this for?'

'Don't,' Tiny screamed as she pressed a large red button.

'F*** a duck,' Debbie expleted as the drone took off like a pocket rocket, shredding her baseball cap into cottonbuds as it whizzed past her nose.

'Go left,' Tiny yelled as Prendergast pushed every button she could find. 'I said left, not right. Oh no... ' He caught his breath and covered his eyes with his scarf.

Debbie pointed to a nearby petrol station. 'Reckon that girl will manage to get out of the way before...?' Her question proved more rhetorical than not as, with an ear-splitting scream, the petrol pump attendant dropped the fuel hose and threw herself to the ground as the drone whirred past her head. Moments later, a sheet of flame engulfed the pumps, and a chariot of fire raced towards a petrol tanker parked on the forecourt. According to the coroner's report, the explosion could be heard in Casablanca and the fireball seen from the dark side of the moon.

'Golly. So, how do I order this thing back to base?' Prendergast asked as the drone emerged from a billowing cloud of thick black smoke and turned towards the motorway.

'You can't. When you pressed that red button, you activated the artificial intelligence. It's gone rogue, so you'll have to abort the mission. Hit self-destruct,' Tiny urged. 'Quick.'

'Which knob?' Prendergast asked, and to be on the safe side, pressed them all.

'Oh my God... you just ordered it to attack,' Tiny groaned as, buzzing like a swarm of angry mechanical hornets, the drone made a beeline for a highway patrol car speeding down the motorway towards a conflagration that seemed dead set on reducing the picturesque village of Merton-on-Wandle and it's chirpy-chappy habitants to a crisp—with the emphasis on dead.

'Crikey, you didn't tell me it was armed,' Prendergast panicked as the drone swooped into the breakneck dive of a kamikaze Stuka and opened fire.

Tiny said, 'relax. They're only blanks.'

'Not sure about that,' Prendergast said nervously as a hail of bullets slammed into the patrol car, sending it swerving into an ambulance—a fitting end for two exanimated police officers and a morted superintendent. 'Oh, no,' she clapped her hands to her cheeks as the drone banked through ninety degrees and, machine guns rat-a-tatting like Gatling guns, headed for an articulated lorry.

As a burst of gunfire shattered the windscreen, the truck driver keeled over with a heart attack and slumped down on the steering wheel with one foot on the gas and the other on the brake. Swerving this way that and the other, the trailer jack-knifed into the bullet-riddled patrol car crushing it like an empty beer can before shunting the mangled ambulance over the parapet onto a railway line, turning a high-speed express into a stationary hearse and prematurely ending life's nasty, brutish and short journey for the driver, a guard and a good many of the five hundred and some-odd passengers on board.

Meanwhile, seemingly in slow motion, the articulated wrecking ball toppled onto its side, skidded along the motorway in a shower of sparks and burst into flames. The mother of all mayhem ensued. The resulting pile-up stretched as far as eye could see as three-score-ten vehicles—maybe more—concertinaed in a whizz-bang-wallop of locking brakes and a snap-crackle-pop of slamdunking metal.

To a cacophonous claxophony of honking horns and a boom-bang-a-bang of crash-bang-wallops, the rogue drone directed its malice at a herd of cattle grazing in a nearby field. Spooked by a burst of gunfire that extirpated three heifers and decapitated a bonnie milkmaid, the herd stampeded through a fence onto the motorway, trampling scores of dazed motorists underhoof. With the drone hovering above their heads like a maniacal mechanical gadfly firing willy-nilly at anything that mooed, the cows careered across the central reservation into the path of an oncoming coach, bringing it screeching to a halt in a squeal of oily tyreburn.

Panic-stricken as a queue of cars, lorries, pantechniwagons and vans piled into the back of his charabanc, the driver leapt out, ran screaming down the motorway waving his arms in the air and was flattened by a fire engine speeding towards the pile-up, bells a-ringing, emergency lights a-flashing. When the firemen jumped out to assist, they were gored *en masse* and their mangulated bodies trampled underfoot by the marauding horde.

As the mad cows stampeded down the motorway towards Merton town centre, bellowing for all their frenzied worth, mission accomplished, the miscreant drone disappeared over the horizon, leaving a trail of gore, blood, death and destruction in its wake.

'Golly.' Heather chewed her bottom lip and gulped. 'What say you we keep this to ourselves?'

'Too right,' Debbie said. 'I'm on probation. There's no way I'm taking the rap for this clusterfug.'

For several minutes, the sleuthsome threesome shuffled, squirmed and sweated, hoping upon hope that the drone would find its way home without further cowtastrophe. They were beginning to give up hope when a cranky whir announced that, like a mechanical fuelpigeon, the dissolute disasterdrone had decided to return to its handlers.

For the briefest of moments, it hovered above their heads before the motor gave up the ghost, and it crashed to earth in a tangle of twisted rotors, blistered transistors, fizzing resistors and smouldering solder.

As Tiny stared at the tangled heap of high-tech scrap, utterly lost for utterable words, Prendergast rooted through the wreckage for the black box recorder. 'I'll check the video footage back at my place to see if there's any sign of Puffball.' She turned to Tiny and said, 'Right. Fix that drone and put it back where you found it. And make sure it looks like new.'

As Prendergast strode off with the black box tucked under an arm, Debbie nudged Tiny in the ribs and asked, 'Is she for real?' When he shrugged, she shot him a wink and said, 'Fancy coming back to my place for a bevvy and a shag?'

Next day, Heather Prendergast turned up at college breezy, bright and early. If there was a spring in her step, it was for good reason. She had been up all night putting the finishing touches to her last-chance salon assignment, as she misnomered it. It was, she fancied, her bestest, bestest, bestest piece of coursework ever, even if she did say so herself. She was sure that Professor Morrisson would agree. No, she was convinced that he would, so much so that she went to his office before class to show him what tumultuous strides she had made in the last few days. However, his reaction was anything but encouraging.

'According to this,' Morrisson said with a thunderous glower on his eczemaed face as he read the first page, 'you seem to think that animals and people are the same. Your entire essay is devoted to the search for a missing cat.'

'Not the entire essay, sir.'

'Speak when you're spoken to, Prendergast.'

'Don't I always?' Prendergast reminded him. 'And really—there's no need to be rude.' She tossed her head and stuck her nose in the air. 'Two can play that game—rotter.'

'I'll give you rotter...' Morrisson growled and turned the page. 'What's this? Park keepers, naked girls in bushes, buttocks stuck in windows... it reads like a work of fiction.'

'Thank you, sir. Most kind.'

'Button your lip. Ah, I see you paid attention to my lecture about drones the other day. Although... ' Morrisson ground to a halt. 'I don't recall briefing the class on attack strategy. Good grief—so, you were the lunatic responsible for the carnage on the motorway last night. The Prime Minister interrupted the final of Strictly Come Dancing on the BBC to address the nation. He claimed that the European Union had launched a surprise attack so he was putting the nuclear deterrent on high alert. By all accounts, we only avoided World War Three by the skin of our teeth. Might have guessed you were responsible.' He tossed the essay on his desk, sat back and crossed his arms. 'I was going to recommend you be suspended, but looking at this, I doubt that will be necessary. My guess is, you'll be spending the next twenty years at His Majesty's Pleasure.'

'Oh, I don't think so, sir. I suggest you take a look at the last page. It's an absolute hoot.'

Morrisson's face turned a deathly shade of pale as he examined a photomontage of high-res photographs reproduced in all their gory glory. 'What's the blazes?' he gasped... as if he couldn't guess.

'The video I lifted those stills from makes Fifty Shades of Grey look like a nativity play,' Prendergast said with a butter-wouldn't-melt expression of virtual virtue. 'Check your inbox.'

Professor Morrisson's hands trembled as he downloaded a file. Five minutes later, having seen more than enough, in every sense of the tense, he powered down his fliptop and buried his head in his hands. 'You scheming little cow,' he groaned.

'Talking of cows, you really ought to take a look at the other video I sent—after you've had a stiff drink.' Prendergast struggled to keep a straight face as Morrisson's went a pasty shade of pastry. 'If you don't me saying, an experienced detective like you should know better than to leave the curtains open when he's having rumpy-pumpy with the guv'nor's wife. I mean, who knows when a drone might fly past? They're all over the place.'

She pointed to a particularly lurid photosnap. 'I didn't twig who you were humping until she took off her pinny. Cook looks rather fetching in the buff, wouldn't you say? I can see why her husband is so jealous. Would you believe, Principal Pratley used to be the Metropolitan Police heavyweight boxing champion? His temper is legendary. So is his right hook. Doesn't bear thinking about,' she said with the mother of all shudders. 'Let's hope your wife, the sumo wrestler, doesn't find out.' She broke into a witchy grin and rubbed her hands. 'I think my essay deserves ten out of ten, don't you? Or should I post my coursework on the World Wide Web and let others be the judge?'

Full of the joys of life, it was with a marsupial bounce in her step that Heather Prendergast left Professor Morrisson to drown his sorrows in whatever he could lay his philandering hands on. She had his assurance—signed, sealed and delivered on official college notepaper—that she would graduate top of the class. Walking on air—metaphorically speaking—she breezed into the dining hall.

She had a gut hunch that after a word in cook's nibbled ear, filet mignon, venison, roast pheasant and smoked salmon would magically appear on the menu. As she pushed through the door, she bumped into a chirpy Debbie Smith arm in arm with Terrence 'Tiny' Bottomley.

'Hiya, Preggers,' Debbie said. 'You'll never guess, but I found Puffball.'

'That's wonderful news, Debbs. Where?'

'Would you believe, he was at Gran's? She gave the surgeon a mouthful cause he was black, so, her operation was postponed, and she's on a ten year waiting list. Her new fella collected Puffball while I was at work. He's a locksmith so he opened my door, no probs. Well, to tell the honest truth, he's a cat burglar. Tailor made for the job. Looks like we got a top result.'

'Yes indeed, Debbs,' Heather Prendergast said with the great-grandmother of all smiles. 'We most certainly did.'

My Moon Landing

by Susie Helme

I own a piece of the Moon. Really, I do. There's a little flag up there with my father's name on it.

The deed is hanging right up there, framed, on my wall. One square foot of prime lunar real estate, right on the shore of the Sea of Tranquillity.

I got it from my dead dad in his will. That was the sort of thing that tickled his fancy. A scheme they ran in the 50s. Purchase your own plot on the Moon, help fund the Space Race.

I choose a piece of cloth just that size, poke it with craters, sprinkle it with sand. The night window is my vantagepoint, where I perch in my one-legged spacesuit, surveying my empire.

On this spot stood Ozymandias, King of Kings. Mohammed waited here, watching ants. Here trod Alexander, Caesar, Napoleon, on their way to conquer. Hannibal's elephants' heavy feet shook the moonsoil here.

I shape my strategy, chart my course, launch my legions, shoot for the stars. The campaign begins.

Atop this narrow post, my rocketship commences countdown.

From this square foot will I conquer the universe.

The Cat's Story

by Elaine Graham-Leigh

The first thing you need to know, human reader, is that this is not a funny story. You humans are remarkable for not finding yourselves ridiculous but cackling foolishly at all sorts of perfectly graceful and dignified feline actions, so let you not do that here. As I will make clear, none of this was in any way amusing.

You may be wondering why I, a cat, would stoop to tell this story to humans. You may also, I suppose, be wondering how.

The how is easy. The Yowl to Text™ app works well to turn sensible feline sounds into something that you humans can understand, and it was a simple matter to download it to one of my human's phones. If you humans realised knew how many passwords and PINs the cats who own you have memorised! But there, I had better not give away secrets.

As to why, the idea came, in fact, from my female human. It was the evening after I had returned to my territory. I had just consumed the better part of the second special-treat welcome-back meal (the gourmet pâté from the expensive stack at the back of the top cupboard, very tasty) and had pushed some of the residue right under the kitchen table in the approved manner so that it could fill the kitchen, over time, with its scent. The female human was sitting in my spot on the sofa as I stalked into the living room.

I fixed her with my best glare and she patted her knees, which I have learnt that she considers, in her foolish human

The Cat's Story

way, as encouragement to jump up. I, of course, disdain such blandishments, but, on occasion, it is true that a human lap can be comfortable. I condescended to board and allowed her to scratch my head.

'You silly old sausage,' she said, 'getting lost like that. What are you like?'

Now, while I can, of course, understand everything that humans say, most of the time I choose to ignore it. This, however, caught my attention—it might have been the mention of sausages—and I pricked up my ears.

'Where did you go, eh?' continued my human. 'I wish you could tell me.'

At that point, ironically, I was rubbing my cheek glands against her hand, which should have given her all the information she could want, but alas, humans cannot pick up such signals. It made me think though that there was another way.

So here, in the still watches of the night, I tell to the Yowl to Text™ app the tale of my Great Adventure. I believe my humans must dimly perceive what I am undertaking, as despite the late hour, they have checked several times that my wants are provided for. I think they are worried it is too much for me, as they have urged me not to continue. But I will not be put off. I am convinced that they will want my tale when it is done, so the yowling will continue. Humans, you are welcome.

My Great Adventure began on Bin Day. This is, as all cats know, the best day of the week, when the delicious treats and enticing aromas from the kitchen bin have reached their ripest. The weather was warm, and my humans, in their trusting way, had left the back door open to the garden, so I had had to neglect my post-lunch snooze to guard the kitchen in case of interlopers.

The tabby two gardens down, Disembowels With One Claw,

(or, as he is known to humans, Mr Tiddles) will attempt to get in if I am not vigilant.

After the Battle Winter two years ago when I first came here, with its famous victories like The Capture of the Water Butt and The Privet Hedge Rout, he should know better than to try to steal my food, but ascendancy is only maintained by eternal vigilance.

I was at my post when my male human came into the kitchen. He scritched me briefly behind the ears, but it was clear that, strangely, this was not his sole purpose. He took the top off the kitchen bin, pulled the bag out, tied it and took it away.

I was weary after my labours and the bin, with its lingering scents of ripening food scraps, seemed a perfect enclosed spot for a little well-deserved sleep. I jumped in and curled up in the bottom.

A short while later, I perceived that my female human had entered the kitchen and was clanking around with something. Humans do this and I pay it no mind. She was muttering to herself.

'Honestly, Ben, don't just do half the job, put the bloody bag in the bin when you take the old one out.'

The notion of a bloody bag caught my attention and I opened an eye. This could be delicious. I felt something descend into the bin. I lifted my nose to sniff for blood, but there was none; it was only plastic, that most boring of human smells. Worse, it was all around me, impeding my movements, settling ON MY PERSON in a most appalling way. I was as outraged as any cat would have had a right to be. I let out a great yawp and attacked the bag.

I am, of course, a more formidable opponent than any mere bag, but in the confined space of the bin, the conflict was a mighty one. I kicked out with my back paws with all my strength, pushing the bag upward until I heard it rip. I yowled a warlike yowl and

The Cat's Story

flipped to get my front paws into play.

The plastic billowed away from my claws. I was winning! I growled my victory growl and struck again, a mighty blow. I felt the bag give way utterly. I had won! I had defeated the bin bag! I was lord of the kitchen! I squirmed around in celebration, and it was at that point that the bin fell over.

I did not, I must make clear, flee. I never flee, not from Disembowels, not from foxes, the stupid Alsatian down the road, the vacuum cleaner or anything. I was merely withdrawing to a secure location to regroup. It is an evolutionary imperative.

I shot out of the back door, down the garden path, over the fence and along the alley. It is a long alley, stretching behind human houses on either side. I galloped along it until I realised that I was out of my territory and had no idea where I was.

You will ask why I could not simply go back down the alley. That is, I must say, a typically human question, a product of your limited, linear minds.

A cat's spatial awareness, our sense of time and place and the interconnectedness of things, is so much more sophisticated than your mere mapping ability that you could not understand it even if I attempted to explain it. Go back down the alley, indeed! That is not how it works.

I sniffed at the gardens behind the fences that lined the alley. They all smelled somewhat of human food—you humans are always surrounded by the scents of your food, it is quite distracting to a cat—but not promisingly. Too tidy, too clean, too much like delicious things shut in that loathsome plastic and 'no, get out of there'.

I prowled along, still sniffing. I was a cat alone now, dependent only on my nose, free and wild, and all places were alike to me, except for the passing pleasure of a stolen dinner that they could provide.

After a little while I came to a garden that smelt more likely. There was certainly something suppurating in there, and with it came the tang of elderly cat food. Cat food is naturally less interesting than human food, but it is often easier to purloin. I leapt with my customary grace on to the top of the fence (I did NOT scrabble) and then down into the garden.

The grass at the bottom of the garden was long and straggly. I slunk through it, swift but silent, deadly as a great cat of the veldt, unseen by all unsuspecting prey. A black and white cat was asleep in a plant pot outside the back door. She lifted her head, stood up, stretched, and looked straight at me.

'I can smell you, you know,' she said.

I froze in place, one paw raised, ears back. The black and white cat jumped out of the pot and arched her back, fluffing out her tail.

'I am Ratsmiter, Queen of all this garden, and the next one along in the mornings unless it's raining,' she went on. 'Cower before me, stranger, and state your business before I tear your throat out.'

I would of course have defeated her in battle, but we free, wandering cats do not fight for no cause like pampered house cats, who have humans to tend to their injuries and even have the last resort of the V-E-T. I puffed up my own tail to show my magnificence but replied politely.

'I am Prowls By Night and all places are alike to me. I was looking for a small snack but I have no desire to rob you of your only cat food. I will pass on and leave you be.'

'I'll have you know that I have many sources of cat food,' said Ratsmiter, offended. 'I once had five dinners from five different bowls all in the same evening. But if you are looking for a meal, I happen to know that three gardens down, the humans have not been claimed by a new cat since old Arse Smells Of Nettles died. You could do worse than try there.'

'I may do that,' I said.

Ratsmiter started washing her paw to show that our business was concluded. I crept under the fence to the next garden.

I found the unclaimed household without difficulty. It had a sagging cat tree in one corner of the garden and many scratches on the fence post, but only a faint lingering smell of cat. I descended the fence and was advancing up the path when I noticed something else: the bright, plastic things that appear wherever you have small humans. I stopped at the realisation. This was a house with children.

Now, I am a cat of the world. I recognise that many cats can live perfectly happily with small humans, just as they can endure the company of such creatures as guinea pigs, tortoises and even dogs. I, I am happy to say, have never had to lower myself to put up with such indignities. I do not do kittens, and I do not like small humans. I looked back and tensed myself to make a run and spring back over the fence. As I did so, a young voice rang out.

'Look, Dad, an orange cat! Can we keep him?'

I bristled at the insult. I am NOT orange; I am ginger-gold. It put me off my leap and by the time I had recovered myself, it was too late. Heavy footsteps were running towards me.

Instinctively I pressed myself close to the ground, but hot hands seized me round my middle and lifted me into the air. I paddled my front paws but could find nothing to get a purchase on. I was a prisoner!

As the small human hoisted me into its arms, I considered my options. It is my understanding that attacking small humans, however much they may deserve it, is something that is frowned upon by any larger humans who may be by. I was also hungry, it having been many long hours—at least two—since I had last eaten.

Sometimes, in the cause of human-feline relations, it is necessary to employ a little dissimulation. I put on my best piteous expression, stared woefully up into the small human's face and said, 'Mewp?'

It had the desired effect.

'Oh, he's hungry!' the small human exclaimed. 'Poor, starving cat! Dad, where's the cat food?'

I found myself carried into the house and placed carefully on the kitchen floor while cat food was located. It tasted a little stale, and it was a brand for which I do not much care, but there was at least plenty of it.

I ate in the persona of a poor, starving cat and then withdrew underneath the small human's bed. It was dark and peaceful under there, with enough discarded garments to make a dusty nest. I was exhausted from the stress of the day and soon fell into a much-deserved sleep.

I was aware that the small human came to look at me several times, but I ignored it, only moving further under the bed so as to be just out of reach of prying arms.

On one of these occasions, I heard the Dad human saying, 'it must have an owner, look at the size of it. We'll have to get its chip read, then they can get it home', but that cannot have been about me. I am not fat, I am pleasantly rounded. In any case, that would be an issue for the morning. I pushed my nose further into a pile of socks and went back to sleep.

The breakfast, when I emerged the next morning, was only adequate, but the small human was, I discovered, quite impressively responsive to mewping and I got an acceptable supply of yoghurt and buttered toast strips when the Dad human was not looking. I was engaging in my post-breakfast toilette under the table in a pleasant state of mind, when the Dad human stood up.

'Your mum will be back from her night shift soon. We'd better get this one's chip read so we can get him back to his owner. Fred, would you get the cat carrier and I'll take him to the V-.'

I sat up, appalled. The V-! The V-E-T! I cannot even now bring myself to yowl the word. It is the horror that must not be named, the darkness that clouds the lives of all cats. I felt my vision blur with the thought of it; the room swam before my eyes. My doom had come upon me!

'Alright,' said the small human. 'It's under the stairs. I'll get it.'

He moved to the kitchen door. I tensed. Could I even now escape?

'Careful, don't let him follow you,' said the Dad human.

The small human turned to see where I was, and I took my chance. I shot like a weasel straight between the legs of the Dad human's chair and through the opening door.

The hall floor was some sort of ridiculous slippery stuff. I skidded, struggled to right myself and galloped almost sideways down towards the front door.

'It's like he knows,' said the small human. 'Come on, Ginger, it's all right.'

He advanced towards me, the cat carrier yawning open from one hand like a pit of despair. I looked frantically around for cover, but could see none. There was nothing in the hall but closed doors. I would have to make for one of the beds upstairs, and I knew there was no way out from that. I was near to giving up, but then a miracle happened. A dark shape appeared in the glass of the front door.

There was the sound of a key in the lock and the door opened.

'Don't let the cat out!' cried the small human and the Dad human together.

'What cat?' said the incoming human, confusedly.

'This cat!' I prrpp'd as I hurtled down the path.

I was free, and I made the most of my freedom. I crossed the road by the approved cat manner of putting my head down and running very fast. Then, I wandered. I was a cat alone in the city and I revelled in all the sights and sounds.

Eventually though, I felt that a post-breakfast nap might be in order. I passed a group of humans working on a telephone pole—which was a welcome sight, the internet service here is decidedly primitive—with their van parked next to them, rear doors open.

They were none of them looking at it. I put my front paws up onto the step and sniffed inside. It was dark and quiet, full of rounds of cables, boxes and other small, enclosed sleeping places. This would do perfectly. I jumped in and made myself comfortable.

I was of course fully aware of when the van started to move. My advanced cat senses are quite capable of noticing movement, thank you. I was however deep in my snooze and saw no reason to disturb myself. I simply curled myself deeper into the coil of cable and tucked my paws over my ears to shut out the sound of the engine.

I stayed like that until I heard the rustle of a crisp packet being opened. I love crisps. Such salty, fatty goodness, to seize and lick and chase under furniture! Such strange, dusty residue to sniff on human fingers, replete with a hundred forbidden scents! Deep in my cable coil I twitched my nose to confirm. Yes, it was crisps, and even possibly the orange cheesy ones which are my particular favourite. I uncurled myself, stretched out each paw in turn, and padded forward to investigate.

The packet was open on the van dashboard, lying with its mouth gaping towards me as if asking me to leap on the deliciousness within. How could I spurn such an invitation? I stuck my head through the gap between the seats. The human driving gave a jump and the van swerved from side to side in what I am sure is not good driving practice.

'F***!' he exclaimed.

'What the—?' the other human shouted. 'Watch it!'

'Woah! F***!'

Humans often have a very limited vocabulary compared to cats, I have noticed this before. The van seemed to be stabilising, so I resumed my quest for the crisps by putting a paw out onto to the gear stick and using that to lift myself towards the dashboard.

'F*** me,' said the driver, 'It's a cat and it's after me Wotsits.' He put out an arm to push me back.

I lifted my paw over it. You won't stop me like that, human, I thought.

'Grab it, Mo!' the driver shouted.

The other human obeyed and seized me round the middle in a most disrespectful manner. I kicked and tried to latch onto the gear stick with my claws, but it was too hard and they couldn't get a purchase.

The Mo human lifted me up and away from dashboard. All that crispy goodness, so near and yet so far! I was beside myself.

'I will disembowel you if you don't give me the Wotsits!' I yowled in fury. I struck out again with my front paws, but met only air. The Mo human held my legs down.

'I will eat your eyes out of their sockets! I will flay you down to the gizzard!' I howled. I was quite put out.

'There, there,' said the Mo human, holding me down onto his lap. 'Nice kitty.'

The driver said that they had better call the depot. 'I dunno what they're going to say. It'll probably invalidate the insurance.'

Mo pressed the buttons on the phone in the handheld cradle, holding me down with his other hand.

'Hi Rina, is Dave around? Would you give him a message? Tell him we've got a cat in the van... No, a cat. C-A-T, like a kitty cat. Big and orange it is.'

I am NOT orange. I do not know why humans keep making this mistake. I was annoyed at the insult and started to struggle again.

There was a pause while the human on the other end of the phone said something, tinnily.

'I dunno.' The Mo human turned to the driver. 'Dave says, what does the cat want?'

The driver snorted.

'How should I know? Wotsits, apparently. Ask him what we're supposed to do with it.'

Mo relayed this and there was more tinny squawking.

'Dave says, if we let it in, can't we let it out?'

The driver turned to look at me, and then at the Mo human.

'Not when we're doing 40 miles an hour on the dual carriageway, no, Mo, we can't.'

'Did you get that?' the Mo human said to the squawks. 'Yeah... OK, I'll tell him. See you later.'

He pressed the button to end the call.

'They say we're to bring it into the depot,' he said.

'But we've got two calls to do yet,' said the driver human. 'How are we supposed to keep it happy until then?'

He looked over at me. I was sitting still now on the Mo human's lap. He was quite good at stroking the right spot on my neck. I was beginning to relax.

'Dunno,' said the Mo human. 'Maybe we should give it the Wotsits?'

The Cat's Story

By the time we reached the second of the two calls, I was feeling quite happy with my situation. The Mo human had supplied me with a handful of Wotsits for myself and had allowed me to stick my head in the bag to lick it out, meaning that I had a substantial deposit of cheesy powder stored on my fur and whiskers for later snacking. I had also had a bit of bacon from the driver human's bacon sandwich, a chicken strip from the Mo human's lunch and a beetle from the floor in the back of the van. All I needed now was a post-lunch snack and I would be set until dinner.

I had had some acceptable scritches from the Mo human, who had clearly been well-trained by the cat who owned him (he had markers all over his shirt saying Property of Bites Your Face Off) and sat on his knee to watch the van's progress as we sped along. It was only unfortunate that the Mo human had thick trousers, so when we arrived at the second call, he was able to ignore me when I dug in my claws to make him stay put.

'Nah, nah, cat, you stay in the van while we go do this quick job,' he said.

The driver human got out as well and went to shut the van doors.

'Hang on,' the Mo human said, 'better leave a door open for the cat.'

'Why?' the driver human asked.

'Well, what if he needs to do his business? After all those crisps...'

'Oh. Ohhhhhh. I got you. Yeah, we'll leave the door open.' The driver human turned to look at me where I was sitting on a curl of cable in the back of the van. 'You got any business to attend to, you get out, understand?'

The Mo human laughed. 'There's no point talking to it, Greg, it's a cat. Come on, let's get this job over with.'

I listened to them clumping off down the road, then settled down for a quick snooze in the cables. I was woken up by quick footsteps outside the van. They didn't sound like either of the van humans, they were too light, and too rapid. They paused beside the driver's door. I heard the handle pull and then a click as it opened.

'Ah, sweet,' an unfamiliar voice said.

It was a new human. I pricked up my ears. Might he have interesting food? I couldn't smell anything, but he could have something in a packet. There was some clicking from somewhere around the steering wheel and then the engine roared.

'Wahey!' exclaimed the new human.

The van jerked forward. From outside, I heard a wail.

'Some little scroat's stealing the van! The whole van!'

The engine roared louder. The tyres squealed as we set off down the road. The speed at which the van was moving was sending the cables and boxes shooting from one side of the van to the other.

This was most uncomfortable and not at all conducive to peaceful sleep. Clearly, this new human needed some instruction into my requirements. 'More food, less speed', should be a simple enough message for any human to understand, I thought.

The van screeched around another corner and the cable roll I was sitting in shot across the floor, nearly bumping my nose against the wall. This was insupportable. I jumped out of the roll and picked my way carefully to the front.

I could hardly see anything of the new human, just glimpses of his head and shoulders in the gap between the seat and the headrest. I yowled for his attention, but disgracefully, he ignored me. To be fair, it is possible that the engine noise was so loud that he could not hear me. I yowled again, but with no better result. I would have to take drastic action.

I positioned myself so that I was facing the new human through the gap between the seats. I measured the jump, swaying forward and back, lashing my tail for impetus. The van was speeding down a straight bit of road. I wiggled my hindquarters in anticipation. One more sway, forward, backward… and NOW! I sprang through the gap in the seats and on to the new human's shoulder, digging in with all my claws.

'Slow down and feed me,' I said.

I still do not understand why this was ineffective. As an instruction it was surely clear, and it was sensible advice, given the velocity of the van and the length of time since lunch. But humans are often strangely slow to heed feline advice, even when it would be to their own benefit, such as in the matter of avoiding claws, cat sick in unexpected places, and other such gentle admonitions.

The human shrieked, 'F***!' and tried to shoo me off his shoulder.

I clung on and shrieked back. There was a confused succession of skids as the van seemed to go round and round. I was flung off onto the other seat. I crouched there, screaming, as for one long, horrible minute, the van appeared to be balancing on only two wheels. Then it righted itself and landed. It turned round once more, rocking, and stopped. The engine noise died away into a plink, plink sound. In the distance I heard a siren.

'F*** this, I'm out of here,' said the new human.

He opened the driver's side door, climbed down and ran off.

I peered through the door after him. I had an impression of approaching humans, and I did not feel like dealing with more new humans at this moment. I was tired and discombobulated, and wanted nothing more than some peace and quiet to consider my position and eat the crisp crumbs in my whiskers. The door was beside the pavement and across the pavement was the opening to an alley.

It looked weedy and overgrown, perfect for cat concealment. I leapt down and sped along it until I was out of human sight.

I padded down the alley, letting my paws lead me whither they would, until I realised that the surroundings were becoming familiar. Surely that was the lilac bush that marked the boundary of Claws On Sight's territory? And wasn't that the bramble clump that covered the rats' nest? Was I... could I be... home?

Now, I am, as will have been apparent, a free, wandering, cat, and all places are alike to me.

However, even for such bold and independent spirits as I, there is an advantage to a familiar territory, where every bolthole and pouncing place is tried and tested. There was also the question of my humans. Humans are, of course, largely interchangeable, and any cat who knows what he is doing can extract food and shelter from almost any of them.

I had to admit, though, that my humans were really quite acceptable as humans go. They had been amenable to training in the important matters of types of cat food, treats and lap provision. I would not go so far as to say that I missed them, obviously, but still, it would be a pity to let all that training go to waste.

I hurried on down the alley until I came to the familiar gate. I turned in, walked up the path and miaowed at the kitchen door. I heard feet running down the stairs inside, then the door was flung open.

'Oh, you're back!' my female human said. 'Where have you been, you bad cat?'

She caught me up into her arms. I was overwhelmed by the familiar smell, the comfort of all the cat hairs and my ownership tags all over her shirt. I pushed my face into her neck and allowed her to carry me in. It was over.

This, then, was the story of my Great Adventure, told to inform humans of the dramas going on around them of which they would otherwise be ignorant. It shows, I think, my boldness and daring in the face of adversity and for humans, carries important lessons, such as: always check the bin before you put the bag in, and: be prepared to supply your crisps to any cat who wants them. Unless of course they are Salt and Vinegar, but over that story is drawn a veil.

My throat is tired now from yowling and I perceive that it is nearly time for my humans to get up for work. I will therefore close here and go and provide my normal morning alarm service for them.

Humans, you are welcome.

Greaper at the Pearly Gates

by em.thompson

The trouble, so I'm told, is that They weren't expecting me. By They, I mean the Greapers. Before you reach for Wikipedia, I should explain that Greaper isn't street slang for a groper or a peeper, it is an abbreviation of Grate Keeper or Grime Reaper. Not sure which. Take your pick.

It had never crossed my mind that the Great Haunters—the high and mighty Guardians of the Spirit World—might be dyslexic. Well, you don't do you... imagine that the Universal Omnipots of The Wylde Ephemeral might have trouble spelling. Or suffer from halitosis. But believe you me, they do. And how. That wasn't my only rude awakening when I crossed the river of Styx.

Take the Greapers' gender as a for-example. I naturally assumed that these shadowy figures in their black cloaks, long white beards, toothless smiles and empty eye sockets were men, or I did until I heard their husky, high-pitched voices. Darling, they called me. Darling, babe, honey, sugar, sweetie-pie. Can you believe it? No one has called me sugar since I took a wrong turning in Tottenham and stopped to ask directions from an accommodating young lady. Actually, being a pedantic pedestrian, in the needs of accuracy, I should say that I was actually a little way from Tottenham—on the Seven Sisters Road to be precise, though to be honest, there were plenty more than seven sisters strutting their stuff at the kerbside. Delicious.

Where was I? Oh yes—the Greapers. So, I walk up to the pearly reception desk and hammer a fist on the counter, as you do when you're in a hurry. Get in the queue, a Thing told me, so, reluctantly, I did. I waited and waited and then I waited some more until, having lost count of how many months I had been kicking my winged heels, I barged through a crowd of bearded blokes with scythes and demanded to know how long They intended to keep me hanging about. I had better things to do, I insisted in the intimidating manner I employ when jobsworths demand I sort out my rent arrears, pay my tube fare, turn up to work on time, that kind of thing.

Well, my bluster cut no ice with the Greaper, I can tell you. No ice, whatsoever. Better things to do, like what, honey? It asked. Time you woke up and smelled the embalming fluid. Well, must admit that had me stumped. I got Important Stuff to do, I bluffed a little feebly. In your dreams, babe; not anymore, you've not, It said. But what if I need a piss, I said, or feel peckish—I hadn't had a Whopperburger and fries since before the accident. He/she/it turned up the bony stub where a nose should be, gave me a derisory look, said, you don't get it, do you, darling? Time to wake up to the fact that pissing and stuffing your face are things of the past, It said, and told me to wait my turn.

So, I rejoined the queue and did. Well, I lost track of time after that, but it must have been... oh, near as not aeons, I guess, before I eventually reached the pearly check-in gate. Name, the Thing asked. John Smith, I replied—with an S and no B. He didn't get the joke. Seems Greapers have no sense of humour. Anyway, It muttered, 'John Smith with no B...' and thumbed through this massive ledger affair, then raised an eye socket, shook its skull and said, 'you're not due yet, sweetie.'

And that brings me to the point of this epistle. You see, much as the Greaper was miffed because I had turned up prematurely,

Its miffment was as nothing compared to mine for having turned up at all.

Let me explain...

I was walking down the street happily minding my own business when I saw a wallet on the pavement. And so, being a conscientious citizen and hoping it might contain a few quid, I picked it up and was having a quick shufty when... biff, bang, wallop. The next thing I knew, I had the headache to end all headaches and was being ferried across the River Styx by a Thing in a smeggy black cloak with a long white beard, empty eye-sockets and a stub of a nose who insisted on calling me sugar.

When I asked what the fug was going on, It showed me the front page of tomorrow's newspaper. I say showed, but it was more of a premonitory thought transfer, not something I would recommend you engage in with a nebulous figure of indeterminate gender who calls you lover-boy. Anyway, be that as it may, the virtual headline screamed... GRAND PIANO FALLS FROM TWENTY-FIRST FLOOR WINDOW.

The article went on to say that the world-renowned concert pianist, Rupert someone or other, was having a Steinway delivered to his penthouse apartment by a massive fug-off crane. Laurel and Hardy and Sons, or whatever the firm of piano movers was called, were manoeuvring the nine-foot grand through piano-man's picture window when the gaffa tape holding it to the hoist unravelled and... well, you can guess the rest. Yup—you got it. Catastrophe followed as surely as night follows day and vice versa.

You see, this wasn't just any old piano. According to The Evening News, it had been made to order with an extra half octave below bottom A, a Perspex lid and go-faster decals on the sides. It was finished in what the newspaper called 'a dashing shade of flamingo pink with translucent ivory lacquer and real mother of pearl and ebonoid keys'. In other words, it was full-on Liberace, bar the candelabras. I hasten to add that this is an abbreviated version of a much longer description. The full monty ran to the best part of a page, including a large before and a tiny after photograph and an airbrushed mugshot of the pianist taken twenty or so years ago when he was still compos mentis. Underneath was a statement from Herr Piano-Mann—he had trans-European pretensions—saying how his life would never be the same without his beloved Steinway.

Fortuitously, it turned out to be insured for twice its actual value, so no great harm done. Quite a result, in fact. Oh, I believe I forgot to mention that tucked away at the bottom of the page were a few lines to the effect that the flying piano landed on a passing pedestrian. According to documents found in the victim's wallet, he was a Mister Archibald Addison of Mile End, London. Death was instantaneous, and he had no known relatives. End of story... and end of me.

'No... no John Smiths on the guest list, darling, with or without a B,' a particularly stinky Greaper said. Did I mention they have body odour? Well, they do. Every last rotting one of them. 'But we're expecting an Artybald Addisson.'

'I think you mean, Archibald,' I said with a knowing smile.

'Look, Baldy,' the Greaper said in a high-pitched voice. 'Don't poke fun at my spelling, and I won't mention that you're a foot taller and twenty years younger than you ought to be according to the Ledger of Life Before Death. And I'll keep schtum about that bit of bother you had with you-know-who when you were thirty-six.'

'But I'm only twenty-eight.'

'Not anymore, you're not.'

Well, I had been in Limbo long enough to know better than to argue with a Greaper. One word out of place and it's back to the end of the queue—a queue that was getting longer by the minute thanks to a renewed outbreak of hostilities in Wolverhampton. So, I just shrugged and said, 'what's in a name?'

'Here, Bill,' the Greaper shouted to a bearded fellow with a quill tucked behind an ear, twiddling his thumbs on a nearby cloud. 'That's one of yours, isn't it—what's in a name? What you want me to do with Baldy... back of the queue till Hell freezes over?'

Bill the Quill turned to me with a kindly smile. 'Well, heaven forgive him and forgive us all,' he said. 'Some rise by sin, and some by virtue fall: Some run from brakes of ice, and answer none: And some condemned for a fault alone.'

'That's all right, then,' said the Greaper. 'All's well that ends well.'

Bill raised a finger and shook his shaggy head. 'Watch it, mush,' he tut-tutted with a roguish scowl. 'That's copyrighted, that is.'

At this stage, I should point out that the process of determining whether a new arrival is allowed through the Pearly Gates or condemned to eternal Hellfire and Brimstone is mired in the most horrendous bureaucracy, or 'procedural pernicketies' as the infinite miles of red tape are humourlessly dismissed by the Grand Greaper. On the face of it, the system is straightforward, or should be. Arrivals are scheduled at birth by the Ides of Fate. When their due time comes, they report to one of Saint Peter's heavenly minions, where their life's ledger is examined, sins and virtues balanced and a decision made.

There is no appeals procedure. It is up or down. Period. Now, occasionally a spanner gets thrown in the works. More often than not, this is down to a mistake on the part of a Greaper—a 'Mick's-up' in Greaper parlance. For example, there's this spook I know—

Jacob Marley, his name is. Well, he turned up at reception one day, not quite sure where he was destined for, to be greeted with…

'You've come to the wrong place, love.'

'Wrong place?'

'We don't take Rastafarians. Try next door, honey.'

'Ratsa-whats?'

'You heard me, Bob. No Muslims, no Hindus, no Scientologists and strictly no Rastafarians.'

Well, of course, Jacob Marley kicked up one heck of a stink. Eventually, he was consigned to Limbo while his case went upstairs to be considered along with all the other 'illegal migrants', as unregistered arrivalistas are called. The process can take forever, and I mean literally forever. Poor old Jacob is still clanking about, miserable as sin. Comes down to earth at Christmas to give kiddiewinks the fright of their little lives. Bless. Must say, he's written a bunch of killer tunes since he arrived, and his dreads are awesome. I know this because, like Jacob, I am wandering the great in-between while I wait for a ruling on my status.

Anyway, back to the sorry story of my mistaken case of identity. The upshot of the confuddle was that I was placed in what is officially called 'Obsivion'—that's Oblivion for alpha readers. Now, Obsivion is a kind of spiritual rubbish dump where odds and sods of unscheduled riff-raff knock about while their credentials are being ratified. This normally takes a few decades, but for some, it can drag on for centuries. We are expected to keep busy. Every morning, a roster of duties is posted on the Pearly Gates. Participation is obligatory. Skive off, and bish, bash, bosh—down the hatch of no return.

Well, I need hardly tell you that this was an unsatisfactory state of affairs, most unsatisfactory, indeed. All attempts to resolve the matter having been dismissed with a snarl and a kiss, I was left with no alternative but to escalate the dispute. Accordingly, I wrote to the Power That Be.

> *Dear Heavenly Customer Services,*
> *I am hoping you can help me resolve an issue that has defeated the best Greaper minds in Limbo, though I must confess that this is not saying a great deal.*
> *I was unexpectedly transported to the Pearly Gates following a terminal encounter with a Steinway Grand piano. Without going into details, I was booked in under the name Archibald Addison of Mile End, East London. I am confined to the in-between while the issue is being looked into, but it is taking an eternity. I am hoping you can speed up the process.*
>
> *Kind Regards,*
> *John Smith.*

It was with unbridled joy that barely a month later, I received the following;

> *Dear Arty,*
> *Great to hear from you. Truly. Rest assured, the concerns of my flock are always uppermost in my mind.*
>
> *Blessings,*
> *Saint Peter*

Wasting no time, I followed this up with...

> *Dear Pete,*
> *Thanks for your prompt reply. I look forward to hearing from you shortly.*
>
> *Stay safe, mate,*
> *John Smith.*

The suspense was almost unbearable, so you can imagine my excitement when barely six weeks later a follow-up pinged into my wing-box.

> *Dear Arty,*
> *Great to hear from you. Truly. Rest assured, the concerns of my flock are always uppermost in my mind.*
>
> *Blessings,*
> *Saint Peter*

Not sure whether to be puzzled, pissed or both, I replied with,

> *My dear Saint Peter,*
> *There would appear to be some confusion. Your last letter was identical to the first. Can I respectfully ask what progress, if any, has been made to address my concerns?*
>
> *Sincerely yours,*
> *John Smith.*

Had I still got eyes, they would have rolled out of their sockets when I read the eventual reply.

> *Dear Arty,*
> *Your letter has been forwarded to me by Saint Peter.*
> *It's great to hear from you. Truly. Rest assured, the concerns of his flock are always uppermost in Saint Peter's mind.*
>
> *Glad Tidings,*
> *Pope Pius XXII*
> *Heavenly Customer Services.*

So that, gentle reader or simple reader, is where I am currently at, or better said, where I am currently not—an itinerant inhabitant of Obsivion. While those with relatively blameless lives join the heavenly host to play harps with virginal angels, eat nectar and suchlike, and villains, thugs and politicians are condemned to eternal hellfire and non-stop lift muzak, I await the outcome of the heavenly secretariat's adjudication.

I am what is officially classed as an 'inbetweener', destined to tramp the netherworld, haunting the living—the 'pending dead' as they are known in the hereinafter. To call it boring would be doing boring a kindness. It is tedium personified. A thankless non-existence. Let's face it, when did you last invite a ghost to dinner, take a spectre to a movie or snuggle up with a spook in front of the telly? With very few exceptions, the possessed tend to throw up their hands and run away as fast and as far as they can. Do they hang about for a chat and a bevvy? Do they, heckers-like, apart from the occasional 'Crankile', as psychics are known to the

Gnoble Breatherhood of Greapers.

All well and good, I hear you say—at least this should mean I get the occasional conversation. You reckon? Yeah, right. Ever met a lifeform who talks to ghosts? Thought not. They tend not to be allowed out of the ward. And so the upshot is that haunting is a lonely, an unforgiving and a thankless task.

The bombshell burst when I was haunting a goat—a goat, for heavenly sake. Not a Billy, not a Nanny, but a Kid—I kid you not... see what I did there? Cute. So, why, I hear you ask, was I haunting a goat? Well, it's part and parcel of the training regime.

The first however long is spent learning how to walk through walls. Think that's easy? Well, think again. What would your natural instinct be when confronted by a solid brick wall? Stop and scratch your head? Turn and walk away? Heaven and Hell no. Do that, and it's down the hatch, pronto. What you have to do is take your courage in both hands and carry on walking.

The first time I melted through a solid object—a fridge freezer, if my memory serves me well—I was chuffed to death—no pun intended—but it's one of those things like riding the four horses of the apocalypse that you soon get used to, and before long you're casually walking through all sorts of hardness without giving it a second thought.

What is more difficult is learning to spook. OK, so according to the Greapers, it's just a matter of flitting about like a blob of manic ectoplasm, waving your hands in the air and moaning like a mad thing. Would that it were so easy. You see, my natural tendency is to be polite, introduce myself with a smile and a handshake and make clear that I come in peace. But if I behaved like that, I would be booted down the escalator to purgatory faster than you can say boo to a goose. So, I've had to spend an inordinate amount of time practicing how to be a convincing 'spoke'—you guessed it, another Greaperism—before being allowed to haunt a house, or better still, to manifest a ruined monastery.

My training went something like this... step one was to bedevil an inanimate object—the aforementioned fridge-freezer or what have you. Would you believe, Jacob Marley tormented a Dansette record player for a couple of years before being allowed to move on to step two—animals. In his case, he was let loose on a cat, but they're canny critters, cats. They can sniff out a trainee ghost a mile off.

As for me, I was given a goat and told that if I could spook it, I would be allowed to haunt a tortoise or an ageing armadillo. Something scaly. And then and only then would I be let loose on an old biddy. Frighten her to death, my mentor—a particularly noxious Greaper—told me, and promotion was pretty much in the bag. Promotion to what, I asked? An apprentice Greaper, babe, It said with a toothless cackle before blowing me a kiss and mincing through a wall.

So, I was trying to spook that bloody goat when I was messaged to report to reception. We communicate by telepathy up here—or down here, depending on your perspective—and a real pain in the ears it is, too, I can tell you. At any time of day or night—not that there's any difference in this infernal place—a telebam can bounce into your head with instructions to do this or not do that. Annoying isn't the half of it. Anyway, there I was, doing my best to spook a goat, not that he cared, when I was instructed to waft up to the Pearly Gates. Accordingly, I made my excuses and fluttered up to see what was occurring.

We got issues, The Grand Greaper told me with the archangel of all scowls. This bloke... he nodded at a short, skinny chap with brand new wings... this bloke reckons he's Artybald Addison. And? I said. Well, sugar, there can't be two of you, the Greaper said. Indeed, there can't, said I, so now maybe you'll believe that I'm John Smith. It don't work like that, the Greaper said. You can't just change your name because someone new wants your old one. It's against the rules.

For Peter's sake, I sighed, this is like something out of a Franz Kafka novel. That's when a little bloke with big ears put down his harp and snarled, 'Pass auf, Kumpel,' in a funny accent and threatened to turn me into a cockroach.

We got the motherfugger of all brain twisters, babe, the Greaper said. See, we have a strict protocol round these parts. Mankind's destiny is preordained, and slots in the hereinafter are allocated from the dawn of creation to The Rapture. There is no leeway. And according to my schedule, I only have room for one Artybald Addison.

Does that mean I get to go back to the vale of tears? I asked. I met this girl, see, in Tottenham. Great legs. I been saving up in the hope of getting to know her better.

The Greaper looked shocked. Well, I think It did. It's hard to tell with a Greaper. Not on your death, sweetie, It said. The last time a cook-up like this occurred, a couple of thousand years ago, some bright spark suggested we balance the books by resurrecting the duplicate. Jesus, his name was. We reckoned no one would notice. Not much, they didn't. So far, the fallout has included the Crusades, the Holy Roman Empire, the Spanish Inquisition, Billy Graham, the Reverend Ian Paisley... Death and destruction like you would not believe. So as a result of that ManAlmighty clusterfug, safeguards have been put in place to prevent it happening again. Then you come along, honey... he prodded my ectoplasm with a bony finger... and it's back to square one.

I hung my head in a show of heavenly contrition. Just my luck to have slipped through a crack in the holy firewall. Damn that accursed Steinway.

Only one thing for it, babe, the Greaper said... an adjudicationary tribunal in front of The Big Boss Man. It looked from me to Archibald Addison, then back at me and said, one of you will be deemed to never have existed. To put it in technical terms, you'll be exorcised. And take it from me, sweetie, it is a fate worse than life.

If I may say, Saint Peter was not at all what I expected. Not one bit. Much like you, I'm sure, I imagined he would be a serene, kindly sort, bedecked in simple robes with an obligatory beard and a halo floating above his flowing locks like an antigravity Frisby.

I was therefore somewhat underwhelmed to be ushered into an ethereal golf pavilion and greeted by an overweight bloke with a peculiarly orange complexion. Sandy-haired—unnaturally so—he was wearing tartan trousers and a polo shirt. And you are, he asked? Before I could introduce myself, the Greaper butted in with, this is Artybald Addison. Trouble, is, so is he—It pointed to the skinny bloke standing beside me.

'Not good,' said Saint Peter. 'Not good at all. Maybe we should classify the tall one as fake news.' He jutted his jaw and gave me the kind of look that spoke for itself.

'Won't work,' the Greaper said with a shake of the skull, 'He's already signed in.'

'This is a bad situation,' Saint Peter—or at least, I assumed the vision of unadulterated nausea to be Saint Peter—said. 'A very bad situation.'

'Gets worse,' the Greaper said. 'Apparently, there's a piano involved.'

'A Yamaha?'

'A Steinway.'

'Beautiful. A classy job.' Saint Peter clasped his hands to his chest and sighed. 'Tremendous.'

'The point is, we've got an extra Artybald, and it's truly put the system out of kilter.'

'Sad,' Saint Peter said. 'I think it's very sad.' Then he stuck up a finger and said, 'Confeve.'

A lightbulb dithered into life behind the Greaper's eye sockets. By Lucifer, he said. I would never have thought of that. Not for one moment.

Saint Peter scowled and shook his head. 'Crooked Lucifer has zero talent. A very bad man. So are we done? I got angels waiting. Hot. Very hot.' He tapped his nose and winked. Then put his golf buggy into reverse and backed into a perpetual bunker.

None the wiser, I cocked my head and asked, 'what the Dickens is Confeve?'

The Greaper turned to a studious man in a frockcoat with unruly hair and a fishtail beard. 'Tell him, Charles, baby.'

'It is the best of words, it is the worst of words. OK?' the man said. 'Now can I get back to work? I've come up with a killer idea to keep Jacob Marley occupied as a Yuletide Wailer.'

Head to one side, the Greaper looked me up and down. Suppose we better get you measured up for a fig leaf, It said. Shame you're a bit... well, tall. Tall? I said. Tall, he said. For a Confeve. Explain yourself, I demanded. Listening, babe? It asked, and when I shrugged, went on to explain that a glitch in the divine order had arisen several aeons ago. Sure, it was brushed under the carpet, but nevertheless, the anomaly had resulted in an ongoing niggle of heavenly instability. Niggle? What kind of niggle, I asked, puzzled, curious and not a little alarmed.

Take a seat, the Greaper said and gestured to a cloud. As you probably know, It said when I was sitting comfortably, we have a host of heavenly angels we wheel out on special occasions—canonical celebrations, crucifixions, ceremonial functions, virgin births—that kind of thing.

'I've seen paintings,' I said. 'Bonnie wee lads and lasses with blond curls, dimples, blue eyes, angel wings and cherubic smiles. But what does that have to do with me?'

'Ah, you may well ask.'

'I just did.'

Well, the Greaper didn't get that I was being tongue-in-cheek. See, Greapers have no sense of humour. Not a sausage.

So, here's the deal, It said. In the need of heavenly symmetry, through the ages, we have had a strict policy of maintaining a quotient of twelve heavenly cherubs and cherubim. One more or one less, and anarchy would break out—the dogs of war, famine, feast, floods, pestilence, plague, Lizz Truss—all the usual. Doesn't bear thinking about, the Greaper said with a shudder and as much of a grimace as Its fleshless face could muster.

In response to my raised eye socket, he ran through what he called the Cupid Crew, or 'The Angelic Massive', as it is known in Rapture Alley... Ariel, angel of natural elements; Barbiel, AKA Barbi, angel of thunderstorms and lightening; Cassiel, archangel of tears; Daniel, the watcher, also known as Snitch; Hamaliel, the housekeeper and kitchen skivvy; Jegudiel, angel of love... a real little cutie; Kokabiel, a kind of a nondescript sort of a heavenly presence; Macroprosopus... have fun getting your tongue round that, the Greaper said; Metatron, the celestial scribe; Muriel, admin; Netzach, eternity and related infinities, not to be confused with Nietzsche who lives a few doors down in the Milky Way; and Confeve.

Confeve? said I. Can't say I've heard of him. Her. Them. It.

The Greaper drew close, looked over both shoulders, shielded Its toothless mouth with a skeletal hand and whispered, 'that's because It don't exist, honey. Saint Peter invented It when our star angel, Gabriel, crossed over to the dark side. It's using the name

Taylor Swift now and refuses to come back—having a whale of a time, by all accounts. So, we had to invent an angel no one had ever heard of to fill Saint Taylor's Jimmy Choos. Hence Confeve. Wicked name, yeah?' It shrugged when I responded with a scowl.

'So, here's the deal, sweetie. We'll transmogrify you into Confeve to fill the vacancy so you won't have to be exorcised. That way, we get to solve two problems for the price of one. Our quota of heavenly angels will be back up to par, and Saint Peter can balance his ledger of births and deaths without dematerialising your prior existence. And the best bit is, Saint Taylor won't have to cancel her world tour... and I've booked tickets in the Gods. Simples.'

What could I do? It was presented as a horse's-head-for-breakfast kind of a done-deal I couldn't refuse; join the heavenly host as Confeve or be exorcised and have all my progenitors erased from the eternal ledger from creation to doomsday. No brainer. The problem was that, to be frank, a six-foot bloke with shabby wings and a straggly beard in the back row of an angelic choir of three-foot fig-leafed baby-faced cherubim stands out like a proverbial sore thumb.

But that aside, it's a pretty cool gig. All the lotus leaves I can eat, a perpetual state of bliss and more fun and frolics than you can poke a stick at. And must admit, I'm partial to a good old sing-song, even if the devil has all the best tunes.

So, next time you are visited by an apparition masquerading as a choir of heavenly angels, rather than burst out laughing at the gangly cherub at the back with a low-pitched gravelly voice, spare a thought for my predicament. After all, I didn't ask to fill a heavenly gap. To paraphrase someone or other, some are born Confeve, some achieve Confeve, and some have Confeve thrust upon them.

Oops, must dash. Seems I've just rubbed Bill the Quill up the wrong way again. Just had a telebam shoot into my head to say he's gunning for me for plagiarism; seems he reckons I've been ghosting his best lines. As if... Anyway, methinks to be or not to be is no longer the question. As far as I'm concerned, it's a done deal.

Keep smiling, stay safe and avoid flying grand pianos.

The Cremation of the Goldfish

by Rajes Bala (Rajeswary Balasubramaniam)

'Oh my God, how awful! All the fish…'

Hearing his wife Kamala's anxious voice, her husband Sundar came up to the fish tank and exclaimed, 'Oh no, poor things!'

The couple was shocked to see forty-six bloodstained corpses floating in red water in the big aquarium, which had been a huge tank-full in past months.

Their youngest son, Shiva, watching his parents, laughed loudly and said in his soft childish voice, 'Very nice, Appa.'

Puzzled, the mother and father nervously smiled at their little boy. Baby Shiva was looking at his parents with a happy expression on his face as if he had done a wonderful adventurous thing. His parents couldn't understand why he was saying, 'Very nice'.

A few hours ago, Margaret and Philip, friends of Kamala and Sundar, had come as guests for dinner. When Philip and Margaret came over, they would bring a bottle of red or white wine or a bottle of champagne as well as a bouquet of flowers.

Philip and Margaret were friends of Melanie and Richard, who had studied together. They met Sundar at an international peace meetings in London, and the couples became friends.

'Very nice,' Philip had said a few times as he drank the red wine. When dinner was over, he picked up the bottle of wine and poured some into his and Sundaram's glasses and went up to the aquarium with the bottle in his hand as he admired the fish.

He may have left that bottle with some excess wine in it beside the fish tank.

After the guests left, Kamala cleared the table and took the plates and dishes away to the kitchen. Sundar was busy talking on his mobile phone. The bottle of wine was next to the fish tank, and some may have been poured into the tank by little Shiva just as Philip had poured it into his glass.

Now the parents understood what Shiva had done. The adults were drinking the wine and saying happily, 'Very nice'. Little toddler Shiva may have felt that he should give some of that very nice wine to their pets in the tank, too. The fish, who were happily floating around the tank as well looked after pets, had drunk the left over 'very nice' red wine offered by the charitable little boy, and in no time they faced a complete massacre.

The parents looked at the tank of fish with pity. The fish had been unable to survive the intoxication of alcohol. They were stunned, lay belly up on the surface. A gruesome death.

In the tank were a goldfish couple called Milly and Rishy, also a black and red coloured guppy couple and their forty-two baby fish, floating in the red water in a horrific state.

Kamala and Sundar had three sons. Nesan, the eldest son, was nine years old and was always reading something. When he was reading George Orwell's famous book *Animal Farm* their second son Amuthan had been six years old, and he would ask his brother about what he was reading.

Since childhood Amuthan was very fond of small animals. He told his brother about the snails, butterflies and earthworms that came into their garden. He often asked questions about nature, animals, birds, snakes or butterflies. He would pick up books on animals in the library and read them. At their school assembly, he gave a five-minute presentation on earthworms. Kamala was proud to see the appreciation shown to her son by the school kids, teachers and some parents who attended assembly that day.

The Cremation of the Goldfish

Little Shiva enjoyed looking at the pictures in the books his brothers read. He would stumble into the garden and feed the birds with the sweets in his hand.

A few months ago Melanie and Richard, their other friends, left London for Liverpool due to Richard's promotion. To be remembered by the boys after they moved, they bought them a present of the large fish tank with the goldfish couple and the guppy couple. Both female fish were pregnant.

All three boys were in charge of the fish tank, but overall administration for the care of the fishes was given to Amuthan, as he was fonder of the new pets than his brothers. He explained to the other boys when the babies would hatch and how to take care of them. Amuthan named the goldfish couple Milly and Rishy in memory of Melanie and Richard.

Today Nesan and Amuthan had gone to the zoo with their uncle (Kamala's brother) and it was arranged that they would spend the night at their uncle's house and return the next morning. 'Oh God, I do not know how my darling Amuthan is going to bear the death of his pet fishes,' Kamala told her husband, almost crying.

Sundar patted his wife and said, 'This is a tragic accident. Whether the fish died due to alcohol or not, we can't bring them back to life. Tomorrow we will buy fresh fish for the aquarium.'

'Please don't say that. Let's call the boys right now and tell the truth.' Nesan and Amuthan had already phoned home to say that they had been thrilled to see many animals at the zoo—birds, fish, crocodiles, turtles and snakes. 'We should call them and tell them the news,' she said.

She immediately called her brother Kesavan and told him about the condition of the fish.

He said, 'Oh, what a pity, I don't know how they are going react. They're in a very happy mood now, as they enjoyed the zoo today.' He handed over the telephone to Amuthan.

'What happened?' Amuthan asked anxiously.

'Oh, my darlings, the fish have had an accident, so sorry, my dears.' Kamala said.

She could hear Amuthan's scream.

'How's that?' Nesan asked.

She found it too hard to explain to them by phone. 'Just come home,' she said.

When they arrived, Kamala carefully told them about the sad incident. She did not say much about how the accident happened, which had so suddenly killed their beautiful pets.

'How beautiful my Milly and Rishy were and their babies that were coming. I was just waiting for their hatchings,' screamed six-year-old Amuthan. Kamala's heart was torn apart to see the sad face of her second son.

The next month after getting the aquarium, 42 babies were born to the guppy couple. Amuthan eagerly awaited the heirs of the goldfish couple. The goldfish couple were still frolicking in the tanks like royalty. They didn't seem to have any thoughts of expecting their future generation.

Amuthan called Melanie frequently and asked when the goldfish would become parents. 'They'll be here soon,' Melanie said, adding that the guppies could have a second set of hatchings the month after that.

The arrival and growth of the fish appealed to many of Amuthan's six-year-old friends. The children went to the library and read a lot of information about fish. Since it was spring, many of Amuthan's friends used to play in a public garden behind Amuthan's house. After finishing their games they came to the garden of Amuthan's house and joined their little friend Shiva to eat snacks, drink *payazham* (Sagoo sweet pudding) and stand for a long time around the fish tank watching the forty-six fishes floating beautifully in the tank.

Kamala was so happy to see that the fish tank provided a wonderful display not only for her three sons but also the small children from the neighbourhood.

'Call Melanie immediately and tell her about this,' Amuthan said with tears in his eyes. It was now 10:00 p.m. However, Kamala understood that he would not be able to bear it if he did not tell his beloved Melanie and Richard about the fish accident.

Kamala knew that her English friends didn't like to be disturbed by phone calls on weekends. Also, calling after 9:00 p.m. would be considered bad manners. However, Kamala, unable to bear Amuthan's pain, called Melanie without noting the late hour.

Melanie asked, 'what's wrong?' She knew that Kamala would not call at this hour unless it was an urgent matter.

'Please forgive me, Melanie. Today Philip and Margaret came over for dinner. There was a little more red wine after we ate. When Philip went to look at the fish, he must have left the bottle near the tank. I think Shiva poured the wine into the tank as a gift for the fish. So, in that drunken state, all the hatchlings died.' Kamala started crying.

'Oh, what a pity. Too bad Philip left a drop in the bottle. Poor Shiva did it unknowingly,' said Melanie.

Kamala put Amuthan on the phone. 'There's nothing we can do about the accident. I will buy you boys some more fish,' said Melanie to him.

'We cannot perform the funeral ceremony without you two,' said Amuthan, weeping.

'Oh, my darling. Tomorrow is Sunday, we are going to see our parents, and we won't be able to come to London before next

Saturday. Until then, if you don't have a problem, you can keep them. Put it in Mum's fridge. We'll all do the funeral when we get back,' Richard and Melanie told Amuthan.

'OK, we will do that,' said Amuthan, drying his tears.

Mother's cooked meals and uncooked food was also in the freezer. One area became the mortuary of the fish.

Kamala's brother Kesavan, who had dropped the boys off in a hurry some time ago, was back at his house. He phoned and asked what was going on.

'Oh, Brother, the children are very upset; especially Amuthan is grief-stricken. He is planning a funeral, but Melanie and Richard cannot come until next Saturday,' Kamala said sadly.

The next day, Uncle Kesavan came to mourn the death of the fish. His approach to animals was in no way near that of Kamala's kids in London who adored little creatures.

He was joined by the neighbourhood children who now arrived to offer their condolences. Kamala hoped that Shiva wouldn't smile and say 'very nice' to the mourning crowd.

In olden days, unlike London, in the villages of Sri Lanka there was no custom of pampering pets. Kamala's family came from a traditional village in in the east of Sri Lanka where animals are usually seen as annoyances.

The River Thillai that surrounds the village, the fields and fields around it, were home to innumerable animals. In the village, the mischief of the monkeys stealing food irritates the old men. Water snakes crawl freely into the houses. Cobras live in the anthills near the temple. It is an area where lizards and wolves roam merrily. The children of the village were fond of catching many-coloured parrots and teaching them to speak.

Kamala's younger brother Kesavan was very naughty as a child, and since then he seemed to see everything in the world differently than others. He was fond of making jokes about things others considered serious. He couldn't help laughing at the tragedy at his sister's house, especially for the dead fish who died due to excessive intake of red wine.

When Kesavan was a child, he would catch little lizards, stuff tobacco in the little creatures' mouths, and in that trance the creature would move with rhythm to the music played by the village boys. Kesavan would think it was a dance and enjoy it.

Young Kesavan's gang used to dress up puppies and kittens in little trousers and T-shirts and let them walk around. Then the crowd of six or seven-year-olds would laugh and enjoy the painful cries of the small animals, until sometime they would be scolded by his grandmother with a wooden spoon for being nasty to poor creatures.

She would shout, 'They are all God's creations for different purposes on Mother Earth. Do not upset them. If you do, you will face the consequences of Karma.'

Sometimes the mother hen screamed in surprise, when he coloured her chicks in multi-coloured paint. The hen would run around in confusion, and Kesavan would laugh at his naughty drama. If a water snake came near the house he would catch it, tie it upside down hang it on a jasmine vine, before getting himself beaten by Grandma with her mighty wooden spoon.

Now in London, he wanted to investigate the killing of Amuthan's pet fish at his sister's house. Kamala suppressed him with an angry look as she did not want her brother to make a comedy drama out of the tragedy. Some of Amuthan's six-year-old friends saw Shiva as a murderer, but Kamala didn't want the little boy to be interrogated by the older boys. She did not appreciate her brother elaborating on Shiva's childish action with funny jokes.

'Forty-six small fish were killed by your little son Shiva giving them alcohol?' Kesavan asked sarcastically.

Kamala looked at her brother angrily. 'Shut up, my little one is not a political assailant massacring his enemies. He just poured some leftover wine into the tank after hearing Philip say it was 'very nice' when he drank red wine.' She warned her brother, 'Don't make fun of this matter. It was Philip's mistake; Shiva acted unknowingly.'

'Well, how is the funeral going to happen?' asked the uncle Kesavan to his nephews.

'We don't know how to do it. We have to discuss with Melanie and Richard, who will be coming next Saturday,' said the big boy Nesan.

'Uncle, tell us what to do, so we can tell Melanie and Richard. We will perform the funeral however you tell us to,' said Amuthan.

Kesavan said, 'I don't know if Melanie and Richard are Christians. I don't know if they go to church or not. But your mother used to go to temples when she was young. Your father Sundar is a non-believer regarding temples, rituals and gods. So, now your mother has stopped going to the temple. However, since the death of these fish took place in a Hindu family...'

Kesavan told his nephews in a very loving voice, 'We should perform the last rites of these fish according to our religion.'

'The fishes' funeral is a religious matter?' Kamala glared at her brother. She knew that Kesavan's mischievous ritual would irritate her atheist husband.

'My dear sister, my darling nephews—particularly Amuthan—looked at his pet fish as human beings. He maintained the care for them in a very humane manner. Let's do this to make him happy,' said Kesavan in a humble voice.

Kamala knew that Kesavan was going to make Amuthan's

misery into a something else. But she didn't want to disappoint the children. Also she knew that her husband would not like any stupid Hindu rituals regarding birth or death. If he saw how Kesavan was trying to make fun of the situation Sundar might be angry.

'Sister, your husband will not be at home next Saturday as he travels around London on Saturdays for meetings to listen to lectures on world peace. Today, there are many wars going on in the world, big and small. This is the world order of the capitalists, who make and profit from the sale of weapons. They are secretly waging wars. I don't know when your husband Sundar will understand that. Next Saturday definitely he will go to some meeting. We will perform rituals for the children as per their wish. Particularly to please heartbroken Amuthan.'

Kamala half-heartedly agreed to her brother's funeral arrangements.

'Uncle, then, what are we to do about the ritual?' the kids asked.

Kesavan said, 'You now isolate the two big goldfish, Milly and Rishy, and keep them separately, as you have given them human names. We have to perform a special ceremony for them, that is, we will cremate the goldfish couple according to the Hindu ritual the same way we would for humans, and bury the other little ones as we do for animals in Ceylon.'

'Oh, Uncle, are you going to throw our beloved goldfish, Milly and her husband Rishy, into the fire?' asked Amuthan.

Then Kesavan, to please his nephews, kept his face very sad. 'These goldfish are both adults, raised in this tank with respect, like leaders who protect the small guppy fish. They should be given the same respect as our elders. That would be only fair. It will be our duty to send those who are dear to us to heaven with due respect.'

'Milly died with her husband. If she had not gone to heaven with her husband Rishy under the influence of alcohol, she would have been thrown into the fire and burnt alive,' Kamala muttered sarcastically in Tamil as she do not want the children to be frightened.

'It's not 1829, my dear sister. We no longer practice the barbaric act of *Sati*, pushing the wife onto her dead husband's funeral pyre, thinking that she had no place in society after her husband's death. The mumbo jumbo mantras chanted by the Brahman priest were just designed to fool innocent people out of their money to fund their comfortable living and control the masses,' Kesavan said.

He said, 'One day, when they understand the cruelties of Hindu rituals, women's place in society and the caste system, they may do something to change these inhumane practices.'

Kamala looked at her brother. Was he trying to make the children to remember this event later in their lives with real understanding of this ritual? Was he projecting a complex religious ideology onto these small kids using a painful experience such as this? She did not want to continue the subject as their uncle Kesavan had already led the kids to anticipate a special service for their dead fish.

The children agreed to their uncle's rituals that day. The two goldfish were carefully wrapped in white cloth and kept in a new plastic box. The guppy hatchlings and their mother and father were wrapped up and placed in another box.

Their father Sundar had gone to a political rally. When he arrived home, Kamala wondered whether she should or should not tell him about the planned ritual. Because he did not believe in God. She knew that he was not going to agree to the religious rituals that Kesavan was planning.

Over the next few days, not only her sons but also their friends were focused on the fish. They came to look at the carcasses in the freezer. They would ask questions while they ate the sweets Kamala offered. The six-year-olds were obviously upset by the death of the fish. Kamala's heart was touched by the grief of the young soldiers. In England, apart from human rights, this culture has taught children from an early age to be kind to all animals.

Some of Amuthan's friends told the story of the shocking death of the fish to their little brothers and sisters who went to Shiva's nursery. Many mothers expressed their sympathy when they saw Kamala with Shiva at the nursery.

When her brother Kesavan heard that the tale of the fish tank massacre was spreading like wildfire in Islington, he said sarcastically, 'Local journalists may come and write about the 'Sri Lankan Tamil house' where the murders took place due to your inappropriate care.'

Philip came with a guilty face and said sorry to the mourning children. He apologised honestly.

The following Saturday came. Melanie and Richard arrived from Liverpool.

On seeing them, Amuthan's cry was pitiful within their embrace. Nesan told the fish gifters in great detail about the cremation that was to take place. They listened to the explanation of death, eating their favourite snacks vada, onion bhajis and sweets, which they had prepared with great sadness. When Philip and Margaret arrived reluctantly to the funeral, Melanie and Richard whispered angrily to their friend Philip.

In Kamala's garden, Kesavan made a funeral pyre for the cremation of the goldfish. Suddenly, Kamala got worried. If anyone saw the smoke of the cremation and called the fire brigade, there would be a big uproar. She was terrified of it.

Kesavan was dismissive. 'Sister, today is Saturday. Some of the neighbours may be having their barbecues too, so not to worry about the police or fire brigade.'

Not only Amuthan's six-year-old friends and Nesan's one or two nine-year-old sympathisers, but also the mothers of some sympathisers, who came from far away with their small children in pushchairs, attended the ceremony with great amazement as they never seen a Hindu funeral service before, let alone a funeral for fish.

The goldfish's funeral ceremonial platform was prepared by Kesavan by picking apple tree leaves. Near the heap, Kesavan lit many candles and prepared to cremate the goldfishes by lighting a special lamps that his sister Kamala had brought from India.

The little boy Shiva, who was responsible for all this, watched all the arrangements with surprise and happily clapped his hands.

'*Amma*, what should we do now?' Amuthan asked his mother.

As per Kesavan's orders, Amuthan's led his army of friends in a procession bringing the fish from the freezer.

Amuthan and Nesan put the goldfish couple together on the funeral pyre. The guppy fish were held by other children.

The atmosphere was sad and quiet. Some on-lookers were in tears on seeing Amuthan's soft cries.

'We pray to God that the spirits of these fish, who have lived with us all this time and made us happy, may rest in peace in heaven,' said Kesavan.

The friends and some of their mothers said, 'Amen'.

'Sister, you should sing prayers for god and the peaceful journey of the fishes to heaven,' Kesavan asked Kamala lovingly. Though Kamala was angry with him for organising this unfamiliar service, which was not understood by any of the children, she did not want to make the children sad and sang the prayer song.

Then he said, 'Sister, you should video this ritual, so the children can keep the memory of their lost fish.'

'Please take a video,' the child soldiers said in unison.

Kamala watched her brother's naughty game of a Hindu funeral. When the goldfish melted in the fire, Amuthan's scream was so painful.

'They have gone to heaven,' their uncle's explanation reduced Amuthan's tears a little. Melanie and Richard, special funeral sympathisers, hugged him.

Next, the ritual of the guppy family took place under Kamala's jasmine tree.

In their memory, small sticks wrapped in white cloth were planted in the treasure as headstones. Some of the six-year-old soldiers planted the souvenir sticks with great sorrow.

'Watch this video when you think of your beloved fish. You will feel relieved,' said Kesavan to his nephews, hiding his mischievous smile.

After the ceremony, there were many types of sweets for the guests. While they ate them they talked at length about the beauty of the goldfish, the way they paraded through the tank, and their disappointment over not having the baby goldfishes that had been expected.

Melanie and Richard watched the funeral with silent amazement. The love these children had for these fish hurt them. Melanie hugged the three of them. She hadn't had a baby yet. To her Amuthan, Nesan and Shiva were lovely kids, and she wanted to have children like them. She was very fond of Kamala's family.

'Does Melanie know that what happened was due to Shiva?' Kesavan said in Tamil to his sister in a soft sarcastic voice.

After the ritual was over Philip and Margaret gave Amuthan their heartfelt condolences and slipped away.

Kamala had asked Melanie and Richard to stay the night.

Melanie had been a vegetarian since she was a child, and Kamala cooked her favourite vegetables.

Staying that night, talking to the children and enjoying the funeral was a new experience for her. 'Thank you for inviting me.' Melanie hugged the children for a long time. When Sundar arrived, the children told their father of their joy that their uncle had performed a good Hindu funeral ritual and sent their beloved fishes to heaven.

Sundar was not a fan of these rituals and the custom of giving gifts to the priests who performed the service.

'Did your uncle ask for gifts like umbrellas and shoes to ensure that the journey to the fish paradise is not hindered?' asked Sundaram sarcastically.

'Oh, *Amma*, you didn't give Uncle an umbrella and shoes. My dear fish will struggle to get to heaven.' Amuthan was sad.

Kamala suppressed her anger at her husband for making the children sadder about the event and said in an assuring tone, 'There was no rain or very hot sun today, darling. And the streets are very clean for the barefoot journey by the fishes as the council street cleaners come every Saturday. Cleaning would have happened on Saturdays in heaven, as well. But the fish will go to heaven by floating on the water. The water tanks on the way to heaven would have been cleaned nicely, just as the pond in our park is cleaned today, and the fishes pilgrimage to heaven will have gone smoothly.'

'Today the cleaners of heaven are not striking for higher wages,' said her husband mockingly. Perhaps it was both an explanation to the children and a conciliatory gesture to his wife. But the kids did not get his tone of sarcasm and were not upset.

Little Shiva took a bite of the biscuit from his baby table as usual. 'Very nice,' he said.

IV Beyond the Bounds

The Wild Man

by Elaine Graham-Leigh

The trees straggle back from the dual carriageway, separated from the layby by a low fence. The ground is strewn with crisp packets and condoms, lager cans and hamburger boxes, the detritus left by the people who park there. It's difficult pulling back out into the road when the traffic is heavy; one of the tree trunks bears ribbons and flowers as a shrine to the latest accident. The top rails of the fence beside the exit have been broken, leaving a barrier only a few inches high. Beyond it, a track of trodden mud leads off into the wood.

The clearing is not far down the track, but from inside the traffic is inaudible, the only sound the constant murmur of rustling leaves. In the centre of the clearing is a trunk of a dead tree. In life the tree would have been massive; in death all that remains is the wide trunk, broken off about ten feet up into a jagged finger pointing at the sky. The bark has been scoured white by hundreds of winters. No ivy grows on it, but here and there ribbons and pieces of paper have been pinned on the trunk like flowering creeper. Apples are piled on the grass around the base, gently rotting into the soil.

There's no one there. There is never anyone there. But sometimes, on still days, the trees lean together like they're talking, or bowing, and the bushes shiver applause. Sometimes, when you look into the leaves, for a moment there are yellow eyes, looking back.

The Wild Man

*****

'I hear them all the time, laughing. I vigil in the church, I scourge myself before the altar till my blood dyes the floor but I still hear them. They should fear to come there, but they do not. When they hear me say the prayer of our Lord in my cell at night it is nothing, just words; thin, slight words with no meaning. I saw them in the window above the altar; at mass the glass moved like faces and said, 'soon'. They blow out the candles when I light them, and they laugh.'

Brother Geoffrey licked his cracked lips and dipped his pen again into the inkwell. Outside the circle of his one candle the scriptorium lay in darkness, but the light was just sufficient to show the bars he had dragged across the door still held. Beyond the empty corridors on the other side all the brothers lay in their cells, ears tight shut against anything but the sound of their prayers. The wind had been high when he barricaded himself into the scriptorium, but the storm had dropped towards midnight and now there was nothing but a thick, waiting stillness.

On the edge of hearing he caught the hint of a giggle, like a bad child hiding. Was it just the candle guttering, or did the bar move? He had struggled just to lift it and now it was chained in place. It could not move. It could not. A moan like wind flittered past his ear, ruffled the pages on his desk. He whipped round.

'Who's there? In the name of Our Lord, show yourself!'

There was no reply. He turned back and watched, unable to stop it, as his pen scratched alone across the parchment, in writing like his own:

'They are outside the door. Jesus Christ protect me, our Lord receive my soul in Heaven, they are outside the door.'

*****

'So that's really how it ends? 'They're outside the door'? That's brilliant!' Claire's eyes sparkled as she grinned at her friend. 'You must be so excited.'

Fenella shrugged, trying to seem offhand.

'New manuscripts are always exciting. We don't find them very often, after all.'

She couldn't quite keep the pleased tone out of her voice. It wasn't often that she managed to impress Claire.

Claire and Fenella had been friends since university, but while Claire had gone to London and got into TV, Fenella had stayed behind and worked as a junior archivist in the cathedral library. Once or twice a year, Claire would invite Fenella to a party with her media friends, and whenever she came back to their university town they'd have dinner in the most fashionable restaurant, Claire holding her elbows in as if the place was too small for her. Fenella didn't usually talk to Claire about her work, but then, it was rare she had anything to tell.

The manuscript had been found by one of the PhD students working in the cathedral archives, hidden in the binding of a volume of fifteenth-century rent rolls. Very unlike the elegant, decorated works that made up most of the library, it had taken the student, Damien, more than two weeks to transcribe the crabbed, spiky Latin on the parchment. Filing while Damien struggled with it, Fenella had felt herself pushing through a thick, brooding silence, hanging over the stacks like mist. For the first time she'd taken to rushing through her work in the afternoon so as not to be the last out.

'I don't know really what we'll do with it,' she told Claire, over the remains of their dinner. 'Poor Damien spent all that time on it, but it's hardly relevant to his thesis topic. Mark—you know, the head of the library—says we'll need to get someone to authenticate it, and then maybe someone will do an edition, but it's just a bit odd, really. I mean, a medieval ghost story. It doesn't exactly fit into anyone's research. Probably it'll never get published and no one else will ever read it.'

In her mind's eye she saw a slim, glossy volume, a moody shot of the cathedral on the cover, and 'Brother Geoffrey' embossed in gold. Piled on the bestselling shelves in the town bookshop, crowds of people leaving with them clutched in their hands. It seemed suddenly such a horrific idea that she couldn't help shivering. She glanced anxiously across at Claire, in case she'd noticed, but Claire was not interested in the problems of academic publishing.

'Do you really think it's just a ghost story?' she asked.

'Of course. What else could it be?'

'Well...' Claire's face took on a sharp, cunning look that her colleagues would have recognised. 'It could be true.'

'Oh, no, I don't think...'

'It could be. It's a first person account. Why couldn't this Brother Geoffrey be telling the truth? And if he was, it would be dynamite. It would make fantastic television.'

Fenella stared at her. 'You mean, you'd be interested in it? You'd want to do a programme about it?'

'You said that PhD student did a translation, didn't you?'

'Yes, he finished it today. He left it with Mark.'

Claire put on her most winning expression.

'Could you get a copy for me?'

'I don't know. I...'

'Please? For me?'

Every thought in her head was screaming at her to say no. Put it away again, let it be forgotten, don't let it out!

'Come on, Fennie. It's me.'

Claire's blue eyes were sharp, brighter even than the shadows. Fenella sighed.

'I suppose I could try,' she said.

*****

Fenella checked her bag for the third time. The plastic wallet with the photocopied translation was cool and reassuring on her fingers, hidden between her book and her umbrella. She'd had to wait until everyone else had gone for the day before she could do the copying, the first time she'd locked up since they'd found the manuscript. She told herself she was foolish to feel uneasy. Leaking manuscripts to the media wasn't exactly protocol, but it didn't hurt anyone. It wasn't as if she was really doing anything wrong.

She opened the office door. The corridor was dim, with only the streetlights outside in the Close saving it from total darkness, but it always was. It wasn't as if she didn't know the way. She turned off the office lights. It was immediately absolutely black. She concentrated on locking the door, trying not to let her handshake. There was nothing to be afraid of, nothing. She would just walk, briskly, down the corridor, then she would cross the nave to the outer door. She did it every night. Nothing to be afraid of.

The door at the end of the corridor swung outwards on its hinges, allowing her a brief glimpse of cathedral, then slammed back, hard. She heard the bolt rattle as it did when it was windy. It wasn't windy. Her hands started shaking and she thrust them into her coat pockets to still them. The door banged shut again and again there was the rattle of the bolt, as if something was trying to draw it across. Something that she would have to walk past. Something that knew.

Blindly she turned back, fumbling for the key. If she could put it back, tear up the copy as if it had never happened... She was six feet away when the office door opened like a jaw and slammed. Stifling a sob she swung round again, forcing herself down the corridor like walking into a gale. When she reached the end, the wood of the door was rough, unforgiving, quivering like a tree in a storm.

'I'm sorry!' she cried. 'I'm sorry!'

The door trembled under her hands. She wrenched it open and fled across the flagstones and out into the Close. She did not look behind her.

*****

When Claire saw her storming through the office, her first thought was that someone had died. Her hair hung over her shoulders in matted clumps, her coat, half off, trailed its belt behind her along the floor. The receptionist was hurrying after her, 'Wait! You can't...'

Claire stood up.

'Fen? What are you doing here? What's happened?'

Fenella stopped, breathing hard.

'What am I doing here? What am I doing here?' She gave a short laugh. 'I'm doing what you asked, what else? Here.' She reached into her bag and flung an envelope down onto Claire's desk. 'There it is. The translation, photo of the manuscript, everything you wanted. I hope it makes you very happy.'

'Fen, wait! What's the matter? You can't just come barging in here like this and then sod off again without telling me what's up. What's the deal?'

'The deal?' Fenella took a breath, composing herself with an effort. 'The deal is I've resigned my job.'

'You've left the cathedral? Because of this? I'm sorry, really I am. I didn't want you to get into trouble. But, you know, you didn't have to do this. I didn't force you. It was your choice.'

'Yes.' Her lip curled. 'It was my choice, all my choice. I knew what I was doing. I tried to take it back, but I couldn't. There's some things you can't undo, you know? Once you've seen it, you can't unsee it. That's all there is to it.'

She sounded on the verge of tears and Claire regarded her with concern. She didn't want her to make any more of a scene. She glanced at the receptionist, hovering behind Fenella's shoulder with one of the security guards in tow.

'Look' she said, 'I can't promise anything, but we're going to need a historical adviser for this film. I haven't gone through any names, but if I told everyone that you're the one who found the manuscript, I'm sure we could find you something. It wouldn't pay much, but...'

'It's not about the money! I wouldn't have anything to do with it if you paid me a million pounds! I never want to read it again, and you shouldn't either.'

She leaned forward, her hands on the desk. Her face under the wild hair was ravaged; Claire had to stop herself from swaying backwards. She caught the receptionist's eye.

'Seriously,' said Fenella.

The security guard took hold of her arm. 'This is the only warning you're ever going to get.' He started to lead her away. 'I'm giving it even though I know full well you won't listen to me. Leave it alone.' The guard had got her to the office door now, nearly out into the lobby. 'It doesn't want to be found, Claire. For your own good, leave it alone.'

The Wild Man

*****

They decided on silver on black for the credits, for the spooky yet restrained effect. They would start with a short historical introduction, explaining that there were medieval English folk tales about wild men, creatures that looked like furry humans, lived in woods and had magical powers. They were sometimes connected with holy men, hermits who also lived outside society and were regarded by the peasants as superhuman. One of the historians they'd dug up to be a talking head had a nice story about a hermit meeting a wild man and giving him an apple. They would put that in, with an out-of-focus reconstruction and a scene of the hermit telling it to a group of suitably awed and grubby peasants, afterwards.

The historian had wanted to go on about how the hermits, and possibly the wild men too, were shown in the stories as defenders of the peasants against their lords, but that was far too complicated to put in. 'This is TV, not sociology,' Claire had said. She wrote the teaser to lead them into the first ad break: 'Historians have always thought these stories were just that, stories. But what if they were true? What if the wild man really existed? What if there was an English Yeti?' From the break they would go straight to the beginning of the manuscript, which Claire insisted on reading herself.

Every time she rehearsed it, it made her shiver. She tried to shut out everything around her, concentrate only on her voice, reading the words of a monk dead for 800 years.

'Yesterday, I heard a story about a wild man in the forest. I was supervising the peasants unloading the autumn tithes in the garth and I heard them talking of it. They didn't want to tell me at first whence they had it, but I pressed them and in the end

they cried out for mercy and admitted that it was the holy man's. They were lucky not to have worse. I said to them, 'so you believe this tale of a wild man, a creature not mentioned in the Bible, not created by our Lord nor saved on the Ark?' They looked at their feet and mumbled as peasants will and in the end, finding no thought in them, I let them go. I should have dismissed it, I know that now. The walls of the City are kept only by ignorance. But I was strong then in belief in my righteousness, and proud. This morning I told the Abbot I had an errand abroad and I went out in search. The peasants watched me from the fields as I passed them by. It seems to me now they laughed.

'I walked all day and as the light was fading I came to the place where the holy man has his hut. He was not there. I called for him, but there was no reply. I was tired and angered, for it seemed to me I had quested far for nothing. I sat down on the ground to wait for him and I felt I had only rested for a moment when I saw it. It came out of the forest with a loping gait, swift, but not straight as a man. It was as tall as I or taller, dressed only in a rough kilt, and all down its back was a brown fuzz that seemed at first like hair, but when I looked again was fur. I stood up and faced it, as my father and my brothers face their enemies on the field of war.

'Are you a true Christian?' I cried. 'Do you accept the power of Our Lord Jesus Christ and His Church?' Awful I felt in my majesty, I was sure it must bow before me, as dumb animals before the saints of old. The creature looked at me in silence. 'Well, do you?' I asked. It raked me with its eyes, right through. It was as if I brought it the world, the City of God and all the great lords therein. It held it all in the balance for a moment, weighing it, it seemed, against its whole chaotic kingdom that none of our wisdom can touch, that is beyond our laws, when I thought the

world had been given over into our keeping. It considered for a brief time, then as if dismissing me it laughed: 'Hach! Hach! Hach!'. Then it disappeared.'

When she first read the translation, Claire had hoped that there would be another encounter, more details about the wild man Brother Geoffrey had met in the wood, but to her disappointment, the rest of the manuscript was devoted to the monk's deteriorating mental state. They argued in the production meetings about how much of the later parts they should use. Will, the co-producer, had a favourite passage that he read out, as if oblivious to the shadows gathering like cobwebs in the corners.

'At first, I heard them only when I was alone. I thought they would leave me alone if I prayed, and I did pray! But they did not stop, whispering words of mockery in a language older than speech, older than death. We think we are proof against them, that our reason and our laws are doors to keep them out, and we are wrong, wrong. I sat at dinner with the brethren in the refectory, and they came to me. They came in the guise of devils riding goats, like the little people of the islands that the great St Cuthbert drove into the sea. They came riding into the refectory at the cloister door, two by two on their black, slot-eyed mounts. They had little spears in their hands, all in a line, upright, with black pennants on them. They leapt onto the table and picked their way towards me, stepping over the plates and dishes as the brothers ate as if they were not there. They rode up the table to me, two by two, and the leader looked down with his yellow eyes from his black goat horse, and laughed.'

'Wouldn't that be fantastic dramatised?' Will said, laughing himself. 'Little goats on the tables! It would be great.'

Claire couldn't explain why she couldn't bear the thought of it, why the very idea of seeing it on film made her retch.

'Yeah,' she said, reaching defensively for sarcasm, 'because if our only Yeti witness was on medieval LSD, that'll really help our credibility. Nice one, Will.'

She usually got her way in the end. They agreed that unless the search for the Yeti failed to give enough footage, they would leave the end of the manuscript out.

'You never know what might happen on location,' said Will. 'It could be anything.'

He caught Claire's glare as she swept past him on her way back to her desk.

'What? What did I say?'

The historical team admitted that they couldn't identify either Brother Geoffrey or his monastery, but judging from the location of the manuscript, they thought he had probably been a monk in the abbey that had been attached to the cathedral itself until the Reformation. In the twelfth century, a famous hermit had lived nearby, in woods about five miles outside the town. It seemed a good place as any to start. As Claire wrote for the voiceover: 'If we wanted to find the English Yeti, we realised there was only one thing for it. We would have to retrace Brother Geoffrey's footsteps, and go in search of the wild man.' They scheduled a two-week trip to the hermitage.

*****

Fenella tried not to go near the cathedral anymore. Most of the time it was possible to ignore it, to flit from brightly-lit shop to shop in the town and never lift her eyes to the stone bulk looming above. But today was different. If she wanted her P45 she had to go to the Dean's office; however much she dreaded it, fear wouldn't sort out her taxes. Her car park pass had gone with her job; she had to leave her car in the multi-storey behind the shopping centre. She walked slowly up the hill, trying not to puff at the incline.

The Close seemed its usual placid self at first, the Georgian houses surrounding the cathedral with their customary incurious stares. Grey scarves of rain drifted lightly across her vision. She reached the corner and started across the face of the cathedral to the Dean's office at the far end. She was tired. The walk had been a longer one than she was used to and she had not been sleeping well. The need for sleep drummed in her ears as she stepped off the pavement, throbbing like a pressure in the air, like an aircraft going over low. Students on their way to class pushed past her, unnoticing, as if she weren't there.

The cathedral loomed in her peripheral vision. She had to keep her head down. She couldn't stop, couldn't stop... Out of her control, she felt her pace slowing, her feet clinging to the tarmac. She stopped and looked at the cathedral. It seemed for a moment as if it looked back at her, as if it were telling her something. Then every door and window on the building, every shutter and latch on the Close began to bang. Forward and backward in rhythm, hitting the frames and the brickwork, splintering, breaking, banging without wind, without sound, because she was held there watching, and all the barriers she'd ever believed in were gone.

*****

Claire put the tape in and sat down. She'd always liked to watch the final version of her shows at home, on her own. She'd always said she could get the atmosphere that way, feel what Mr and Mrs Joe Public would think. This wasn't the finished programme; there never would be a finished programme, now. But she wanted to watch the footage once before she destroyed it, see it once through the dispassionate eye of the camera as well as in her memory every time she closed her eyes. She curled herself into the corner of her sofa, sitting sideways so that the window was on her left and not behind her. She didn't like having anything behind her, not anymore.

The entryphone buzzed as she turned the TV on. She didn't get up to answer it. All the flat doors in the block had double locks, complementing the massive steel door at the main entrance and the electric gates by the porter's lodge outside. When she'd bought the flat it had been a selling point, how secure it was, and that was before a spate of burglaries had led the residents to put the CCTV in and add the spikes to the walls round the courtyard. She could put yet more locks on the door, but she knew that wouldn't make a difference. There were some things not even gates could shut out.

The footage started with the crew in the restaurant. It had taken them much longer to get out of London than they had expected, accidents and road works delaying them one after the other until Will joked that God was trying to tell them something. It had been almost dark and raining by the time they reached the town, and they'd decided that they would wait until the next morning to find the hermitage site. They'd checked in to the best hotel and gone out to what they'd decided was the only decent restaurant.

She couldn't remember why they'd done so much shooting at dinner. Something about engaging the viewer with the filming, she thought. She watched the flushed faces of the crew, ensconced in the lights of the restaurant as if it was the very expense of it that separated them from the dark streets outside. After a while they'd put the camera down on the windowsill, but it had kept on filming.

Opposite the windows a group of youths was hanging around, their hoods over their faces against the rain. On the film they looked not aimless but organised, as if they might have stormed into the restaurant, might have seized the plates and the half-empty bottles of expensive wine and handed them out to the town. She hadn't seen them at the time. She hadn't ever noticed people like that, then.

The sunlight slanted onto the corner of the screen; in half an hour it would be right across it. If she sat up they would see her. She could feel their eyes even now, when the back of the sofa was hiding her. She reached up quickly and twitched the new, heavy curtain across the window, ducking back down as soon as it was done. It made the screen more visible, but she could still feel their eyes on her, looking through her. She knew they were watching her.

She and the crew had set out the next morning for the hermitage. It didn't take very long to get there, nothing like the full day's journey poor Brother Geoffrey had had. A few miles up the dual carriageway, then a bouncing ten minutes down a single-track road, following a wooden sign so worn it could hardly be read. There was no house left, of course, whatever hut the holy man had lived in was long gone, but at some point after his death, the locals had built a stone chapel on the site. The camera scanned the one remaining chapel wall, the moss-covered stones and ivy waving in the small arched window. There was nothing else left of the building, but a stone cross set into the grass marked where the tomb of the holy man had been. All around, the wood stretched off into the distance.

They'd set up the tents against the chapel wall; three of them, an individual one each for Claire and Will and a larger one for the camera crew. They could have stayed in the van, but they'd decided that camping would be more dramatic. There was nothing that audiences liked more than the idea of presenters in the wilderness, in jeopardy. They'd taken lots of footage of them all in camp; sleeping, chatting, cooking rudimentary meals over a campfire, which off-camera would usually be thrown away in preference for takeaway fetched from the town. On the tape they all looked so small, so temporary against the stones and the grass, the bright cloth of the tents clinging to the wall like fragile, alien blossoms. Claire hadn't let herself notice then how the trees had loomed over them, how they circled the light around the cameras like actors waiting for their cue. As the tape played on she was surprised the camera hadn't caught the eyes.

They watched her all the time, just looking for a way in. She'd thought she was so safe, with her locks and bars, her degree and fancy job. She'd thought she didn't have to think about them, that it didn't matter how much she had or how much she flaunted it because they were powerless. They weren't powerless. She'd lived as if they would never come for her, but even though she hadn't seen them they had always been there. The journey to the office to get the tape had taken all the willpower she had, she knew she couldn't go out among them again. The stillborn film was the last programme she would ever make, and they were just biding their time.

*****

Fenella's parents paid for her stay at the centre.

'It's not a mental home,' her mother said. Fenella could hear the echoes of all the times her mother had told herself this, imagining the comments of the neighbours.

'It's very nice, really. It's just a place where people can go and have... a rest. When they've been overdoing things. Lots of famous people go, apparently.'

She tried, manfully, to smile. 'You don't know who you might

The Wild Man

meet.' The staff said, 'anyone can have a breakdown. It was all in your mind. You can recognise that. It's nothing to be ashamed of.'

Fenella fixed her eyes on the windows, watching the trees beyond the gate bending in the wind. She didn't have any more episodes, as everyone insisted on calling it. After a month her mother brought her back to her childhood home, just outside the town.

Her mother thought she might be able to get her old job back.

'That nice Mark from the library called while you were... away. He said he'd heard you weren't well, that he quite understood. They haven't found anyone for your post, he said. I think he was missing you.'

She shot a pointed look at her daughter, maternally watchful for any glimmerings of romance. Fenella imagined returning to the cathedral, kneeling before the altar in penance, resting her head on the cool stone. It didn't feel impossible, just pointless, like cowering behind a broken wall when she could be outside and free. The cathedral was built as much for defence against the locals as for worship, she was enough of a historian to know that.

She remembered some of the stories her friends used to tell, before she got the scholarship to the private school, where all they talked about were exams and skiing holidays, and had forgotten them. She borrowed her mother's car for an afternoon and headed for the dual carriageway. She pulled over into the first layby after the services, stepped over the broken fence and followed the path into the wood. At the foot of the broken trunk she laid the apples she'd brought onto the grass. There was no sound, no sign of recognition or rejection, only a gust of wind in the trees around that made them lean briefly over her, then away again. That was all.

Halfway back to the car, she met a youth in a hooded top, hurrying the other way. She stepped off the narrow path to let him by, and as he came past she found herself catching his eye and smiling 'hello'. He half-smiled back at her, muttering 'Awrigh'. As soon as he was out of sight, it began to rain. She had an umbrella in her bag, but she didn't use it. Fenella walked on to the road through the wet wood and let the rain fall on her, like forgiveness.

*****

It had come on the fifth day. Claire had been sure at the time that the camera had been on, but it wasn't on the film; there was no footage from the last day at all. She had been the only one to see it, and after they'd checked the film she didn't know if the others believed her. Will said he did, but he'd had a careful, concerned tone to his voice that was worse than scorn. 'Are you alright, Claire?' he kept asking, all the way back in the van. Watching her, his 'Are you alright, Claire?' running through her head like pain.

She didn't need the film to remember. It had been cold all day, raining in spurts as the wind drove the clouds along. In the late afternoon, Will and one of the crew had taken the van into the town for pizza. The other two had walked down to the road so that they could swig whiskey and smoke: although the chapel was ruined, none of them felt comfortable drinking in it, as if the hermit could still disapprove of their vices. She'd sat on a ground sheet outside her tent and the sun, coming out from behind a cloud, had slanted suddenly into her face. She'd closed her eyes for a moment, dazzled, and when she'd opened them it was there.

The wild man stood slouched at the edge of the clearing. It was about six feet tall, with a dull brown skirt round its hips and fur all over its chest. Its eyes under the tangle of black hair were yellow and angular like a goat's. It strolled across the grass to where a ridge marked the missing chapel wall and stopped and looked at her.

The Wild Man

She had planned so many things she was going to say to it, but none of them would come. It looked at her and it seemed that it saw everything, saw right through her to the world. The mobile phones and fancy restaurants, the money and power and gates and locks and bars. The city and everything in it. It blinked, once, then the yellow gaze returned to hers. It looked scornful, and maybe a little disappointed.

'Hach! Hach! Hach!' said the wild man and, turning, faded back into the trees.

Cunntrahayam

by Susie Helme

'What do you think? Fraahd Chicken, Patata Salad, and we got us a Cunntrahayam,' says Mama, planning the menu for the big day. 'And I'll make a Breakfast Casserole.' Naturally, Mammy's contribution doesn't get a mention.

'Oh, goodie, your famous Breakfast Casserole,' says Kelly Anne, sounding complimentary.

Mama's 'famous Breakfast Casserole' consists of one layer of sausage (Pepperidge Farm—don't imagine that we have anything organic or from a real farm), a layer of scrambled eggs (white shells), a layer of bacon (bits not rashers—they are synthetic, not even made from real pork), a layer of toasts (white), decrusted and cut into cute little rectangles, a layer of cheese (not real cheese, mind you—'American cheese', the slimy orange stuff that comes out of a spray can)—then repeat: sausage, egg, bacon, toast, cheese. Ad infinitum, ad nauseum. Literally.

Behind Mama's back Kelly Anne puts her finger in her mouth and makes the 'vomit' sign. There is no other corner of the world where such perfectly revolting food goes down as *haute cuisine.*

Before I introduce the cast of characters, let me first go through the recipes.

First, Cunntrahayam, as that's my title. It is a roast ham, cut into circular slices around the bone by one of those circular saws, and it's so dry that it crumbles between your fingers and so salty you gag when you put it on your tongue. It is served on Beat'n

Biskits, which are made of white flour, the dough beaten so hard and for so long that they are as hard as rocks, literally. They are completely tasteless. Then you slather on a whole heap of butter (which I 'llow probably does comes from real cows) and slap your slices of Cunntrahayam on top of that.

The liquidness of the butter contrasts with the dryness of the ham, and the tastelessness of the biscuits contrasts with the saltiness. When your teeth manage to hammer through the biscuit, you're rewarded with a sudden mouthful of salty hammy butter. But let's face it, if you're not a Southerner, you are going to retch.

Mammy was up to her black elbows in white powder (and not the good kind) yesterday beating that biscuit dough. She was all 'Miz Geraldine this' and 'Miz Geraldine that', giving me 'sugar' (kisses) and calling me 'chile'. I couldn't stand it if she came out carrying serving trays with a white cloth napkin folded over her arm. Paul is a socialist. I would just die for him to find out we have *slaves*! Kelly's husband Jermaine is black. How would he take it?

Fraahd Chicken is pure trans-fat, with some meat underneath the grease.

Patata Salad is what you would think, except that every ingredient other than the potatoes comes out of a jar. Nashville jes' don't do real food.

This is the first time all the Turner girls have been together in one place since Betsy Lee's wedding ten years ago. It is the first time ever that all the husbands-in-law and boyfriends-in-law are here and the first time anyone in the family has met Paul. Plus, it's a rare grown-ups-only event, as the kids are all at summer camp.

Mama only talks about our clothes, but we know underneath all that, she wants to show off her girls and her sons-in-law. She loves them, she really does—Jermaine, too. He passes her usual racist bar, you see, because he is 'edjacated'.

We're out back in the pantry, digging out the additive-infested ingredients required for our recipes, and Betsy traipses in.

'So, who wants what drugs?' she says, big smile on her face. She's Munchausen's (at least, I think so) and doctor-shops for a fully-stocked pharmacy in her bedside table, and her husband Hank deals drugs for a living (don't tell Mama). She holds out a selection of pill bottles and small plastic baggies. 'I've got Valium, Percocet, coke, Oxy…'

I drag Paul into the bathroom to smoke a spliff—what these Amurrc'ns call a 'joint'.

'Remember, they're all lunatics,' I warn him.

'You're the craziest of the lot,' he jokes.

'No, Mama's the worst.'

'Aw, come on, she's a lovely lady,' he says, and I love him for it.

My story began with the recipes, but don't imagine that's where it begins for Mama, aka Miz Geraldine. These ladies, our invitees, are people from her church. Did you get that? Church! Secondary to whatever food we serve, secondary to whatever men we marry, secondary to all the law and the prophets is, 'what are you gone ta weahh?'

The first thing the church ladies are going to notice is not our pretty dresses, nor that some of us—shock horror—have black or foreign menfolk. They won't notice that everything we've put on their plates is disgusting at best, poisonous at worst. They probably won't notice that the daughters are coked to the nines. The first thing they will notice is that their hostess Geraldine is blotto. Yes, the pillar of the church, the ordained deaconess, she's pretty much blotto every day by about 3pm. The Turner girls are so used to this we don't even mention it anymore.

Our mother is a drunk; our brother in law is a drug dealer and wife-beater; our sister has some new invented illness every week, on top of the regular bruises from her husband. I've barely even told Paul any of this. And that's just the fun stuff.

There are dark secrets in this family that no one is allowed to talk about. Our brother is so obese he can't fit into an automobile. He hasn't been invited today. We didn't even tell him it was happening. For all our nostalgic talk about home, Belinda and I both got as far as we could from Nashville the minute we turned 18. And Kelly, it's not that there weren't any nice white boys on her dance card. She deliberately chose a black boy to p*** Mama off. But hey, none of that bears attention. What's important in life is—what are we going to wear?

As toddlers, Mama dressed me in blue, Kelly in red, Betsy in yellow and Belinda in green. Ridiculously, as adults, we more or less stuck to this colour code.

So, the Turner girls have decided for the occasion we'll all wear 'frocks'. 'Just like Southern Belles,' says Belinda. We do our hair in buns and follow our colour code.

Dressed in our frocks, the Southern Belles, we're going, 'You just set there in the rockin' chair, Mama, we'll do all the work.'

I'm thinking, yeah, sure. Mammy did most of the work, yesterday. But I don't say anything. Something happens whenever I step off the plane in Nashville. Suddenly, my mouth goes as dry as Cunntrahayam, and any thought of being a 'tribune of the oppressed', which, as a socialist, I am supposed to be, goes right out the window. I leave my political conscience back in London and just go along with whatever BS is going down.

One example is Belinda's husband, Kristofer. Though it is not his name that resonates in the cultural memory. What Nashville remembers is that he is 'furrin'. OMG. Call out the exorcists! Worse than Jermaine. We'd already done processed his blackness.

Bel was out of the kitchen for some reason, and Betsy whispers, 'Where is he from? I'm so embarrassed. I forgot.'

Sitting in her rocking chair, chugging Bloody Marys, happily letting her girls and Mammy take care of everything, Mama goes, 'Somewheah in Yurrp.'

So, it's not me. My 'tribune' mouth shuts up. It is Kelly, 'There are 44 countries in Europe, Mama.'

'One of those Commanist ones,' says Mama. Her church ladies haven't even shown up yet, and she is already sloshed.

'Estonia,' says Kelly, just as Bel comes back in.

'Well done, Kelly. Shall I get out the map?' says Belinda.

Paul will undergo similar scrutiny, I reckon, but maybe not so much. The English speak our language; they're kind of honorary Amurrc'ns, only posher, sort of an adopted nobility. Bereft of a royal family, we've adopted theirs and follow the wardrobe choices of Princess Kate by the day. Mama tried to dress Betsy's little boy like Prince George, in those short, smocked cotton overalls, but Hank wouldn't have it. 'My son is a boy,' he said.

By this time, Betsy's drugs are kicking in. Plus, we've started on the booze, too. Mama has ice cold vodka on tap. This luncheon is going to call for some serious substance abuse.

The ladies arrive, and the Turner girls are on form, trotting out in our colour-coded frocks, introducing our well-behaved husbands and boyfriends to all and sundry. I introduce Paul, Kelly introduces Jermaine, Betsy introduces Hank and Belinda introduces Kristofer. Mama is just beaming.

All the paper plates have got their neat little cubes of Breakfast Casserole, a greasy leg or breast of Fraahd Chicken, a pile of Patata Salad and a Beat'n Biskit smeared with butter and Cunntrahayam. The Turner girls, high as kites, flit from one lady to the next, charming as all get out. We top up their little crystal glasses with sherry.

Our frocks are admired. Our husbands and boyfriends, of various colours and nationalities, are the stars of the show, and the church ladies just can't get enough of how wonderful we all are. The ladies ooh and aah over Paul's 'purty acceyant' and find they love Kristofer's, too.

Jermaine is the only black face on the terrace. I noticed it, so I'm sure he did. But Paul and Kristofer are outsiders, too, so they give each other moral support. The Turner husbands and boyfriends are bonding.

Mammy has remained diplomatically in the kitchen, because, hey, my potential embarrassment is the main thing, right?

Mama has had one of the best afternoons of her life and goes to bed absolutely plastered.

In the yard after everyone's gone, the Turner girls top up their drugs. Paul and I pop into the bathroom again.

Kristofer has been unable to touch most of the food on his plate. 'His X-ray vision sees all the E-numbers,' Belinda confides to me. Nary a one of us has touched the Breakfast Casserole, but Paul makes a valiant stab at the Cunntrahayam.

Kristofer has brought some posh Estonian beer called Saku. Betsy's husband Hank, a good ole' cunntra boy from East Tennessee, is scornful. His poison of choice, Budweiser, Kristofer calls 'piss'.

'Make ya a deal, bozo,' says Hank. 'You take a baaht o' this-shere Cunntrahayam, and Ah'll take a swig o' yo' fancy furrin beer.' The two of them chomp biscuits and ham and swig beer for the next half hour or so. These men barely even have a language in common, yet they are having a whale of a time.

Hank gets his guitar out of the car and starts picking. He keeps it down, though, so the conversation doesn't stop. Jermaine and Paul are talking about the upcoming election, each as horrified as the other about Donald Trump. Paul tells Jermaine about the rise of fascism in France and Germany and how we're fighting the British Nazi Tommy Robinson. Betsy and Kelly are telling Kristofer and me about the crazy insane things that happened last Christmas.

Hank starts playing 'This Land is Your Land', and we start singing along. Kristofer sings the words in Estonian, and he knows every goshdang verse. Jermaine and Paul vie with each other to produce a tenor harmony like a Sacred Harp gospel. The result is magic.

Mama gets up from her stupor to hang out the window, and Mammy opens the porch screen.

The Turner girls, we're so moved we start crying. We talk about how much we've missed each other, how much we love each other's husbands and boyfriends, how we promise to all come back next Christmas. I cry about missing 'my land', America.

Just when things are at their most sombre and emotional, Hank starts up, as loud as he can pick, on 'Nashville Cats', and everybody cracks up, belting out 'thirteen hundred and fifty-two guitar pickers in Naayshfeeyul'.

Kristofer can't get the words out fast enough to keep up, so we let him practice it a few times, coaching the Europeans, him and Paul, on the accent (not Nashvülle, Kristofer. Not Nahshville, Paul. Naayshfeeyul). Then we start back up again, louder than ever. Everyone puts their right arm on one shoulder, their left arm an another, and we Conga sideways around the backyard until Belinda trips and almost hurts herself.

We're yelping, 'clean as cunntra wawderr', 'waahld as mountain doo-ooo' like we're a pack of howling wolves. Mama doesn't even mind 'cause all the church ladies are gone home.

Betsy and Belinda break away from the Conga line and actually start clog-hoppin'. Hank takes his cue, picking 'Foggy Mountain Breakdown'.

'You playin' our number, Hank,' yells Belinda. She and Betsy are tap, tap, tapping, and slapping their thighs with all due vulgarity, and Betsy jumps up on the picnic table. The rest of us rush to clear off all the beer cans, sherry glasses and plates of leftover Breakfast Casserole.

They finish on a tandem jump. Betsy leaps off the picnic table and Belinda swings her, she lands thud, both feet square on the ground. She yells, 'The South shall raahz again.' Then Belinda jumps up and Betsy swings her. Underpants in yer face, y'all. She lands equally ungracefully and roars, 'Raaah-aawww', with such force that she wobbles a bit and falls against one of the benches.

Paul has never seen anything like this in his life—he has never even heard of anything like this in his life; his mouth is just wide open. He's seen Riverdance, but Riverdance ain't nothing like this. Clog hoppers flail their arms around like they's fightin' somep'm. It ain't graceful. Nobody ever learned this s**t at ballet school.

Though he's equally awe-struck, it's Kristofer who interprets this rare slice of Americana for Paul. 'I think that was a Rebel Yell,' he says.

So, you got it. We ain't elegant, y'all. For all our pretty colour-coded frocks and our educated and European husbands and boyfriends and our little crystal sherry glasses and our talkin' purty for the church ladies, underneath our lily-white skins these Southern Belles jes' as common as possums, and you c'n kiss our frilly underpants.

Kelly has read the room. She yells, 'Ladeez, choose yer partners,' and it's Sadie Hawkins Day in the Turners' backyard as we lunge lustily for each other's menfolk. She grabs Paul; Betsy grabs Kristofer; Bel grabs Jermaine. I grab Hank, and he has to put the guitar down, so we continue 'Foggy Mountain Breakdown' acapella, singing, 'diddle diddle diddle, woo, woo'.

I join the party. I yell, 'Allemand left, and do-si-do.' We show the boys how to do it, and we're square dancing around the picnic table. We girls hitch up our hems so we can get dem knees right up high.

'Foggy Mountain Breakdown', after umpteen repeats, is breaking down, and our drugs are wearing off. The boys agree that they've met their match—what man can keep up with the Turner sisters?—and we decide to call it a night. We give them big smoochie kisses regardless of whose partner is whose.

As all the craziness dies down, we start tidying up the mess in the yard before anyone really gets hurt; we don't want to leave it all for Mama tomorrow. She's sure to wake with a hangover.

Then Paul does something wonderful. He asks Betsy if he might 'take away a box of Beaten Biscuits and Country Ham'. Goodness knows there's enough left over; we've all shunned the stuff at lunch. My sisters and I are flattered—*tickled*, as we Southerners say—right down to our frilly underpants.

Paul puts one hand on my shoulder as the other lifts a suitcase into the car. 'For a bunch of lunatics, you're not half bad,' he says, in front of all my sisters. All three of them give him big smoochie kisses.

'Welcome to the circus, Paul,' says Kelly.

And we realise.

He has passed induction. For better or for worse, he's a Turner, now.

Footprints

by Brian T. Marshall

I spotted them on my third day there. A question mark in the sand.

First off a little background. I was never supposed to be there all alone, walking on that beach. But Karen had decided, two weeks shy of departure, that she wouldn't be going. That we weren't a couple anymore. And no, I don't want your sympathy, it happens all the time, and compared to any real disaster, a car wreck or bout with cancer, it was hardly worth a blink.

Still, along with the usual crap, the regrets and recriminations, it left me with a problem. Do I stay or do I go? Once, back in college, I'd decided to head north, thumb my way up 101, only to discover that traveling alone wasn't what I'd imagined. That being in a place where nobody knew you felt less like life and more like death. But there was the money I stood to lose, cancelling that close to departure, and the time I'd already blocked off, and the longer I thought about it, the more it appealed to me. A big f***-off wrapped up with a bow. Who needs you, anyway?

On the flight over, I got mildly sloshed. Drinking for two, not one. With the eyes of the flight attendant flitting right past me as if I wasn't there. And then, once we'd touched down, all of us bleeding out into the terminal, lining up for our luggage, it really started to hit. I was somewhere else. All along, I'd been pushing for the Greek Isles—clean light and chilled retsina—but Karen, she'd insisted on not being a tourist, opting instead for a tiny republic on the east coast of Africa, a name I still couldn't quite pronounce. The night-dark skin of the taxi drivers. Air so thick it came out of a jar. And over it all a sweet, pungent stink, like fruit that had started to spoil.

I let my driver pick the hotel. A room was a room was a room. Over-tipped him once we'd pulled on up, earning a big flash of teeth. Like him, the woman spoke good English, asked how long I'd be staying there, and seemed surprised when I merely shrugged back, admitting I wasn't sure. As for the view from room 206, it required no translation. An alley, a brick wall, a truck on blocks. Moonlight catching on broken glass.

It took me two days to scout out the town. To establish a routine. That compulsion every animal feels when confronted with new turf. For better or worse the place had no draws, no attractions or destinations, which meant I earned my share of keen looks, a white man with nothing to do. The very next morning I found a spot where they served a decent breakfast. Another place, two blocks over, where afternoons meant a bottle or three of the local lager, sweat beading on the glass. In between the two there was always the market, or an hour spent in the square, a dusty expanse of dying grass shaded by what looked like banyans.

And, of course, there was always the beach.

For me it had always been the Pacific. The only coast I knew. And so this new thing, this whole other ocean, it took a while to get used to. For one thing there was the color. A listless, washed-out grey. Like seeing the tail-end of something, a curtain lowered after the show. And the waves, the breakers, seem tired somehow, they were just going through the motions, an endless climb up a long steep hill, and then their quiet retreat. Pirogues anchored just past the swell. Piled fish-nets, swarming with flies. Even the men, working since dawn, seem immune to time's slow passage. Knowing themselves as quietly insubstantial as the waves lapping at their feet.

The town, it turned out, was near the southern end of an immense, sweeping bay, and with nothing better to do one morning, I set out to test my legs. Once past the row of fishing camps, the country opened up, thick stands of brush, the occasional road, pounded soil as red as rust. For the most part I stuck to the beach itself, the firm sand at water's edge, finally tucking my shoes in a bush for retrieval on my trip back. Wet granules, like sugar, that stuck to my toes. My shadow spilling before me. Just for a moment, it felt almost right, like being there wasn't a mistake, and I wondered if one day I'd have to thank Karen for stranding me on my own.

A day slips by. Then two, then three. That blurring from one to the next. Only to find that even more than my coffee, or that first sip of beer at dusk, it's these lonely walks along the coast that soon define my stay. That give my life some purpose. On my first trek, I spot a sand dollar. On my second, a piece of sea-glass. But it's not until my third hike north that the true prize is offered up.

Footprints.

What stands out first is their sudden appearance. The way they've popped up out of nowhere. As if whoever left them there simply fell out of the sky. And then there's their size, much smaller than mine, which means they must have been cast by a woman, or a child. But what's most striking is how they're not matched. How one of them, the one on the left, seems malformed somehow. Defective. Following along, I reach a spot where their owner must have grown careless, strayed a little too close to the surf, and the impression left in the wet sand is even cleaner, more distinct. And I realize then what's missing. That whoever it is I'm pursuing has only got one big toe.

Tantalised, I scurry forward. Like a dog that's caught a scent. Wondering if what I'm seeing is a birth defect, the result of an accident, or courtesy of the local sharks. With the tide near its low point, I decide the prints must be recent. And yet when I look up to scan the horizon, the beach is deserted, like always. Which might be a kind of blessing. Sometimes as I sit there, on my bench in the square, a flock of young beggars will find me, and if one has a defect, a flaw of some kind, I feel compelled to give that child more. So do I really need yet another cripple, nagging away at my conscience? No, of course not. And yet here I am, back bent, nose forward, squinting into the wind. Determined to follow this meandering track, wherever it may lead.

It's hard to say how much ground I cover. A few hundred yards, give or take. And then, just like that, there are no more footprints, the sand is undisturbed. I come to a halt. Perform a three-sixty. Might even scratch my head. Already I'm at it, wracking my brain, trying to conjure up some explanation. A boat, shallow-hulled, hugging the shore, spiriting my friend away. Or no, more like that old tracker's trick, retreating in your own footprints to throw off a pursuer. But why? What would be the point? And backwards or forward, this way or that, both ends of the trail lead nowhere. Leaving only a question behind: where the h*** did their owner go?

Later on, over beer, I ponder this trick. Like worrying away at a tooth. Or else that mosquito, circling your ear, as you lie awake at night. Every day, every moment, we see countless things, things that don't make sense, that cry out for an explanation, and yet we're too busy, too distracted, to give them a second thought. Only now I have the time. More time than I know what to do with. Which means, once again, I'm left to thank Karen for giving me what I needed. For leaving my life so barren, so empty, I can spot where God missed a stitch.

I endure six hours of not-quite-sleep, then hurry my way

through breakfast. Find myself on the beach so early half the boats haven't yet made it back. They probably wonder, the few people there, why I'm studying the sand so intently. Why my eyes seem to hug the ground, as if searching for some clue. Fine. Let them wonder. Heading north, I scour the beach, a fierce sun perched at my shoulder, with a second orb, its reflection, its twin, winking back from the shallow water. I must be walking faster this morning, a stride instead of a stroll, and pretty soon I've reached my first landmark, the ruins of an old fishing shack, turning back into dust.

But still no footprints.

And then, just like that, I spot them, twenty feet down the beach. A trail of breadcrumbs, left behind, or the string that threads a maze. And maybe it's my imagination, but the prints seem different this time around. Still small, still misshapen, but the imprint itself is altered, deeper at the front end, near the toes, and shallower at the heels. Meaning, perhaps, that whoever left them was running. Sprinting. Or no. The pattern, the rhythm, first shallow then deep, is too uneven, too playful. So let's make that skipping instead.

And as soon as I think of that word, skipping, I can see her in my head. A girl, maybe eight or nine. Kinked hair and beanstalk limbs. With some kind of shawl clutched in her hands, stretched tight above her head, as if she's hoping to snare the wind, to float off past the horizon.

I pause. Blink. The girl is gone. Only the footprints remain.

Now, I'm the one who's running. A clumsy, ugly thing. Breath rasping through my shopworn lungs, knees creaking with each lunge. As if to taunt me, the prints dance ahead, twisting and weaving along, burning through a dozen steps where I barely manage one. How does she do it, I ask myself, half cripple that she is. What could inspire her, one of life's victims, to skirt across the sands?

Maybe all my questions blind me. Maybe I'm just out-of-breath. I've probably gone a dozen yards before I finally stop. Realize that she's done it again. That there are no more footprints to follow.

Day three.

I've asked the woman to wake me early, a good hour before the dawn. Just in time to hear them rumbling off, trucks headed for the capital. I snag a packed bus at the stop on the corner, the only white man waiting there, the eyes of the workers, the shop boys and maids, staring at this pale apparition. Riding to route's end, five blocks from the beach, I finish my journey on foot. To the east, the sky is clear. The air is cool and fragrant. That stillness, like a breath held tight, that comes before the sunrise.

The sand is dotted here and there with a half-dozen flickering campfires. Men sipping tea, and warming their bones, and readying themselves for the day. As for me, I'm already scheming as I set out for the shack, hoping the ruin will provide some cover, like a hunter tucked in his blind. But don't get me wrong. It's not like I really expect to find anything, to catch her at her game. Because, I've decided, none of this is real. Not the girl, not the footprints, not even myself, the same self that knows he's a fiction. The tree that didn't fall in the forest, never once making a sound.

Gradually, the sky starts to color. Light seeps back into the world. A hush of hope, of anticipation, at the place where the sun will appear. This will be, I belatedly note, the first time I've ever seen it. A sun rising, not setting, over the ocean. Which should make this whole farce worth all the trouble, no matter how it ends.

I reach the shack. Settle down in the sand. At some point, I must nod off. Only realize that I've been asleep in the instant I snap awake.

Footprints

Laughter. Childish laughter. Bells pealing, but rendered small. I don't think I've ever heard a sound so sweet. So impossible to resist. Sitting up, I rub my eyes, eager to find its source, then spot her in the narrow band where sand gives way to sea. She's even smaller than I suspected. As fragile as a bird. And instead of holding the rag I'd envisioned, she's hanging onto a length of rope, the same coarse strands of braided fiber the men use for their nets. As I watch, she snaps it once. The knotted end leaps in the air. Another laugh, even more raucous, a surrender to delight.

And then, somehow, she feels my gaze. The doll's head whips around. Two small stones, dark and gleaming, bore into my own. She doesn't look frightened, not in the least. More like angry, or aggrieved. As if by being clever, by getting there early, I've broken some kind of rule. There's a second or two of hesitation. Each option is carefully weighed. Then, with a shrug, an air of dismissal, she scampers off into the surf.

Without even thinking, I cry out. A voice that's not my own. If she'd brought her bells, I've stuffed them with cotton, melted them back down to slag. And hearing that sound, hearing me bellow, she retreats even further, the water almost reaching her chest. A thing so tiny, so insubstantial, one good wave could knock her down.

Before that can happen, I stand up. Take a few halting steps. Tell my face to deliver the message: I am friend, not foe. And maybe, just maybe, it's working, because at least she's stopped backing away. Seems content to wait me out, this oaf from another world.

The first wave grazes my ankle. The second one hits me mid-thigh. Seeing my approach, she paddles off further, bobbing aloft with each swell. Despite all my walks, I haven't yet done it, haven't yet risked the surf. Which must be why the tug I feel, that horrible, blind hunger, catches me off-guard. One second the sand is there, at my feet. The next I'm floating free. Turning to find the shore pull away, like a film run in reverse. So, not just a tide. A rip tide. One of those things that they warn you about, but that I've never once had to face.

Don't panic, you moron. That's what they say. You'll only wear yourself out. So instead I just lie back, keep my head above water, seeing where the journey takes me. Kind of like life itself. And the girl? The girl, of course, is nowhere in sight. She's pulled her vanishing act. Sucked down to her doom, a watery grave, or maybe just back up on shore. Laughing her fool head off.

For a good long while I float along, gradually drifting northward, until, at last, I can feel a shift, a recalibration of the currents. Testing it, I start to paddle, aiming again for the shore. My feet plunging downwards, desperately searching, hoping to find solid ground.

Only something finds me instead.

'So. You have a good trip?'

I turn away from the plane's window. See a stranger smiling back.

'Not good, not bad,' I tell him. 'More like interesting.'

He motions then towards my left leg. The plastic boot I'm wearing.

'And what's that about?' he wonders. 'Do I even want to know?'

I see a footprint, one toe missing. Hear a burst of girlish laughter.

'Like I said, it was interesting.'

The Concierge

by Marie-Lise Mullen

This is it: an ordinary block built in the 1950s, 72 Rue de la Résistance in Montreuil, just outside Paris. I'm the live-in caretaker, the concierge. I also work for the building behind, which looks onto the Rue des Clos.

It may not look like much, but with the six stairwells, two courtyards and twenty-four wheely bins—it's a lot of work! Not to mention all the other duties I have to handle: storing the bulky parcels, and people's keys and pets and sometimes children. Then there's watering plants, chatting to the older tenants and to the pregnant women, work accident victims, or people under house arrest, and supervising removals, showing people around, accompanying bailiffs and plumbers, meter readers and census takers, ambulance drivers and undertakers, and all that.

Oh, but I love my job, I do. And I love the people who live here. I never get tired of hearing them all tell me about their lives, of watching them come and go in the courtyards, (sometimes with the strangest of companions), of seeing them in the evening behind their flimsy curtains, of hearing their music, their cries and the complaints of the neighbours. You get attached to them. Rather than just the concierge, I feel like I'm the guardian angel of all these beautiful people. I'm always on the ground floor, often looking up like little children do, but I still feel as powerful as a load-bearing wall. I don't know what they'd do without me.

And you, my poor Arlette, what would you do without them?! That's where my bloke comes in, Jean-Pierre. He's a plumber by trade, which comes in very handy for my residents. He's also a philosopher at times and a grumpy old so-and-so the rest of the time, even if it means him losing customers.

Without the residents, I wonder what I'd become, where I'd end up. I think about it sometimes, and it sends shivers down my spine. That's why I don't take well to people leaving. When someone moves out, I get upset. Deaths in the building upset me, and I'm in mourning for months.

Today I'll be getting out my black dress again: it's Monsieur Meyer, whom his sister found dead when she came to visit him this afternoon. Monsieur Meyer wasn't very old, but he was very ill, and over the last few months he'd made a spare key for his sister, because he had trouble getting to the door. He was half-deaf, and even the food delivery man had given up trying to get his door to open and left his meals on the doormat. René, as he was known, had collapsed while eating his dessert, and I can imagine the shock for his sister, who wasn't that young, either. In addition to his diabetes, deafness and his rheumatism, René had a weak heart, and everyone assumed he'd had a heart attack.

The ambulance arrived in no time, followed by his doctor. He contacted the police, who requested an autopsy, and they took the body off to the forensic institute in a police van. Wow! We weren't expecting that. But it was the next day that the real upset began, in other words, the investigation: you see, they found that Monsieur Meyer hadn't died of natural causes, he'd been killed.

And the murder weapon? Poison! Monsieur Meyer had been poisoned. What a story! Everyone gathered in the courtyards to share their excitement and speculate. My Jean-Pierre was one of the first. He wasn't being gruff, now.

If you think about it, being a plumber isn't very different from being an investigator. You have to find the leak, you have to work back to the source, and it's often quite a convoluted business. I looked at my man differently.

Especially when the inspector, a lady inspector, arrived in the yard. She stepped forward with authority and introduced herself. After that, it was mainly me she spoke to. Of course, as the concierge, I was in a key position.

No, I hadn't noticed anything, no stranger had knocked on my door (but, silly me, no murderer is going to announce himself like that), besides, at mealtimes I'm quite busy with my husband, it's not every day but just that day we were eating together, I'd prepared him steak and chips, you have to concentrate with steak and get the timing right.

An army of busy hands had taken over the scene of the crime—the scene of the crime! As you might have guessed, the poison had been added to Monsieur Meyer's food. But what poison? And how was it administered? The inspector was keeping everything about the investigation secret.

The first suspect was the sister. 'It's much more common than you might think, reporting a death you caused yourself,' Jean-Pierre told me. You can see why: no need to go away and hide, and you can keep an eye on the investigation, perhaps steer it in the right direction if need be. But the poor sister looked so lost and so genuinely sad that she wasn't suspected for long.

But shortly afterwards we heard stunning news. Monsieur Meyer, that scruffy old man with his flat needing a coat of paint, this Meyer had a fortune stashed away. Just a figure of speech, of course it was all in the bank. Monsieur Meyer was a millionaire! And it was all going to his heirs.

How do I know all this? It's because the sister came crying to my place on the first day, where she found someone willing to listen to her. Two of us really, because Jean-Pierre couldn't get out of the building, so she came back the next day and, one thing leading to another, she told me all her secrets.

So, the family had quite a motive. Now, it wasn't just the sister who was under suspicion: there were three stepchildren, too, each one more destitute than the last. And grandchildren, as well—they were at that age when you're just starting out in life, when you need a little nest egg, of course you do.

Let's start with the sister: she was a respectable lady of 84 who had had an incredible life. You could still tell she had once been very beautiful, and a woman's beauty, especially in the old days, was always a source of trouble. In those days, there was no higher education for women, no stories of travelling the world, of breaking through as an artist or any of that. The only dream they had was of Prince Charming, the only success, that of the family. I'm talking about women from my background, from my mother's time.

My mother didn't fall for the wrong kind of guy, she was lucky. But Nicole—that's Monsieur Meyer's sister (it was already after the war and the war had killed her father), being really pretty, attracted the wilder boys very early on. And, at the time, it wasn't as easy as it is now to protect yourself. At the age of fifteen, she ended up pregnant, with the father nowhere to be seen, and she entrusted her child to her aunt, who had no children of her own.

She got off lightly that time. But her next great passion, 'the love of her life', she whispered, wasn't much better. Sure, he stuck with her faithfully, and 'he was good at everything, he could do anything with his hands', but he fell into drinking, and alcohol made him mean. Because he was all repentant and lovey dovey after he beat her, it took her decades to get out of the relationship.

Then she was with a Romany guy. He was like a king, who showed her a good time, no expense spared, especially at night, because he was married. They hung around in slightly dodgy nightclubs and spent money which came from God knows where. It wasn't easy for her to break his grip, either. Then, late in life, she took up charity work, combining the pleasures of hiking with the pleasures of pilgrimage, on the road to Compostela, and singing hymns in the choir of Notre Dame de Saint Cloud.

For months, she had been travelling from halfway round the Paris suburbs every day to help her brother out. She knew he was careful with his money, but she hadn't known he'd made a mint. When the solicitor told her how much there was, she was gobsmacked just like the rest of us. By 'the rest of us', I mean everyone in the building, because I like to pass news around.

So, our inspector was very interested in Nicole. What could be simpler than for her to come a little early to add the poison to his meal—fish, yes, that's what was on the menu that day. But Nicole has eyes like the porcelain eyes of a doll, that you can read like an open book, so our inspector's suspicion didn't last long.

Especially since if anyone was aware of René's poor health, it was Nicole. She had followed his various illnesses from day to day, and she knew that he didn't have long to live. Why would she take such risks to hasten his death? Even if she had known about his fortune, all she would have had to do was wait a little while to collect it. Unless he had threatened to disinherit her and give it all to some charity. Can you disinherit your sister?

Before moving on to the rest of the investigation, I need to say a few words about the investigator. Our inspector. When I say 'our', I mean Jean-Pierre's, really. I could see straight away that she caught his eye. She's certainly not younger than me, but she's much better dressed, more dolled up, as they say, ready to do anything, as I'd say, to seduce everyone around, to get the information out of them, to solve the crime.

She's tall and blonde, well put-together, with a shy but sporty look, a fine figure of a woman, isn't she, Jean-Pierre? She moves so lightly, you can't see her coming, and her voice is strangely soft, so you have to strain your ears when she asks you a question.

Well, I've got mixed feelings about her. I do think she's a big shot, and her elegance is a credit to our building. But my heart sinks when I see the looks of admiration on Jean-Pierre's face and the respect shown by all the residents, whereas sometimes they treat me like I'm just a skivvy.

Well, they show respect, perhaps a little fear, too, because, my dear friends, at the moment our inspector is interested in the family of the victim, of course, but she's bound to come on to the neighbours next, and when she does, everyone's secrets will be on show.

In the meantime, let's continue with the family. I see each of the children come and go, and some of them I haven't seen for years.

'But how can they be suspects?' Jean-Pierre asked the inspector, 'they didn't have a key to their dad's place.'

'Yes, but remember, Monsieur Calabret,'—that's our name—'the meals-on-wheels man leaves the food at the door, on the doormat, so that anyone who could get that far there could have added the poison, and the children did have the code to open the gate, didn't they?'

Now, the inspector comes to the caretaker's lodge to do her debriefings. She's not coming to gaze into Jean-Pierre's beautiful eyes, is she? He has small brown eyes and they're ugly.

On the one hand, the children, or grandchildren, as they didn't often come to visit their father or grandfather, had no idea that René was in such bad shape.

On the other hand, we already knew that they weren't his biological children, they were from his wife's first marriage—René had married late—and we learned, well, Jean-Pierre and I did, from the sister, that they had no rights to the inheritance, because René hadn't made a will, and they had married with the standard separation of property clause.

Were they aware of this? 'No, I don't think so,' the sister blurted out, 'they're taking it very hard.'

Questioning the family went on for a few days. But everyone was in the clear, I guess, because the inspector then turned to the neighbours. Well, especially his next-door neighbour. Because everyone knew that she and René rowed like cats and dogs. They were the two oldest residents in the building, and, as if by design, they lived on the same landing, side by side, and could hear each other coughing through their kitchen walls, until they went deaf. And they'd been there for fifty years. Naturally, if that doesn't create a bond between the two, it can end up infuriating them.

You see, ours is a nicely kept residence, but that doesn't make the walls any thicker, and rows between neighbours are quite common. Those two even came to blows once, and it was Jean-Pierre who had to separate them. You should have seen it: the old lady, even older than him, all shrivelled up and shabby, grabbed René's arm and was kicking him, and he, despite how ill he was, had thrown his hat and his glasses at her and was now attacking her hairdo... And there was such screaming in there. To make sure that their old ears would hear the insults. This time, it was the old lady's cat, which had gone to pee on the old man's doormat.

'And the delivery boy puts my bag of food there,' he lamented.

I think it's the delivery man who's at fault in this story—it's not human to leave the food on the doormat. Other times it was the old man's TV that kept the old lady awake. Or the old lady's grandchildren, who knocked on his door so insistently that he ended up answering, to receive his delivery of pulled faces. I don't know when the disagreement started, I've only been here 15 years, but there's always been a bitter fight between those two. Another elderly resident told me that there had been something going on between their spouses, but I haven't been able to find out anymore.

Whatever the case, Madame Sourat, the old lady, had every reason to be angry with Monsieur Meyer. Might she have been angry enough to kill him?

'That's what the investigation will have to determine,' Rose told us—because by now we knew the inspector's first name—'the meal waiting on the doormat, every day, at her feet, so to speak, could have been quite an invitation.'

'Yes, but how could she have got hold of the poison?'

'Ah, the poison, that wasn't very complicated.'

'It wasn't?'

Then, it was my turn to be investigated, and I have to admit that I didn't do very well.

'It's just a formality,' Rose told me, and, in fact, the questions were very simple and might have come from an investigator's training manual. What was I doing at the supposed time of the crime—in fact, most of the morning, since it was established that the delivery man had dropped his bag off at 10am? OK, I went through it all, I was ready for the questions. Had I noticed any suspicious comings and goings? Oh, dear, with 80 residents in this building alone, there are too many comings and goings for me to suspect any. What was my relationship with Monsieur Meyer? He was one of the half of the residents who had entrusted me with their keys, in complete confidence. When was the last time I saw him? Did I know any of his enemies? No, apart from Madame Sourat, I can't think of anyone. Thank you, Madame Calabret, we don't have any more questions for now. It was like being in a TV series.

Then they interviewed all the residents on his staircase. Many of them were at work that day, but they might have overheard a scene or a burst of conversation as they passed his door—Monsieur Meyer lived on the first floor.

Everyone had something to say about how well they got on with their good Monsieur Meyer.

'You never know, Arlette, they might get the idea of framing me for all this,' said Madame Vitez, the neighbour upstairs. We didn't know where the investigation was heading, but we had the impression that things were going pretty slowly, anyway.

It was when she questioned my husband that we found out a little more about where it was heading. How did he manage to get into Rose's good books? It wasn't his charm, that's for sure. There's no doubt that the murder weapon was poison, but she wouldn't tell him what poison. 'You understand, Monsieur Calabret, you have to keep a few secrets if you want to catch the culprit.'

As for the '*modus operandi*'—he speaks Latin now, my man does—the most likely thing is that the substance was added to his meal, but no one knows when.

But it was the motive that posed the real problem. Often it's money. But they had to accept that that was not it this time. René's financial situation, though surprising, was quite clear: no will, no tricks, everything went to the sister, and the sister, whichever way you look at it, was innocent. Perhaps her children were after the inheritance, but their ignorance, their unremarkable and distant lives, and above all, the fact that every one of them, the parents and the children, had a solid alibi for that morning, put them, alas, out of the frame.

Once the money motive had been ruled out, the only motive left was revenge.

Madame Sourat was the obvious culprit here, although we shouldn't get carried away, either, the team realised, she wasn't as bad as all that. So, there we were. Who could have been so angry with Monsieur Meyer that they killed him? Who could have been so angry with him that they wanted revenge before he died of natural causes? That's a bit rich. Monsieur Meyer had lived a long life. Perhaps we shouldn't have confined ourselves to studying his last few months.

As for me, I don't know much about René's life, he wasn't a very talkative sort. What I did know was that he was born in a suburb on exactly the opposite side of Paris, where his sister still lives. And that he moved to our town when he was very young, because it had a Communist town council—his sister told me that. As far as I could see, he'd left such ideas well behind him.

He was one of the first residents of this building, which was quite classy at the time. He was already retired and a widower when I took over the lodge, but he was still full of energy and very active in the neighbourhood voluntary organisations. You could see him storming out of his building, always with a little satchel under his arm, to settle some row or to do the accounts. After all, he'd been an accountant all his life, and I think even a chartered accountant towards the end. So, perhaps it's not surprising that he'd made his own accounts grow.

Now that he was plagued by rheumatoid arthritis, he hardly ever left his flat. A little physiotherapist came twice a week to get him out and about a bit. But he continued anyway to deal with a few issues, even launching civic initiatives and getting neighbours to sign petitions. Once, he set up a petition about the bulky waste collection by the council, and I have to admit that it made my life a lot easier. He was still an elected member of the residents' council, too, and they used to meet at his place.

Apparently there were papers all over his flat, and it was madness to sort through them, but you have to find the clues. In fact, I've been there a few times, in his flat, and I've seen the papers, but I didn't really pay any attention to them. I really didn't think they would attach such importance to them. Let them find him dead and bury him, that's all.

This Rose, who appeared at all hours at the door of my lodge, was beginning to make me nervous. Jean-Pierre bent over backwards to please her and always made her a cup of coffee. He was passionate about the case, and as if bewitched by the inspector. He drank in her words: 'How is it, Monsieur Calabret,' she said, 'that someone's gone to the trouble of getting rid of an old man in bad health who wasn't going to last much longer, when all they had to do was give him time?' (In a way, she'd come to the same conclusions as me). 'No, no, Monsieur Calabret, I don't really believe it was for revenge. No man would be foolish enough to take such risks. One might have thought it was to make the victim suffer, but no, the poison they used kills almost instantaneously when you have a weak heart.

'Well, I was saying a man, but I'd say it's more likely a woman. Poison is a woman's weapon, you know that as well as I do, Monsieur Calabret.'

And my feverish Jean-Pierre replied, 'A woman, yes, Madame Inspector, a woman, I think so, too.'

'Why end his life now? When we find the answer to that, Monsieur Calabret, we won't be far from finding the killer. Next week, I'm going to investigate the voluntary organisations whose accounts he managed. He may have uncovered something very dishonest, something sufficiently dishonest...'.

'On that note, I wish you a good Sunday,' she finished (because this conversation was taking place on a Sunday morning; there's no rest for the wicked, when a murder has to be solved).

On that Sunday, the weather was lovely, Jean-Pierre and I went out to the woods like the young people do, he even hired a boat, and we went canoeing on the lake like lovers. But we were both still in our own thoughts and in our own stiffness. I wasn't exactly jealous of the beautiful inspector, but their conversations didn't mean anything to me, and sometimes their asides... why was she hanging around him like that? It seems to me that ever since Rose came into our lives, he's been pulling away from me, hardly speaking to me anymore, avoiding me, with pensive looks. At the end of the day, he took me by the shoulders, exclaiming, 'Arlette, Arlette,' and buried his big round head in my neck.

On Monday, just like on Sunday, the inspector was in our lodge. They had been working all Sunday at the police station. In short, nothing fishy had turned up in the papers about the voluntary organisations. But we did learn something important: the poison that had been used was antifreeze.

'Yes, Monsieur Calabret, I had to tell you about it, because as a plumber, you're bound to use antifreeze.'

'That's for sure, Madame Inspector, I've got plenty of antifreeze in my stocks, but it's a non-toxic formula, it's clearly stated on the packaging, it wouldn't even kill a cat.'

'Yes, we know that, Monsieur Calabret, but this was antifreeze for car engines, a much more dangerous formula; just one spoonful is enough to cause serious problems, and if you have a weak heart, well...'

'Well, Inspector, we're not the only ones with a car in the residence, or in the town, so that doesn't get us very far.'

This time it was me who intervened and shut her up. Let her

go and investigate somewhere else and leave me my Jean-Pierre. 'Monsieur Calabret' here, 'Monsieur Calabret' there, why can't she just leave us alone?

She must have got the message, because she didn't come around for the next few days. It was Jean-Pierre who was moping about. He wandered around the flat like a lost soul. And, as if on cue, there was no work to do, no customer in distress, not the slightest little job to distract him. I've never seen him like that before. Things are usually hectic, and Jean-Pierre doesn't know which way to turn. Was he saying no to everything just so as to stay close by her?

Rose doesn't come to our door anymore, but she's still in the building, in Monsieur Meyer's flat, and it seems she's decided to set about going through all his files. The other evening, I saw her silhouette behind the bedroom curtains, bent over the papers. I was at the gate when she left. 'Madame Inspector, can you tell me what it is you're looking for?'

As tall and powerful as she is, she flinched when I stepped forward. 'I'm sure I'll find the killer's motive in those documents, Madame Calabret, I'm not far from getting there.'

I didn't say anything to Jean-Pierre; there was no point in exciting him. I put on my thinking cap and thought things through. Because the investigation had suddenly taken off.

'Madame Calabret, we now know how the murderer administered the poison. Everyone thought it had been added to his meal, but no, we've had more detailed conclusions from the laboratory: it was poured into a glass of alcohol. This corresponds exactly to the time of his death, as it takes about half an hour to act on the heart. We also found two whisky glasses on the kitchen drainer, which had unfortunately been washed. The victim knew his killer well, so he opened the door for him and offered him a drink. Also, if you think of the difficulty he had getting about, if I'm to believe his doctor... it might be that the killer had a key?'

I carried on sweeping the yard, quietly. I put away my broom and turned back. 'But why are you telling me all this? Here, in the courtyard, just passing by?'

She still couldn't find the key piece, the document that would prove motive.

Myself, I've never paid much attention to papers, and I'm even a bit disgusted by them, it goes back to my time in school. I guess that was wrong of me. She was poking around, and I was sat there thinking.

And with Jean-Pierre, things weren't going well at all, his mood was getting darker by the day, as if he had something to be ashamed of. The other evening, I heard him crying in the bathroom. He didn't say anything to me about it, but he hardly ever talks to me anymore. Gone are the bad jokes, the surprise tickles and the sex. But last night he held me close before he fell asleep.

I waited until her assistants had left, but she was still up there, so I kept a close eye on her. It was a busy time of day in the courtyard, with residents coming home from work, then leaving again to do the shopping, people coming and going, doors slamming, tired or hungry children crying, noise everywhere, a muted agitation. But it was still daylight, and in the daytime you can't see the silhouettes behind the curtains. I took the key from my cupboard.

What Rose, the pretty inspector, didn't know when she confiscated the key was that I'd had a duplicate made ages ago, like I do with all the keys entrusted to me by the residents, you never know if they're going to stop trusting you. So, I have two key cupboards in my house, one in plain sight in my lodge, and one hidden away.

The other night, I sneaked into René's flat, wearing gloves—you never know—so as to track down the damned document myself. Jean-Pierre is a heavy sleeper, he's always taken medicine to help him sleep, in drops, and I'm the one who gives them him. I have an advantage over Rose, too, because I know what I'm looking for, but I haven't found it any more than she has, because, unlike her and unlike everyone else, I can barely read, and it takes me a huge amount of time to decipher stuff.

That's what made him start on me, René: I made too many mistakes in delivering the mail, he said. Then he went on, did Mr Thrift himself, about the caretaker's lodge being too big—selling it off would help finance the refurbishment, you know, and this salary paid out every month, we could probably find cheaper. All in all, I was costing the owners too much, my job had to be done away with.

'Don't get me wrong, Madame Calabret,' he went on, 'I've got nothing against you, it's a question of common sense.' He had nothing against me? And he dared to say it to my face. With his honeyed ways and his cold little eyes.

I was boiling inside with anger and terror. I'm not going to tell you about my miserable past life, or all I had to put up with to finally get him, my Jean-Pierre, and to get this job, which is my pride and joy, and to hold both of them tightly in my arms. It had taken me years to build up this little safety in my life and that bastard would just smash it with a little snap of his tongue, 'Tsk tsk, Madame Calabret, we can't just go on wasting money like this.'

I had to act quickly, as the general meeting was to take place the following month, and the building management company would soon be collecting proposals from the committee.

Monsieur Meyer, with his background as an accountant, had a lot of influence on the committee. But he was as stingy with his confidences as he was with his money, and, with a bit of luck, he wouldn't have told anyone yet about his idea. When I turned up to plead my case to the top man, I had everything I needed in the pocket of my apron, and the bottle of whisky in my hand.

Everything I needed was in the pocket of my apron, just as it is tonight, when I snuck into the flat as discreetly as I could, because, given that the inspector is bigger than me, I will have to rely on the element of surprise. There are no firearms around me, it will have to be hand-to-hand combat. I find this distasteful; that's why I hesitated for so long.

We don't have any guns, but there are sledgehammers, hammers, spanners, as many tools as I could want, in my husband's storeroom. But I didn't want to get Jean-Pierre involved. So, I had a clothesline in my pocket, and this was the idea: I was going to come up from behind and pull the rope tight with all my might, squeeze until she collapsed, and then—I couldn't think of anything else—I was going to set fire to the papers and make the body and the evidence, the motive and the accuser disappear in one fell swoop. And perhaps myself as well, I don't know, I couldn't see any further than the blaze.

But it didn't go at all as I'd thought it would. Opening a front door and walking six yards down a corridor makes a lot of noise, no matter how careful you are. And there was no noise in the room where Rose was working. It was when I took the rope out of my pocket that everything changed.

Suddenly, two big, muscular arms grabbed me by the shoulders and turned me round, pinning me against a warm, solid chest, a chest I knew well—it was Jean-Pierre's. He was crying. Rose rushed over, almost as upset. I just stood there, frozen, transfixed, my thoughts racing but understanding nothing.

I didn't understand what had happened. I mean, just that it was over now, that I was free of that secret, and I was so relieved that all of a sudden I started sobbing, too, clinging to my man like a life raft.

I'd thought I was so smart, I'd lied to everyone, and to myself. too. I was so proud to have pulled it off. And I'd held on, all alone, all these days as if nothing had happened. But inside it was like a flood of despair, dark waters rising, rising to engulf me. Kill Rose, confess or throw myself into the flames, but it had to end. But how did you know about it, Jean-Pierre?

'Arlette, my darling Arlette, I've been so unhappy. Little by little, I began to get suspicious. On the day of the murder, when I came home for dinner, you smelt of alcohol, but you never drink. I didn't say anything, but I couldn't find our bottle of whisky, either, so I told myself you were going through a bad patch.

'Then, with the murder, I stopped thinking about it, until the detective told us how the poison had been administered. And then there was the antifreeze, I know we've got a can of it for the car, but the can wasn't in its usual place, and the cap had been unscrewed a while ago, so when the inspector told us I went to check. And then I remembered how worried and depressed you looked in the days before the murder. I remember teasing you : 'a penny for your thoughts', but you would just shake your head with a mean look as if to say, 'mind your own business'.

'When Rose contacted me discreetly and I went to the police station...'

'You went to the police station without telling me anything?'

'I couldn't, Arlette, I couldn't take it, anymore. The inspector hesitated before telling me her suspicions. But I was way ahead of her, and heartbroken with it.'

'What you didn't know, Madame Calabret,' the inspector added, 'was that I discovered the compromising document, the written proposal to abolish your post, some time ago. But I didn't have enough proof, which is why I've been acting as bait to trap you for a week, now. I knew I could count on your husband's love; he wasn't going to let you out of his sight.'

In fact, I ended more like a cabbage than a wolf. Throughout the trial I just felt like a big cabbage from which you remove one by one its big stupid leaves, and all that's left is a stupid core.

There's one last thing I want to say: I shouldn't have mistrusted Jean-Pierre. Because Jean-Pierre has always been on my side. I've thought about it a lot since I've been here. I don't have much to do other than think, mind you. If I'd told him how heartbroken I was when Monsieur Meyer spoke to me, before it all happened, we would have found a solution together. Because Jean-Pierre never gave up on me. And he'll be waiting for me when I get out, I know he will. And that certainty is the feather pillow on which I rest my guilty head every night.

Translation from the French: John Mullen

The Widow's House

by Brian T. Marshall

Every small town has its stories, its myths. Tales passed down from hand to hand. And if you'd grown up in Edynwilde, Pennsylvania, you'd know them all by heart.

That spot on the MacKenzie River Bridge where some teenager, his name long forgotten, had climbed the rail and then leapt outward, ending his stay on earth. The rumors every fifth-grader shared about the old Ansyler Mine. How once a year on May 7th, the day of the disaster, you could still hear the cries of the men trapped inside it, echoing through the abandoned shaft. And, of course, there was the Widow's House, perched atop Stantler Ridge.

It was a simple saltbox, built by the Stantlers years back, a stern and grudging scab of a house, situated on old orchard land. At some point in the distant past it must have been new, well kept up, but for anyone still alive in town it had always been a ruin. Peeling paint on weathered clapboards. That crack in the kitchen window. A sagging porch with a crawlspace beneath it, where animals would nest, emerging at night to feast on grubs, or fallen fruit from the cragged Winesaps. Seeing it there, forlorn and alone, you'd assume it was long abandoned. Unless, of course, you lingered a while. Noted how, each day at dusk, a single lamp would flicker on upstairs.

Ask Tim Withers, who'd just turned nine, how he first came to hear of the place, and all you'd get back was a shrug. I don't know.

Somewhere. Probably some other kid at school, or maybe it was my dad. But ask that father the very same question and you'd get the same shrug back. Because, it turned out, he'd learned about it from his own father, and that father, in turn, from his, with the chain extending back through time to when the land was still wild. As if the house, the widow who lived there, had always been there, always would be there. Persisting into a future when those same fathers, and their children as well, would themselves be dead.

Flesh turning back into apples.

*****

That year Tim was an astronaut. Had his eyes dead-set on Neptune. A watery orb in the black of space, taunting him like some jewel. As for Brad, he was a cowboy, again, and Jay was some kind of robot, and Kevin had put things off for so long he was stuck wearing an old sheet. They'd hit up the usual houses downtown, the ones that had store-bought candy, and were trying to figure out where to go next before it was time to head home.

That new neighborhood across the River. The town's one cemetery. And then somebody, probably Brad, gave voice to what they were all thinking.

The Widow's House.

A two-mile hike out to the Ridge. No sidewalks, just a narrow gravel shoulder. The occasional car, drunken high-schoolers, pretending to swerve right towards them. Once they'd taken the old turn-off, the traffic petered out, just a two-lane track snaking up to the highlands, tattered weeds and broken glass. Being boys, they all told their stories, each trying to outdo the others, severed limbs and dug-up graves and skeletons, pale as moonlight. Until Kevin, in the lead, halted mid-step, his hand thrust into the darkness. All four of them freezing, staring as one, with the house staring back at them.

There was no need to name their game. To spell out the rules or restrictions. Whoever got closest, stayed the longest, would walk off with the prize. Slowly inching past the wrought iron gate, traversing the cracked cement sidewalk, a tennis shoe finds a worn cedar step, provoking a cry of complaint. Kevin, their bravest, was already lagging, leaving Tim to take his place. When he glanced back from the porch, deeply shadowed, his friends had somehow disappeared.

So, what's scarier? The fact he's alone? Or suddenly knowing he isn't? Knowing that rattle is an ancient brass doorknob, with what must be a hand clinging to it. Against his will, he slowly turns, turns just like that knob, and now there's a narrow band of light where door and jamb should meet. As he watches, the crack slowly widens, there's something waiting just past it. A twisted shape, stooped by age. A lesson in bad taxidermy.

What's your name?

It's not a voice, more like two stones, being slowly ground together.

Tim, he whispers back.

So, turn around, Tim, the stones demand. Let me get a good look at you.

Meat on a spit, he does what he's told. Two sockets drink him in.

You'll do.

Now, finally, he dares it. Dares to regard that face. The parchment skin, and the sunken cheeks, and the wrinkles as deep as a creek bed.

Do what? he asks.

The cackle of a dying crow. Whatever I tell you to.

*****

A year creeps by. A boy grows older. Nine candles give way to ten. Tim has entered a whole new world, defined by two digits, not one.

He rarely thinks back to that Halloween night. The fact is he can't quite remember. The way, one moment, he was there on the porch, and the next safely back with his friends. And it looks like this year, this Halloween, will be just as forgettable. Kevin, along with his whole family, had moved out of town months back. Brad has the stomach flu. And when Jay calls up, all alone just like he is, Tim claims to feel sick, too.

The same hike up that narrow, two-lane road, only this time there's no costume. No bantering boys, no tortured tales, no companion but his own thoughts. If you were to stop him, shine a light in his eyes, he'd probably blink a few times. Ask where he was, how he got there, maybe even what day it was. The cold, blank stare of a man, sleepwalking, old beyond his years.

The house, of course, hasn't changed one bit. A place that's immune to time. Forever frozen in disrepair, both the amber and the fly. Climbing the steps, there's no call for silence. She's expecting him, after all. An appointment he'd made and then forgotten, or at least until that very moment.

The twisting knob. The tortured hinge. A bulb that never needs changing. Her shadow spilling across the porch and bleeding into his. Perhaps his memory's playing tricks, but she doesn't seem quite as withered. Still a stick, but not nearly so bent, so inclined to the horizontal.

Has it really been a year where you come from? Feels more like a day to me.

Even the stones are softer, he notes. Chalk instead of slate.

So, this is how it will work. Each year, in your world, you'll grow a year older. No surprise in that. Only here, in my world, I'll grow younger instead. Ten years to your one.

Like most boys, he's fond of counting. Tallying up the score. Ready to pounce the moment he sniffs it, any sign of impropriety.

That's not fair, he replies.

Fair? Fair is for maidens. And I am still a crone. Or at least, for now.

Already he's starting to work it out. Years forward and years back.

And what'll happen later on? When we finally meet in the middle?

A laugh like before, only not quite as cruel.

Yes. Exactly. What.

*****

In five years anything can happen. Anything at all. Worlds are discovered, empires collapse, the new becomes the old. And something as fleeting as a boy soon wakes up a man.

Tim Withers now has a learner's permit. He can almost handle a clutch. Makes sure to shave at least once a week, more for practice than anything else. He's too short for the court, too small for the field, so he settles instead for the diamond, just nimble enough to cover shortstop or steal the occasional base. And girls? He now realizes there are two forms of terror, as distinct as night and day. The kind that comes out on Halloween, or plays at the drive-in each week, and the kind that renders him deaf, dumb and blind every time a skirt strolls by.

As for her, it's been a journey, too, only one that proceeds backwards. Peeling the long years from her flesh like a bug sheds its chrysalis. One year it's the hair, from grey to gold. The next finds her crow's nests departed. Her limbs growing taut, her breasts distending, the sags recast as curves. Is that his grandmother, there at the door? No, look again, it's his mother. Or that very last visit, what came as a shock, an older sister this time around. And yes, he knows, or at least suspects, that those years aren't coming from nowhere. That somehow she's siphoning off his future and winning back her past.

Sixteen candles. A new Schwinn bike. A weekend trip down to Pittsburg. And then fall descends, as sharp as an axe, and October draws to a close. The walk that once seemed an expedition is now just a country stroll, and the few kids he passes in their sad little costumes clear the sidewalk as they see him approach. The rusted gate. The moldering steps. Everything is the same. Except, this time, the front door is already cracked, despite the chill night air.

Seeing that, he sees an old bear trap. Rusty jaws eager to close. But rather than turn, flee back to his life, he slips into the house.

The room, a parlor, is frozen in time, an old daguerreotype. A diorama with no glass, no partition, separating the then from the now. He stares at each relic, each quaint artifact, hearing a voice in his head, one he can almost recognize, so sly and cool and mocking. Cold, it tells him. Prodded by that single word, he takes a halting step, homing in on a narrow staircase that leads to the second floor. As he does, the voice sounds again, a bit louder this time. Warmer.

Each stair-step sounds its very own note. Climbing up is a melody. The tempo of his footfalls slowing as the glow from the parlor recedes. By the time he reaches the second-floor landing, he can barely see his own hand, the only light a guttering candle in the room at the end of the hall. He stops. Hesitates. A fly contemplating a web. Only then, for a third time, the voice sounds out. Whispers a new word.

Hot.

Her bed smells like cold ashes. Her sheets are cloaked with dust. But as for the woman, the girl wrapped within them, she's sixteen, just like him. There should be words, awkward glances, a fumble of shoelace and knot, but their bodies quickly move past all that. Find a new agenda. Surrounded by crumble, by rot and decay, they glory in the moment. An insistence that blood and seed and soul will always outwit death.

Afterwards. Sweat cooling on damp skin.

Did you like that?

What do you think?

He moves his leg. The bedsprings squawk. Swallowing, he tastes her.

So, was I the best?

You're all the best.

Not exactly what he'd wanted.

And you know happens next.

No. What?

We get married.

What? No way. How come?

You don't want to make me a fallen woman, do you?

He pauses, thinking that over.

And besides, if we don't get married, how can I be a widow?

*****

One week later the fliers appeared. You could see them all over town.

Brian T.Marshall

MISSING. CASH REWARD.
TIMOTHY WITHERS—AGE 16.
LAST SEEN ON 10/31.
VICINITY OF ROLLINS MARKET.

Like every small town, Edynwilde has its share. Stories, or call them myths. Passed along from hand to hand, like a trick, or perhaps a treat.

Our Bios, Our Books

Susie Helme

I'm an American ex-pat from Nashville, Tennessee, living in North London, after sojourns in Tokyo, Paris and Geneva. Though I've kept my accent, I identify as a Londoner, and I write UK English.

My passion for the historical fiction genre is driven by a curiosity for ancient history and a desire to portray human beings who want to change the world, with a side interest in aberrant psychology. In real life, I'm a socialist and political activist.

Once a journalist and editor of mobile communications magazines, I was subeditor for several years on *Dignity* magazine. I now am an Editorial Consultant with Reedsy Marketplace offering Developmental Editing, Copy Editing and Proofreading. You can hire me to be your editor on https://reedsy.com/helme-susie.

I write book reviews for *Historical Novels Review, Reedsy Discovery* and *GetBooksReviewed*. Please check out my book reviews on Amazon.co.uk, Goodreads, Reedsy or BookBub. I have been a judge on the Killer Nashville Silver Falchion and Claymore Awards and the Historical Novel Society's First Chapters Competition.

I am convener and founder member of Bounds Green Book Writers.

I am a fiend for Mah Jong, though I rarely win.

My daughter lives regrettably far away (New Jersey), and my son and his wife (Stratford, East London) have just had their first baby—Kira. A grandchild for Susie!

My Books:

The Lost Wisdom of the Magi
(The Conrad Press 2020).

- Winner: 2021 Killer Nashville Silver Falchion Award for Best Historical.
- A first century runaway from Babylon becomes an Essene, then joins the Zealots to fight for the Freedom of Jerusalem.

'The forensic research… the detail… is amazing'
—Brendan Gerad O'Brien

'An immersive work, detailed with such richness that a full appreciation of it demands… one finger on the search button of Wikipedia'
—Martin Bird

'A tour de force, like no other book I have read'
—Christophe Medlar

The Genizah Codex
(The Conrad Press 2024).

- Finalist: 2022 Killer Nashville Claymore Award for Best Historical.
- Murders occur in three timeframes—2008 Jerusalem, 165 CE Alexandria, 1307 Al Quds. An ancient document may hold clues to solving the crimes.

'The layers of dust are peeled back to illuminate a treasure'
—Charles Cordell

'Alive with mystery and mythology. Detailed knowledge of Middle Eastern history is evident with the turn of every page'
—Tony Bassett

'If you're big into the scholarly-research-with-huge-stakes genre, you'll go wild'
—Niki Holmes Kantzios

Please look forward to the publication soon of *Dreaming of Jerusalem*, which was a Finalist for the 2022 Claymore Award for Best Historical, and *The Receptacles of St. Annianus*. I am also writing a genealogy of my mother's German ancestors.

WEBSITE . . . https://www.susiehelme.co.uk

~~~

Elaine Graham-Leigh

I'm an activist and writer of history, politics and fiction. My historical works, on medieval Languedoc, are: *The Southern French Nobility* and the *Albigensian Crusade*, (Boydell and Brewer 2005) and *Revolution in Carcassonne: The story of a fourteenth-century rebellion*, (Whalebone Press 2025).

My politics books are: **A Diet of Austerity: Class, Food**

and Climate Change, (Zero Books 2015) and ***Marx and the Climate Crisis***, (Counterfire 2020).

My science-fiction novel is *The Caduca*, (The Conrad Press 2021).

My science-fiction short stories, many of which are set in the same fictional universe as ***The Caduca***, have appeared in various zines including ***Jupiter SF, The Harrow, Bewildering Stories*** and ***Theaker's Quarterly Fiction***; all are also accessible from my website www.redpuffin.net. I write and speak regularly on a range of political issues. You can read my political articles and book reviews, and see some of my speeches, on Counterfire.

In 'real life', I'm an accountant (because even radical movements need someone doing the books).

My Book:

The Caduca
(The Conrad Press 2021)

- When the major power in the galaxy invades a poor colony planet, two women, an alien diplomat and a human guerrilla fighter, confront how neither of their causes are what they seem.

'Glitteringly good'
—The Morning Star

'A political and thoughtful novel... an entertain-

ing and exciting book about a serious subject'
—Theaker's Quarterly
'A brilliant book, with an unbelievable level of complexity, that really makes you question right and wrong'
—The Book Suite

'The best ending in a sci-fi book ever'
—Judalon de Bornay

'A science fiction-loving feminist's dream'
—Reader's Favorite

WEBSITES:

https://www.redpuffin.net
https://counterfire.org

~~~

Rajes Bala (Rajeswary Balasubramaniam)

I am from Sri Lanka, the author of 23 books in the Tamil language—including 8 novels, 9 collections of short stories, two books on health education, one research book on the Tamil god Murugan and three collections of articles. My books and stories have been translated into Sinhalese, English and French, and I have won 16 literary awards in India and Sri Lanka, and two Sahithya Academy Awards in Sri Lanka. My writings have been taken by university students for research studies for BA, MA and PhD.

I am a human rights campaigner, staunchly opposed to the dowry system, caste system, Tamil separatism and genocide. I'm a founder and chairperson for the Tamil Refugee Action Group, the Tamil Refugee Housing Association from 1985-88 and Tamil Women's League in London from 1982. I have campaigned all my life for reconciliation in Sri Lanka, attending the UN for four weeks in 2012.

I have an MA in Medical Anthropology, BA in Film & Video, Certificate in Health Education, RM, RGN, RSCN, and worked in the NHS for many years. I produced a documentary **Escape from Genocide** in 1986 on the Sri Lankan atrocities against Tamils.

I have given lectures on many subjects at universities in England, India, Sri Lanka, Switzerland and Holland, and I regularly give Zoom lectures on various subjects in Tamil, which are broadcast all over the Diaspora.

My Books (published in English):

The Banks of the River Thillai
(The Conrad Press 2021).

- Published in Tamil twice in India, first in 1987.
- Three Tamil girl cousins, Gowry, Saratha and Buvana, grow up near the beautiful River Thillai in the old-fashioned village of Kolavil, which is turned upside down by racial violence in 1958. This gorgeous, funny novel is a must-read for Tamils, but non-Tamils will adore it.

'Transports you to another time and place in Cey-

lon when new political troubles were brewing. A feminist book, with girls and women at its heart'
—Archana

'An affectionate portrait... many anecdotes of village life and village customs... tinged with sadness. A convincing picture of the sleepy village on the cusp of far-reaching change'
—E. Graham-Leigh

'You can almost taste the coconut prawn curry and smell the incense wafting from Ganesh's temple down the sunset-coloured lane'
—S. Helme

Journey to Jaffna
(The Conrad Press 2024).

- Published 1981 in Tamil in Sri Lanka and later in India. It was the first work of Diaspora literature published in Sri Lanka.
- Param, a Tamil immigrant happily married in London, journeys home to Jaffna, answering his duty to conduct his father's last rites. There he faces the ghosts of his own and his country's past. Three women—his English wife Mary, his former girlfriend Karthiga and modern-minded journalist Liz—influence his life and his decisions. Where do his loyalties lie?

'A cautionary tale, a must-read for Diaspora Tamils. Param's struggle will be familiar to many immigrants. While still holding onto the values of the home world, his new world faces him with

different challenges and possibilities'
—S. Helme

'Bala's unpretentious narrative style is punctuated with poetic insights about the contradictions faced by the very human protagonist. Confronted by the ghosts of his past, he is forced to question his values'
—Mark Thompson

~ ~ ~

Mark Thompson (em.thompson)

I'm that old bloke who needs a haircut, leaning on a lamppost watching the world go by. Curious. Always curious. Because every picture tells a story.

I didn't always write. When I was young, I read. I read plenty. Lots of history. Lots of politics. Lots of philosophy. But mainly Agatha Christie and George Orwell. And plays. A passion for Shakespeare and Brecht. Some Neil Simon. Each in their own way understood.

Then, swept away by Old Man River, I set out to chase moonbeams and make music. Succour for the soul. A neat guitarist, doubling on sax and flute, I made a decent living before waking up one morning on the other side of the creative fence.

And all the time, I watched, sometimes understanding, often not, but always watching. Curious.

I travelled. I ran a record company, I managed bands and record producers, I built recording studios, I made records. Some sold. Some sold very well. I won glittering prizes. Hollow trinkets.

The best sold hardly any. But they told a story that needed telling. But when music became a digital commodity to jog to, commute to, or drive to, I hung up my guitar and turned my mind to committing a lifetime of curiosity to paper. A new passion.

WEBSITE . . . www.em-thompson.com

My Books:

Elliefant's Graveyard—
The Curious Case of the Throatslit Man
(Eccentric Directions 2023).

The Happy Thistle—
The Curious Case of the Katenapped Girl
(Eccentric Directions 2024).

Murder on the Ordinary Express—
The Curious Case of the Butcher of St. Mary Nook
(Eccentric Directions 2025).

The Sinisterhood of Celebrity Psyclones —
The Curious Case of the Swiss Alacatrazamataz
(Eccentric Directions)

Krill
(Eccentric Directions 2024).

Also seven more rib-tickling short stories in *The Stoat Hall Legacy Book Club* are available to download at, https:www.em-thompson.com

Brian T. Marshall

Brian T Marshall lives 'half a geographical globe away but merely a virtual creative whisker from Bounds Green in North London'.

I was born on Tuesday, September 3, 1956. And no, you're not seeing double. I really am that old. All these years later, and the quandary remains: how does an author explore their most personal issues without losing the power of The Story? How does one tell a tale? For me, it has always begun with a voice, one that speaks with total conviction, even though the journey and those who inhabit it are nothing but make-believe. If we're lucky, we'll spot a few gems along the way—the perfect metaphor, an exact turn of phrase—and everything else is just bubble-wrap. All the crap, the tumult of words that drag us along in its wake. On the way, we'll meet fellow travellers, some real and some imagined. Each one carrying their little bag of tricks, half of it borrowed, the rest of it stolen outright.

    Pointing fingers. Saying thanks. Or just painting a pretty little picture. All that matters is you've still got a choice, in the hours or minutes that remain. A choice. Because that's what writing is.

WEBSITE . . . https://www.briantmarshallauthor.com/

Marie-Lise Mullen is French, a retired nursery school teacher living in the Paris region. She is mostly interested in reading, cinema and migrants' rights.

Kay Towers was Mark's grandmother.

I was rummaging through some family papers earlier this year and came across this brief account of my maternal grandparents: Reg and Kay Towers—courtship before the First World War. As well as offering a charming window into another age, Kay's story has a sting in the tail. Truth or fiction? I have no idea, but my grandmother was not given to flight of imaginary fancy.

—Mark Thompson

Susie Helme, Elaine Graham-Leigh, Rajes Bala (Rajeswary Balasubramaniam) and Mark Thompson (em.thompson) are members of Bounds Green Book Writers. You can check out our novels and our blog on writing techniques on: https://boundsgreenbookwriters.com/category/writing-advice-and-comment/).

If you write books and live within traveling distance to Bounds Green, consider joining us.

If you enjoyed our stories, please leave us a review, buy/read/review our novels, check out our websites and join our mailing lists.

Printed in Dunstable, United Kingdom